Beneath the African Sun

MARIA LYNCH

 FriesenPress

Suite 300 - 990 Fort St
Victoria, BC, Canada, V8V 3K2
www.friesenpress.com

Copyright © 2015 by Maria Lynch
First Edition — 2015

ISBN
978-1-4602-7485-9 (Hardcover)
978-1-4602-7486-6 (Paperback)
978-1-4602-7487-3 (eBook)

1. Fiction, Historical

Distributed to the trade by The Ingram Book Company

Contents

////////////////////// **Part One** //////////////////////

////////////////////// **Part Two** //////////////////////

Part Three

for my late father, C. P. Joanes

"Exclusion is never the way forward on our
shared paths to freedom and justice."
—Desmond Tutu

ACKNOWLEDGEMENTS

Many have contributed to the writing of this novel. I thank Margrit Eichler, Sharon Crawford, Susan Glickman, and Carter Sickels for their encouragement, critiques, and lessons in creative writing. I am grateful to Warren Layberry, my editor, who presented invaluable insights and assistance. Pip Wallace and her team made beneficial and varied contributions. I lovingly appreciated the support of my sons and most especially my husband, Tim, who embraced every aspect of my creative writing endeavour.

This is a work of historical fiction. Thus, while the setting and many of the larger events that form the backdrop of the novel are drawn from historical fact, the characters of the story are the author's inventions and should be recognized as such. Though many sources informed the author's research, three books in particular were helpful.

Anderson, David: *Histories of the Hanged The Dirty War in Kenya and the End of Empire* Publishers: W. W. Norton & Company, NY, 2005

Elkins, Caroline: *Imperial Reckoning The Untold Story of Britain's Gulag in Kenya* Publishers: Henry Holt and Company, NY, 2005

Kariuki, Josiah Mwangi: *'Mau Mau' Detainee* Publishers: Penguin African Library, Oxford University Press, 1963

And so it is that I can now look back over all that has happened and see the pattern of my life and the lives of my wife and children chalked out in careful strokes beneath the African sun.

Part
One

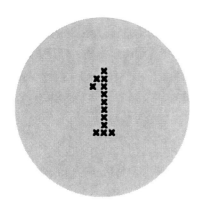

GOA, PORTUGUESE INDIA

The sun's rays were streaming into the sewing room, making it hotter than usual. It was a Tuesday afternoon, and there was a slight breeze coming in through the windows, but it brought very little comfort to us, the two apprentices, pedalling away at the sewing machines. We were hot. The shop's tailors were also at their machines in front of us. There was a wooden cabinet counter top separating the sewing room from the front of the shop. Mr. Fernandes, our apprentice teacher, was sorting out the suit lengths on the shelves against the wall in the shop. He turned around to walk towards us in the sewing room at the back of the shop.

He observed us—his apprentices—encouraging us to continue sewing. I stopped and pulled out my handkerchief to wipe the sweat from my forehead. Dominic did the same. Mr. Fernandes noticed this and told us to go to the front to have a drink of water that he laid out for us in small tin cups. During this break, he pointed to the suit lengths on the shelves. He asked both of us to come to the table where he had rolled out three suit lengths. He explained the quality of the cloth by letting us feel and touch each one.

"Notice the differences in these cloths. Touch each one for its smoothness, and note the type of cloth it is made of. Feel these differences to help you select the right suit length for the customer's needs. Get to know each suit length. Decide whether it will be appropriate for a formal event or not. This is part of becoming a good tailor."

We listened with great interest. He instructed us to pick out a suit length from the shelves. Dominic and I each brought a suit length to the table. We touched and felt the suit length and then described the quality of the cloth and our recommendations for the suit lengths we examined. Dominic described his suit length and its use. I took my time and carefully told Mr. Fernandes the quality of my suit length and my advice to the customer. Mr. Fernandes smiled approvingly and then explained why Dominic's description was right on the quality of the cloth but not on the recommendation to the customer. He explained the reasons. He took us to the other side of the shop to the counter top and opened up the customer book. He pointed to the date and then moved the pencil down towards the name of the customer and measurements for the customer's suit.

"A new page for each customer. Look at the title for each measurement of the different parts of the suit."

We read through the measurements for a moment. Then Dominic looked up.

"When do we get to do these measurements?"

I too looked up at that point, for I had the same question.

"In two or three months," said Mr. Fernandes, glancing first at Dominic and then me, "when I think you are ready to take a customer's measurements. First you must sew the different pieces of the suit together. Learn how the pieces fit together."

Dominic and I continued looking at the different pages of the customer book.

"You will do the measurements followed by the cutting of the cloth for a suit or a woman's dress. This is the most important part of your training that will make you a good tailor or a bad tailor. I will show you how to be a good tailor," he said. "But it takes time, and you must be patient."

We eyed him impatiently. "Thank you Mr. Fernandes." I added, "I want to be a good tailor; I like this kind of work." Without responding, he sent us back to our sewing machines.

I was sewing the second sleeve of the suit jacket when Mr. Fernandes came by on his rounds again. He assessed my work and then, with a serious look on his face, told me that I was doing a good job. I was relieved. I thought he was going to correct me, but he didn't. I carried on sewing feeling really proud of myself.

At closing time, we put away the suits in the cupboard on the side wall. I hurriedly tidied up my workspace around the sewing machine. I arranged the chalk pieces, the pairs of scissors and different sewing threads and needles in the boxes on the right of the worktable.

It was late Saturday afternoon. Mr. Fernandes let us go home on Saturdays; we didn't have to come back at four o'clock to finish the day at seven o'clock. I had to walk home to Pedda where I lived with my parents; usually one hour, sometimes less when I had the energy to run part of the way. I planned to meet up with my friends Anton and Menino at a snack shack nearby. We hadn't seen each other often since we finished school.

I found myself dodging the people on the street to get out of Margao and onto the mud pathway that led to Pedda. Almost alone on this pathway I drifted into my own thoughts. It was late January 1913, and I was fifteen years old.

Mr. Fernandes was my teacher at his shop, Fernandes Tailoring Company. I was learning how to do tailoring. It was designing the suit, cutting of the cloth and using the sewing machine to firmly stitch the different pieces of the suit together. We sometimes worked on women's clothing. It was slightly different because it brought in the creative part of dressing up a woman. This kind of tailoring had more details and flexibility in cutting and shaping the cloth to dress a woman's body in different ways. There was imagination and cleverness in making women's clothing. When the time came to work on a woman's dress, I thought of different ways to design the dress. I spent more time designing the dress than sewing it.

I arrived home in time to help Mai; we went to the well to get water and after two trips to the well and back there was enough water in our home. I freshened up and changed my clothes. Mai insisted that I had something to eat before I left for the evening to be with my friends.

There was not much light, for it was beginning to turn dark on this hot night in January. I made my way to the snack shack where Anton and Menino were waiting for me. Menino was sitting on one of the stools at a small table and looked up at me, broadly smiling, his black hair smoothed down, with his straightened back and his hands around a coconut shell; he was drinking coconut water. Anton was there. He was much shorter than Menino, slightly heavier in weight. He glared in my direction, quite impatiently. He raised his hands signalling me to hurry, reserving the stool for me before anyone else took it away.

I sat on the stool, and we tried to talk in the crowded dimly lit place. We stopped talking; Anton and I walked to the far end of the snack shack to get our coconut drinks. After waiting awhile, we picked up our drinks and returned to our table. We huddled closer to each other so we could talk and hear each other.

"Well Sabby," said Menino, "what's it like at the tailoring shop? What do you learn?"

I was excited and answered without thinking. "Lots. I learn how to make suits, fine men's suits. Now I am sewing the different pieces of the suit together. Then we will learn how to take measurements and the most important part is cutting the cloth. That's what Mr. Fernandes says. He is a good teacher, and I will learn to become a good tailor."

Anton smiled and sipped his drink. "I never thought you would like doing this kind of work."

"Look, I didn't know what to expect when Pai took me to this tailoring shop in Margao. I was worried; to be in a shop where they make suits for men and some dresses for women."

We straightened ourselves on our stools and thought back to a Sunday at Benaulim beach, two days after we finished school. On that Sunday we talked about what we would do with our time. There were no jobs in Goa. My parents didn't have the money to send me for any more schooling. But my Pai arranged for me to do tailoring.

Menino and Anton shook their heads and smiled because they remembered what I said to them on the beach.

I was nervous and didn't know what to expect. I followed my Pai. It seemed a long time ago, and yet it was only a month. And now I was comfortable doing tailoring. They both jostled me around at my enthusiasm. We stopped to gulp the remaining drink, and I scooped out the juicy pulp from the coconut and let it slither down my throat. It tasted good.

"You really like tailoring, Sabby? While you are gone, Anton and I meet and walk on the beach wondering what to do next. It's boring," said Menino.

"Yes, I like tailoring. Mr. Fernandes tells us about the different cloths. There is much to learn. I can't explain it all now. But I can tell you I see myself becoming a tailor, and a good one too." I confidently glanced at both of them.

Menino shifted about on his stool and looked around at the people who were laughing and talking loudly. Across from me, Anton's deep brown eyes narrowed.

"Tell us what makes you excited about tailoring."

I leaned in closer so they could hear me.

"It's about creating a suit from a straight piece of cloth. I keep imagining how I will cut the cloth into the different pieces to sew together to make a suit. Right now, I'm only sewing the pieces together. I will learn how to cut the cloth according to the measurements of the customer."

"That would be difficult for me," Menino said in a loud voice, trying to make himself heard.

Anton shouted how it was a special skill. I nodded.

"But maybe," I said, "I became interested in sewing from watching Mai sew at home."

I told them my memories of watching Mai sew ever since I was a little boy. When she would sew, my brother Miguel and I would not disturb her, and I particularly would watch her. She would softly hum while she would move the cloth around, fluff up the curved cloth around the neckline, position the dress in front of her to examine its look in the mirror and then make small sewing adjustments until it looked perfect to her. As I grew older, I would ask her many questions about how the dress was made. She would eagerly tell me that it was a special skill. Mai said that I had to be imaginative when drawing the design on paper and then chalk the design on the cloth according to the measurements. She showed me the measuring tape. Over time, I learned the numbers on the tape and saw how she would measure me for a shirt, write down the numbers and then use the numbers to chalk out the cloth. Menino and Anton listened to me without interruption. With dismayed looks on their faces, they wished they could become enthusiastic about something.

"Of course, Mai and Pai are happy that I like tailoring. When I'm in the tailoring shop, I watch the tailors do the cutting and sewing. The work is very interesting and not tiresome. But, it gets very hot in that sewing room at the back of the shop with all of us pedalling away at our machines. This is when we get rest breaks. Enough about me, What about you two? What do you think you will do? Now we have to do something for a job."

We looked at each other without saying anything. After a while, Menino sat upright and told us stories from his uncle who lived in Bombay. Our people were leaving for Africa. Some went by ship from Bombay while others left directly from Goa in the dhows. They were going to Beira in Portuguese Mozambique or to Mombasa in British East Africa. As I listened, it seemed strange that people left Goa to work in faraway places. Menino could read the look in my eyes.

He said, "That is a long way to go for work, I know. But it is better than doing nothing here. I wish I would have the courage to leave home and work on a ship. I would like to do that; work on a ship. Who knows, I may do it someday. Think about it, Anton and Sabby, you could be sitting here in this snack shack while I would be working on a ship. Tell me. Could I do it?"

Anton shoved at him. "I can't see you doing that. You love it here too much, and besides your parents will never let you go. What do you think, Sabby? Could you do it?"

Anton and I observed Menino, wondering if he would really leave Goa, but I accepted his plan.

"Maybe," I said. "Who knows? Goans are leaving to find work elsewhere. In the past, they would go to Bombay, but now they are going to Africa. Let's see what happens at the end of my apprenticeship. I have to sew a suit from the beginning to the end and some dresses. Then I have to take measurements and cut the cloth. This will take some time." I took a deep breath, impatient at the thought. "The whole year."

"See, you keep talking about tailoring," Anton said. "You love doing this work. But will you do it here, or will you go to Africa?" He stood up to stretch his legs. Menino and I did too. We looked around us, and there were a few people left in the snack shack.

"I wonder what it would be like to live somewhere else," I said. "Different from Goa. My parents talk about Africa. They know of young people going there to work for the railway company in British East Africa. But there are other people who go to Portuguese Mozambique. Who knows, if we keep talking about it, maybe we'll actually do something about it."

We walked out of the snack shack into the night.

Menino gazed into the sky as we started down the dusty mud pathway that led from the snack shack.

"Sabby, I remember overhearing some of the older folk at your place when we were there for Sunday lunch—who is leaving and who is coming back. Are we too young to leave home? What do you think, Anton?"

"I don't know, Menino. I'm not sure. I don't even know what I want to do with my life. How can I even think about going to Africa? What would I do there? Sabby is learning to become a tailor. I suppose he can find work as a tailor."

We didn't say much to each other in the darkness of the night. We went our separate paths home.

That night I had dreams of being on a ship bound for Africa. They were beautiful dreams of a very different life. But there were also dreams of things going wrong and getting mixed up with different kinds of people who were strangers to me. The morning brought me back to being in Goa.

When I wasn't at the shop, the days and nights passed as they usually did. I continued improving my tailoring skills with Mr. Fernandes, and he liked my work and offered praise. By April, I was taking measurements for customers, chalking out the cloth according to the measurements and then cutting the cloth. This was very interesting, and though, at first, I made a few mistakes, with practice I became good at it.

The Monsoon season, in June, brought heavy rain almost all day and all night. It was very hot. But we lived through our routines. Back at the shop and with Mr. Fernandes watching over me, I was now able to make a suit. I was very happy and proud of myself. Mai and Pai were very glad that I was doing well in tailoring. When a customer came in asking for me to do a suit for him, Mr. Fernandes told me that this was a sign that I was becoming a good tailor.

One day in September, with only few more months of apprenticeship remaining, I spoke with Mr. Fernandes about going to Africa. It was after closing time. We were alone in the shop. We sat down, and he told me that he knew of people who had gone there. Some had liked it and stayed, but others found it difficult to adjust and returned to Goa.

"Here," he said, "we are all the same people, but in Africa there are the Africans, as well as the European and Indian settlers. You will have to learn to live and work with these different kinds of people and customs."

I listened to everything he knew about living outside Goa. He said it was more important to take the advice from my parents, for it would be a big adjustment for them. He cautiously told me that we sometimes hear talk from people who come back and this is turned into stories; but you cannot know if those stories are true or not. It was difficult to say how any one person would adjust to living in Africa. I thanked him for his advice and walked out of Margao and onto the pathway to home, thinking it was time to talk to Mai and Pai to help me make a decision.

Regularly I had been meeting up with Anton and Menino at the snack shack for our Saturday evening discussions and sometimes arguments. On some of these nights, we would go dancing at the local dance hall. We cheered on our local teenagers who would stand in front of the crowd to sing. And when

Menino did his song and dance number, we would shout as loud as possible. It was always fun on these Saturday nights. The next day, we drowsily saw each other in the church pews of St. John the Baptist Church in Pedda and tried to properly participate in the Sunday Mass.

After Mass, Mai was into her routine of preparing a big Sunday lunch. Some friends, relatives or neighbours would drop by to eat, drink, talk and sing. Sometimes, I brought Menino and Anton to our Sunday lunches. We joined in the conversation, while at other times we only listened to the stories. The best part was when we would sing and dance. This was enjoyable. I knew that if or when I did leave Goa, I would miss those Sundays. I would be with different people, and who knew what kinds of activities I would do. I knew that I would miss Mai and Pai and, of course, my brother, Miguel. He was younger than I and still at school.

On Sunday afternoons my friends and I would go to our favourite Benaulim beach. On one of these beach afternoons, Menino talked about working on a ship again, while Anton talked about doing carpentry at a shop in Margao. Sometimes I met up with Anton on the pathway on our daily walk to Margao. That day, however, we were sitting on the sand, looking out onto the Arabian Sea.

"My uncle from Bombay will be visiting us soon," said Menino, his eyes on the horizon. "I am going to find out about working on a ship. He may be able to tell me how I can do that. There's no one here who would know this information. What do you think?"

I couldn't imagine being at sea for long periods of time.

"Menino, you are serious about working on the ship. I think it will be very different. You'll be on the ship most of the time, and then on your days off you'll come home. You will be between the ship and home. I wonder what that will be like."

"Yes Sabby, it'll be different all right. I have to find out more. My parents tell me that they have heard of young fellows working on the ship as stewards. I think I would like to do that. I will have to be trained. You know as I say it out loud, it feels exciting and terrifying at the same time. I'll be on the ship day and night." Menino sounded worried and looked to the sea in hopes of an answer.

Anton too was looking off into the distance and not saying anything. I wondered if he still liked doing carpentry work.

"Anton, why so quiet?" I shoved him on the sand. "Do you think Menino will make it on the ship? And what does a steward do anyway?"

"I don't know. If that is what he wants to do, he can always try it out. Who knows what is good and what is not until you try it out. I am still not sure that I like carpentry. I do not know if this is the kind of work that I would become good at, and I'm not sure if this is what I want to do every day of my life. It's very confusing for me. But now I'm listening to Menino talking about leaving Goa and doing work elsewhere. I have to think more seriously about carpentry," Anton said, making circles in the sand with his fingers.

"Anton, the more carpentry you do, the better you will become at it," I said. "As for leaving Goa, I'm considering it. I often wonder what it is like to live on the other side of the world. The more I think about it, the more I want to explore other places. It'll be different with other kinds of people. I've been talking to my parents about leaving Goa. They seem to think that I would be better off in another place rather than here. They talk about Pedro being in British East Africa. He's from our village. My parents know the family. He misses Goa very much, but he likes it there and will stay there for a while. He likes the work he is doing for the railway company in Mombasa. I think he is a mechanic."

I looked down and realized that I had been drawing dress designs in the sand.

We continued our discussion about leaving Goa. We exchanged bits of stories we heard from other people who talked about living in Africa and what it was like there. These people received letters from Beira, Nairobi and Mombasa. It seemed to be a big adjustment from life in Goa. This was gossip from the villagers. It seemed risky to go some place faraway to live and work.

At home, the dinnertime discussions were quite different. Mai and Pai wanted Miguel and I to go to Africa for a better life, but they knew that once we were there they might never see us again unless we came back on holidays. But that would only happen once we had jobs and were able to save enough money to make the journey back to visit them. It could be as long as two or three years before they saw us again. It was distressing Mai very much, but Pai seemed confident about us going to Africa. Then the big question was around the choice between British East Africa and Portuguese Mozambique—which like Goa, was under Portuguese rule. These discussions came from the rumours and gossip in the village. We heard there were more jobs in British East Africa than in Portuguese Mozambique. But I wanted to do tailoring and, therefore, would it make a difference where I went? Would there be the same amount of tailoring work in both countries?

Then there were other considerations that my parents talked about constantly. The British had been in India since the sixteenth century and were still ruling the rest of India—except our Goa since the Portuguese would not give it up—would I adjust more easily under Portuguese rule or would it be difficult either way because both these places were in Africa? There was too much to sort out in my mind before I made my decision to leave Goa. In the meantime, I knew I had to continue working on my tailoring skills.

FAREWELL TO GOA AND SEA VOYAGE TO MOMBASA

When January came around again, it was the end of my apprenticeship. Mr. Fernandes was very pleased with my tailoring skills and kept me on as a junior tailor at his shop. This was excellent as I was able to gain more experience.

Late Saturday night, Menino, Anton and I, in a happy mood, walked to our favourite Benaulim beach. The night sky was covered with stars shining brightly. We seemed to be the only ones on the beach. Our voices carried through the night. We found a spot to sit and talk. At times I drifted far away. I could barely hear the conversation around me because I was in my own world, thinking of my decision.

At one instance there was silence. Menino and Anton were glaring at me—I could see their mouths moving. I shook my head to get back to what they were saying. I said I was now ready to leave Goa and that my parents supported my decision. Pai was very encouraging, but Mai was anxious. They spoke with friends and villagers about the best way to get to Africa. I would go to British East Africa. My parents would have been more comfortable with my going to Beira in Mozambique since it was Portuguese Africa. But I was thinking of British East Africa because it would be different, and I was ready to try something that was not like Goa. Also, Mr. Fernandes said he heard that there were more jobs in Nairobi, its new capital. Without interrupting me, they listened with great attention, with their jaws dropping. It felt strange. I stopped talking. They both jumped on me, pushing me around, shouting and yelling. Quickly we settled down on the sand and began a serious conversation.

"There are big differences there, already," said Menino. "British rule for one."

It was ruled by the British which made it an English speaking country. Beira, on the other hand, people spoke Portuguese. We were more familiar with the Portuguese, for they had ruled Goa for hundreds of years while the British ruled the rest of India and we were not familiar with British ways.

"What do you think, Sabby? Are you ready for this change?"

I sat there cross-legged on the beach with my hands drawing out images of different designs of clothing into the sand, trying to come up with some kind of an answer.

"Yeah, yeah, it will be an adventure. But we are teenagers, and this is the best time to learn, to explore, and adjust to a very different life. If I can make clothes for people, I will be more than happy. The other adjustments will come in time." I tried to hide my anxiety about leaving Goa.

"But Africa is newly discovered," said Menino, looking out at the crashing waves. "I wonder what the Africans are like."

"My question is how do the British treat the Africans? We know how the Portuguese invaded Goa and how they continue to rule us," said Anton and drew what he considered an image of the African map on the sand. We could hardly see it in the darkness of the night.

I wandered off in my own thoughts again. The two of them continued talking. This was too much to take in, and all I wanted to do was to make clothes even if it was in a country far away. In Africa, I would meet different kinds of people. I would explore the country and make many friends. This made me want to leave Goa. I was used to the people, the customs and the activities here and thought that it would become boring in the future. I wanted to live in a place unlike Goa.

Mr. Fernandes said I had proven to be a good tailor. After my apprenticeship, I made a suit a month and a few dresses. I chalked the design on the cloth from the measurements. I carefully cut along the chalk lines and then sewed the pieces together. With much patience I did it, and it felt very good to see each suit I made on the men who had ordered them.

I thought, *I am good at this, and most important of all, I feel proud and happy to see that I make the men look good in the suits I sewed for them. But I think I like designing, cutting and sewing women's dresses better than the men's suits or shirts. I like using my imagination when I am designing a dress. This is the best part of being a tailor.*

I was interrupted when they pushed and shoved me about to get me out of my thoughts.

"Look, I think it's about politics and what the rulers do. And I'll learn how to live under British rule. Menino, I remember your neighbour once telling me about his uncle's trip to Bombay. It's different there. Everyone speaks English as their second language, and the laws are created from British law.

That's what foreign conquerors do when they take over the land. The local people have to adjust. Our ancestors did that when the Portuguese conquered Goa. There are horror stories of what the Portuguese did to our ancestors too, right?" I waited for them to say something.

We were silent. Our heads turned towards the horizon. Dawn was breaking, for we spent the whole night on the beach, talking, dozing off, and talking again. We saw the sun gently bringing in daylight onto the beach. Menino and Anton both looked at me, but it was Anton who said what both of them were thinking.

"It looks like you are definitely going on a long voyage to Africa."

I closely looked at them and smiled broadly. "Will you see me off at the port when the day comes?"

My parents told me that there were dhows leaving for Mombasa but that it depended on the monsoon winds. The dhow captain would talk with the port authorities and accordingly they would choose the best day and time for sailing across the sea towards Mombasa in British East Africa.

"When are you going?" Menino asked.

"Oh, I still have the rest of the year with Mr. Fernandes." And though it seemed a long way off, I could feel the excitement of leaving Goa. "I want to be an experienced tailor before I leave Goa. I need this year of experience and maybe more. I will have to talk with Mr. Fernandes."

"Yes, yes," said Anton. "We will come to see you off when you are ready to go."

The three of us stood up and stretched for a bit. Looking towards the sea, I wondered what awaited me on the other side. We shook the sand off ourselves and drowsily walked towards home. We continued our conversation. Menino told us about the possibility of working on the ship, while Anton would continue working as a junior carpenter in the shop in Margao. He said he was beginning to like carpentry and looked forward to the big furniture jobs. We were finding our different ways to make a life for ourselves.

At home I talked with my parents about getting more tailoring experience in Goa. They advised me to check with Mr. Fernandes. This I did when I was at work. He thought it would be better for me to be more experienced before I left for British East Africa. He looked pleased and recommended that I stay on for two more years. This surprised me.

He took me aside and said that more and more customers requested that I sew their suits. This made me very happy. He added that he would give me more responsibility with the customers. He would let me work with the customer from beginning to end. This past year I worked on the suits under the direction of Mr. Fernandes. But he advised that he would observe and only interfere if necessary. It was up to me to continue to prove customer satisfaction with no assistance, but only advice and support from my teacher. And thus I became a successful tailor.

During these years of staying behind, I thought about Goa, our people, our customs, and traditions. Some of my customers were Portuguese; they lived in different parts around the country. But here in Margao, we'd walk by their big houses with beautiful gardens. They ruled over us. When they conquered Goa in 1510, they allowed the Hindus to keep to the caste system, but they had to convert to Catholicism. If not, they were tortured and killed; apparently these were the Hindus that could not bury their dead—they were accustomed to cremation.

No one talked about the Goa Inquisition that began in 1560. During those early days, the newly converted were put on trial in the courts because it was supposed that they were secretly practising their old beliefs. And then there were those who stubbornly continued to practise their original Hindu or Muslim religions. Many were tried in the courts; yet very few were sentenced to death and executed while others were burned. But it was not known what happened to the remainder that were tried. The Inquisitors wanted to control the people of Goa and seized their property. This Inquisition ended in 1812; most of the records were destroyed. These were very difficult times for our ancestors.

The caste system survived through the years; the Goan brahmins maintained their status. For the church celebration of feasts, the brahmins wore special cloaks and were in the front pews of the church and led the processions. Each village had a feast celebration day that always began with a Mass at the church followed by a festival in the village with plenty of food, music, singing and dancing. Our family always participated in these feast festivals. It was a time to have fun and mix with the villagers.

We were bound by our faith and followed all the obligations of the church. We did what the Pope commanded with no questions asked. We had a deep faith and it worked for us. As I made up my mind to leave Goa, I thought more and more about what I would leave behind. And these two years of experience gave me extra savings that I would take to Kenya.

Of course, Anton and Menino were thrilled that I would be around for a while. They assured me that time would go by very quickly; they understood my decision to delay my departure. I absorbed everything about being in Goa and wondered how much I would miss it. While at the beach, we talked about the way of Goan life; fishermen who went out daily to bring in their catch of fish. We remembered the time during our school holidays when we used to watch them bring in the nets full of fish; sometimes we helped them pull on the rope to bring in the net from the sea. That was hard work in the heat of the sun.

The two extra years I spent at the tailoring shop was mostly interesting and sometimes difficult. I did well, and according to Mr. Fernandes, I matured and became very confident with the customers. They appreciated my tailoring.

On my last Sunday in Goa, we went to Mass at St. John the Baptist Church to pray for my safe sea voyage. After Mass, relatives, friends and neighbours came over to our place for a farewell party. Mr. Fernandes was there, wishing me the best on my journey and my settlement in Nairobi. He put a small envelope in my hand. As the party ended, people left wishing me a safe trip and good luck. Some gave me money while others gave me small tailoring tools that I would need.

As I prepared to leave I sensed the emotion and tension in our home. My parents gave me some extra money, and Miguel was very thoughtful perhaps wishing he was going with me. It would have been too difficult for Mai and Pai if both of us left together. Besides Miguel needed to complete his tailoring training. He tended to spend less time on tailoring and more time socializing with friends. I told Miguel that, when I was settled in British East Africa, I'd send for him when he was finished with his apprenticeship. He accepted that and then said that he might come on his own when he was ready. That was a surprise remark, a way of showing his independence I assumed.

My departure date was the next day, Monday January 24, 1916. The journey was expected to take three or four weeks depending on the cooperation of the winds. The dhow that would take me across the Arabian Sea was called the *Monsoon Wind*. A small dhow with a crew of ten or twelve, it would carry half a dozen passengers and likely some trade goods destined for the port city of Mombasa.

It was a perfect day for the start of a sea journey. I packed a small suitcase with clothes and tailoring tools. I looked around our home one last time and then hugged my parents with much love and gratitude. Mai was crying and Pai was quiet while Miguel was at a distance looking anxious. Neighbours dropped by to wish me well. It was time to go.

We arrived at the port to find a few fellows boarding the dhow *Monsoon Wind*. Menino and Anton rushed towards me, hugged and wished me well. I promised to send letters to them with people coming back to Goa. Before I boarded the dhow, I went to Mai whose tears were streaming down her face. Pai cautioned me to stay safe. I hugged and kissed them both and then I embraced Miguel, Menino and Anton with very few words said between us. I jumped on board, turning around to wave. And with that, the *Monsoon Wind* slowly made its way towards the sea.

I was eighteen years old.

I continued to look back, waving at those I was leaving behind. We were asked to sit down and keep steady, but I continued looking at the shore. The tiny figures there grew fainter as we drew away, and soon I could no longer see them clearly. Tears filled my eyes.

I turned around and saw the four other fellows who would be travelling with me. The crew members were busy working the sails, as the wind appeared to be just right to move forward. Another crew member directed us to the cabin below. We climbed down with our suitcases. There were six low beds laid out in a row with very little space in between—we would learn that there had been a last minute cancellation. At the head space of each bed was a small cupboard with a key hanging out. I chose the bed nearest me at the end of the row and closer to the rung of stairs leading to the deck. I slid my small suitcase under my bed and put my light jacket in the cupboard, locked it and put the key in my pocket. We introduced ourselves. My fellow travellers were John, Paulo, Caetano and Tony. We dashed back up on deck since it was still daylight. The waters were calm with a wind moving our dhow along.

The sails looked stretched and were upright in the wind. We were moving fast. I continued turning back peering at the dwindling Goa coast. John was standing next to me. He was tall with a light complexion, light brown eyes and a broad smile.

"Are we doing right by leaving Goa?" he asked, turning to look at me.

"At this very moment, I'm not sure." Waves were gently breaking across the bow. "I'm more concerned about this sea voyage. Hope we get to Mombasa safe and in one piece."

"I'm not worried about that," John said. "Look at the crew. They seem to know what they are doing. They do this voyage frequently enough. I trust them to take us safely across these waters."

With the wind blowing through his thick hair, he looked confident enough.

"I am nervous about the voyage," said Paulo. "I'm not very good in boats. Every time I tried fishing from a boat I would always become seasick. In fact, I gave up fishing and never thought I'd be on this sea voyage. So far I'm okay. Let's hope the waters don't get rough."

He was my height and had a similar chocolate brown complexion to mine. He had narrowed his eyes and spoke softly in an unsure way, and I wondered what made him come on this journey.

Tony and Caetano were on the other side of the deck. They seemed to know some of the crew members and were busily talking to them. We walked over to join them. It turned out that Tony and Caetano had uncles in Mombasa. They would be working for the railway company as arranged by their uncles who were well settled in Mombasa. Paulo looked dismayed at that, for there was nothing certain waiting for him, and he *hoped* he could find a job in Mombasa or Nairobi. John and I were with Paulo in that we had no one to greet us in Mombasa and no jobs.

We were silent. We felt the cool breeze on deck. We rubbed our arms to warm ourselves. Night had fallen. We looked up to a sky lit up with many stars, and way out in the distance we saw another dhow or small ship with its lights shining. We were interrupted by the dinner call. We sat at the table next to the very small galley. I didn't have much of an appetite but ate the dinner and turned to see Paulo picking at his dinner while John gobbled up what was on his plate. We soon stood up, cleaned our dishes and rushed back on deck.

Tony and Caetano went to the cabin while John, Paulo, and I lingered on deck. We talked into the night. I shared with them my desire to work as a tailor in Nairobi. John didn't have any skills and was hoping to pick up any kind of work. Paulo was eager to become friends with Tony and Caetano because he wanted to work for the railway company. The night air was getting colder, and slowly we made our way to the cabin. Tony and Caetano were playing cards. John and Paulo joined in the game while I watched. I never liked playing card games. As the game became intense, we could feel the dhow heaving up and down. Paulo gave up and crawled into his bed with the hope that he would not get sick. The game ended, and we laid in our beds, holding onto the bed frames to the heaving of the dhow. We fell asleep. I dreamt about becoming a successful tailor; about the women I would dress and the suits I would make for the gentlemen of Nairobi. Next morning I thought about my dream and hoped I could make my dream come true.

Two weeks had gone by and we were still at sea. The calendar that Tony had stuck on his cupboard door pointed to Monday February 7. The voyage seemed endless. Sometimes we would see a ship or a dhow far in the distance—some would pass by near enough that we waved to their passengers. The crew informed us that we were more than half way through our journey. Depending on the wind we would likely see land in a week or so, but if the wind was not with us then it could be longer. I was getting bored and restless, as were the other fellows. But sometimes we were able to keep jovial. John was good at this.

On this one particular evening, we were in our cabin space telling jokes. John stood up and acted out his joke. He made different gestures with his hands, raised his eyes, and broadened his lips showing his teeth with every joke he told. We laughed loudly and with great joy as we encouraged him for more and more antics. Without warning, the tide turned, the dhow started heaving very high and it crashed down on the waters. We were thrown about in our cabin.

John went down with a thud. I was knocked back towards the cupboard at the head of my bed. Our suitcases slid from under our beds. Paulo unsteadily rushed to the bathroom. A crew member called from above, yelling at us to get into bed and hang on tightly to the edges of the frame. John finally came around and dragged himself to his bed with Tony's help. We clung to our beds as the heaving continued for hours—at least that is what it felt like. We eventually fell asleep to the gentle swaying of the dhow. Thank goodness for that.

The next morning, we woke up to the strong smell of vomit.

Paulo sheepishly told us that he didn't make it to the bathroom during the night. We ran up the stairs to tell the crew who silently gave us buckets of water to tidy up the cabin. Down we went and sent Paulo up to the deck to breathe in the fresh sea air while sipping on warmed ginger water to relieve his seasickness. With the cabin tidy and smelling clean, we joined Paulo on deck.

We checked out the vast horizon. The waters were unbelievably calm with the sun glistening on the gentle waves of the water. All was calm and normal. We gathered around on deck. We were back to telling stories, having lunch downstairs and the others spending the afternoon playing cards in the cabin. This time they were playing for money. I walked up to the deck and looked to the horizon, getting a bit worried about what awaited me. I watched the crew managing the sails. It was a puzzle to me to see how they moved this dhow along. There were men working the sails into perfect positions. I marvelled at them doing this job. My peaceful thoughts were interrupted by the loud noises and shouting from below. I went down to see Paulo and Tony arguing with each other while John and Caetano were standing back in silence.

"Stop shouting," I yelled at them. "Why are you arguing? You're playing a card game, no?"

"I lost, and I think it's because Tony is cheating." Paulo looked very angrily at me.

"How can you tell he's cheating?" I shouted back getting closer to Paulo.

"Sabby, you don't play cards, and you don't know what it's like to lose especially when you put money down."

I stepped back, and John took over. He grabbed Paulo by the arm and led him onto the deck while I talked with Tony and Caetano. They were not happy with the way Paulo reacted. They shrugged their shoulders and we walked up to the deck.

It was too hot and cramped down in the cabin area. There was not much air circulating. It felt damp most of the time. And that led to tempers rising when in the cabin area. Mostly, we were tired of being stuck in the dhow. So far, John's happy personality had helped us to get along with each other. He made light of every discomfort we experienced. The previous week we had an argument about the bathroom not being kept tidy and we could not figure out whose turn it was to clean it up. We accused each other until it came to a point of shouting and yelling while at the same time pushing each other around in this small cabin. We fell on our beds wrestling with each other. It had become tense. We were frustrated, sick and quite fed up with being in the dhow day in and day out.

John came to the rescue. He untangled himself from us, raised himself up as much as he could in the cabin without hitting his head, and in a deep loud voice he yelled that we were in this together and there was no way out until we docked in Mombasa. There was silence after he spoke. Caetano went to the bathroom to clean it up.

Our group was split in two. Tony and Caetano stayed together most of the time while John, Paulo and I were always together. Many nights we would climb up to the deck to take in the air and have some quiet time among ourselves. The cooler night air made it easy to sleep on deck. We whispered to each other, watching the dark sky lit up with millions and millions of stars. We'd fall asleep when the waters were calm. The crew was always very busy and did not like us staying on deck at night. They kept telling us to get back to our cabin.

It was easy to lose count of days at sea. I asked John how many more days and he shrugged his shoulders as though it didn't matter—and in a way he was right. We would get to Mombasa when the wind blew us there. But he informed me that the calendar showed that it was February 15. Even with the calendar, we might have lost track except that, thank goodness, every night Tony drew a line through the day that had passed. The trip would take as long as it would take, and the five of us were stuck together until Mombasa.

Then, one morning, we awoke with the crew shouting something about land in sight. We rushed up to the deck, and there in the far, far distance, we saw glimpses of land. We were hysterically happy. All five of us were hanging over the edge of the dhow. We broke out into singing as though our combined voices could push us more quickly to land. The crew was energetically working the sails to catch as much wind as they could. It was Thursday February 24, 1916.

At the far end of the deck, I watched this strange land in the distance and grew nervous. John came over and leaned against the rail beside me

"I wonder what'll happen to us in the new country, Sabby."

"Yes," I said. "I wonder too. We have to make it work for us, John. There is no going back without a lot of trouble."

On the other side of the dhow, there was Paulo getting sick over the edge. We left him alone until he came around. He had his ginger water close at hand. The crew had been a good lot and looked after us very well. Each one of us arrived in one piece with no lifelong scars or bruises, and our memories of this voyage would last a lifetime.

It took most of the day to get to Mombasa. As we drew nearer I looked at the dock. There were many men there. It stretched for miles. We steered to a slip on the far side of the dock, passing by the big cargo ships. We watched the men unloading boxes and boxes onto the dock. The *Monsoon Wind* was very tiny next to those big ships—it felt like a miracle that we made it across the Arabian Sea alive and well. We were now in the Port of Mombasa beside the Indian Ocean.

"Isn't this amazing?" said Paulo, marvelling at the activity.

"Yes, that was exactly what I was thinking. It looks very busy. I've never seen anything this grand. And, Paulo," I said putting my arm around him, "I'm very happy that you are feeling better."

"Incredible," said John. "There's no mistaking this for Goa."

I knew what he meant. The port in Goa was a fraction of the size. It had seemed busy to me as we left, but it was nothing compared to Mombasa.

The *Monsoon Wind* made its final jolt and it was securely tied up. It was time to find our land legs. We gratefully shook hands with each of the crew for bringing us across safely. We jumped out of the dhow with suitcases in hands. Each of us faltered. We caught ourselves feeling unsteady on land. We stopped for a while and found a bench to sit on until we were used to being on solid ground. Tony and Caetano came over to wish us well and walked towards their uncles who were waving to them on the other side of the fence. We decided to stand up and walk as slowly as possible until we felt steady with our land legs. It was hot and very humid. I looked at John and Paulo whose faces appeared wet with sweat just like mine. I wiped my face with my handkerchief, and then John, Paulo and I walked towards the main street to find a place to stay.

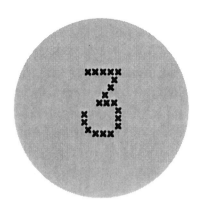

MOMBASA

The smells, the sounds and everything around us were unusual. It was sweltering hot, making us feel that the heat from the ground would swallow us. We continued walking on the main street. The people looked different. They weren't like anyone in Goa. We stopped to talk to some of them, but we didn't understand each other. Instead our talking with them became gestures, smiles and words spoken that neither understood. The surroundings were not anything like Goa. The street was crowded with people walking back and forth who seemed to be in a rush. Paulo, John and I stayed close together. We were confused and couldn't think properly. We walked for a while and then we saw the sign Mombasa Lodging. This had to be for us. Thankfully, we found a Goan at the front desk, and he put us together in a room on the second floor.

There were three beds with a chair next to each bed. In the corner was a large wardrobe divided into three sections with keys. A mirror was hooked on the door. There was a small table just below the window. In the distance, we could see the shimmering waters of the Indian Ocean. We took turns freshening up in the common bathroom in the hallway. Before we went out again, we stood in front of the mirror looking at ourselves. Paulo's face was back to its normal dark brown complexion, his black hair was neatly puffed towards his forehead, and with a change of clothes, he looked ready to face the world. As always, John appeared smart looking with a perpetual smile on his face, standing taller than either of us. I wore a sky blue shirt and a pair of navy blue trousers, and my face was cleanly shaven. All three of us, in our teens, looked courageous and ready for adventure. It was time to head out.

There were shops on either side of the street: groceries, a fruit and vegetable shop, an Indian sweets shop and small restaurants. Some were still open while others were closing up. We walked for a while trying to make sense of our surroundings. It would soon become twilight. We stopped at a small Indian restaurant. We ordered some food, took it to a round table, and quickly ate the chicken curry with rice and green beans covered in shredded coconut. It tasted very good. We drank many glasses of water and then had ice cream to cool us down. We didn't say much to each other. Instead we took in our surroundings and watched the people talking in a language unknown to us; though we did hear some familiar English being spoken. We watched the night sky from our table.

The server came over to tell us that it would be closing time soon. We talked with him. He pulled up a chair and sat down with us, sensing that we were new customers. He told the other fellow to close the restaurant while he listened to our stories.

We were alone with him. After about an hour, we left and thanked him for listening to us. We told him we would return for breakfast because he promised to introduce us to some other people who would possibly be able to help us out with our many questions.

We walked back to our lodging, inhaling the sea air; *this* at least felt the same as in Goa. But the atmosphere and people weren't the same. We had to be careful walking these streets only because we couldn't understand what was going on around us. It was foreign. We kept reminding ourselves that we were in Africa. We made our way to our room, as we continued talking. Once inside the comfort of our room, we prepared for a good night's sleep. We were tired and were soon in dreamland.

I awoke to loud sounds coming from our open window. I didn't know where I was, and it took me a while to realize that I was in Mombasa and not in Goa or aboard the *Monsoon Wind*. I eyed Paulo and John. They were more wide-awake than I. John was dressed while Paulo was partially dressed. I jumped off my bed and hastily put on my clothes. It quickly came back to me. These were my new friends.

"Sabby, it's time to explore. Paulo wants to go to the railway company," said John. "What do you want to do?"

I brushed past him and walked to the door heading for the bathroom.

"Remember, we're having breakfast at that same place we ate last night, and I want to find out about getting to Nairobi." I said, disappearing into the hallway. Hurriedly I returned, finished dressing, and we stepped out.

We stopped at the front desk to get directions to the railway company. I decided it would be a good time for me to find Pedro while Paulo was making enquiries about working there. I had a small parcel and letters for him from his parents. Our instructions were to turn left for a long walk towards the railway company. First, we stopped at the small Indian restaurant.

The server from last night recognized us and brought us chai and chapati.

"I'll introduce you to Kumar who will be here shortly," he said. "He'll tell you how to get to Nairobi. He knows people here." And with that he hurried off to serve other customers.

We waited and waited, but there was no sign of Kumar. Paulo became impatient. He stood up to leave. John decided to wait for Kumar while I joined Paulo.

"Let's meet up again at the lodging," John said, "later this afternoon if not sooner, for lunch maybe."

We agreed and walked in the direction of the railway company. Paulo appeared to be keeping pace with the crowd. People were in conversation, some were shouting while others were gesturing and talking in loud voices. This was very strange to us. We didn't say much to each other; instead, I tried to keep pace with Paulo. We passed by a street with many cloth shops.

"Look, Paulo," I said slowing my pace. "Some of these shops have suit lengths for men's clothing, and I can see a shop with brightly coloured cloths for women's clothing. I have to stop here."

"You stop. I'll carry on. I'll see you at the lodging this afternoon."

I watched Paulo go, moving with the people on the street. He had a spring to his walk and became part of the crowd. I turned around and went into the cloth shops. I talked with the men there, asking them about tailoring. During our conversations, they let me examine some suit lengths that were placed horizontally, one on top of the other. There were the varying shades of grey, blue and other light coloured suit lengths. At the back, I could see the tailors. One was at the machine while another was at the worktable chalking out some part of the suit.

While talking with the shop owners, some of whom were tailors, I found out that Nairobi was a bigger city and that there were places where one could work as a tailor or open up his own tailoring shop. I thanked the men for spending time with me and walked onto the street. The sun was brilliantly shining onto the pavement. I shaded my eyes with my hands; I wanted to see where I was going. I could feel the humidity, making it uncomfortable to walk.

I stopped by a shop that only sold cloths for women's clothing. These cloths were in rolls placed side by side and on top of each other. There were many different colours and patterns on each cloth. Some were plain solid colours while others had different kinds of patterns or flowers on them. This reminded me of the cloth shops in Margao, in Goa. I couldn't wait to get into tailoring. With my head filled with ideas and dreams, I continued walking towards the railway company, but I was distracted again as there were more tailoring shops to go into. This was where I belonged. I wondered what it would be like in Nairobi. It seemed as if the sun's heat was slowing my pace. I was getting very thirsty. I stopped at a small restaurant, bought a coconut drink, and sat on a stool at a table, sipping it. A couple of fellows joined me.

"Hello, my name is Joyoti. You are new around here. I haven't seen you here before. You see we come here regularly for an early lunch."

"I've just arrived from Goa. My name is Sabby. I'm finding it very different here. How long have you been living here?"

"I was born here. My parents came from Bombay when they were younger. By the way, this is my friend, Prateek. He too was born here. You said you came from Goa, that is Portuguese Goa, right?"

"Yes, yes. You know Goa, then?"

"A couple of fellows at work are from there. We hear their stories about Goa. Did you see the fort when you docked at the port? That is Fort Jesus, built by the Portuguese in 1593. Later it became a prison and still is."

"Oh my goodness, the Portuguese were here in Mombasa as well? That is good to know."

"When did you arrive?"

"Yesterday. That sea voyage from Goa was long and sometimes it became quite rough. But tell me about this place. There are many people around here, and everyone's in a hurry. I get tired seeing them rushing up and down the street. I want to go to Nairobi. How different is Nairobi from Mombasa?" I sipped on my drink waiting an answer.

They both laughed. Prateek's face lit up, and he began answering my question with great enthusiasm. I was told that it was very hot and humid in Mombasa but that Nairobi was at a higher altitude and the climate was much cooler. Because Nairobi was the capital, the people were more sophisticated there. The British had taken over the farms outside of Nairobi, and the main banks and offices were in Nairobi. Mombasa was a typical port city, and because the ships come and go, so do the different kinds of people who work on the ships. There were many Arab traders living in Mombasa. The freight trains transported goods from Mombasa to Nairobi and beyond to Uganda, its terminus being on the eastern shore of Lake Victoria. The line, known as the Uganda Railway, was only completed in 1901. There was a large railway depot in Nairobi.

"How long does it take to get to Nairobi by train?" I asked, watching them both sip at their sodas.

"It takes a whole day to get to Nairobi, but you can do it overnight. Some people take the risk and travel by freight train, but it can be tricky getting on a freight train. Isn't that right, Joyoti?" Prateek said, turning to his friend who agreed.

"Yes, you have to know who to contact, as few passengers are allowed to travel on these freight trains. Mind you, it's very uncomfortable in the freight trains," Joyoti said cautiously and in a disapproving voice.

"Tell me about the passenger trains," I said.

"Well, they are segregated of course and—"

"What does *that* mean," I asked.

They looked at each other for a moment before explaining it to me; I was shocked by what they told me.

Under British Protectorate rule, the Indians were allocated to live in designated areas. The Arabs were in another and then, of course, the British and the Europeans had taken over the best parts. The Africans were ignored and were left to their rural areas or the slums on the edges of Mombasa. As Indians, I was told, we could not socialize or mix with the British or the Europeans. They kept to themselves, and under pain of severe punishment, I was not to socialize with them or go to their areas. This segregation applied to train travel as well. The first-class section was reserved for the Europeans only and was positioned at the front of the train. Then there was the second-class section, for the Indian travellers. The Africans were at the back of the train in the third-class section.

I was sitting there looking at my feet because I didn't know what to say. It was like being hit in the stomach. I silently gasped for air taking in this information. Did I make the right move coming here and not going to Portuguese Mozambique? I understood train travel in different classes, but surely those who could afford it should to be able to travel in any class they wanted to. Joyoti interrupted my thoughts.

"Are you okay? It'll take you time to get used to it. We are used to it. We don't know any other way. But, be aware."

There was a long pause. Many questions came to my mind, but I did not say anything. Joyoti and Prateek tapped me on my hands, assuring me that I'd get used to this kind of living. They wished me well, and I watched them leave. I regained my calmness and observed my surroundings. There were no Europeans walking on the street. I put away my thoughts and re-entered the hustle and bustle of the crowds heading back to the lodging. It was too late to meet up with Pedro. I walked for quite a while and was hot and bothered with this liveliness around me. In the distance, I could make out John and Paulo, and there seemed to be someone else with them. I slowly ran towards them. Paulo was almost running towards me.

"Look who I found while I was at the railway company," said Paulo. "A fellow from your village. What do you think of that, huh?"

I could hardly believe it. I grabbed hold of Pedro's hand and we back slapped each other. It was good to see him. He was taller than me, had his black hair tightly combed back, and wore navy blue pants and a white shirt. His dark tanned face was radiant with a broad smile.

"I suppose Paulo told you I was distracted and stopped by the cloth shops. You're looking good. Living here agrees with you, huh? Come, come, let's go upstairs. I've something for you from your parents, some letters and a small parcel."

On the way up to our room, Paulo said, "Pedro wants us to go to his place on Sunday. He's going to introduce us to some Goans living here."

"That is wonderful of you, Pedro," added John with a wink.

I could feel the joy in Paulo's voice as the four of us climbed the stairs.

"Yes, we'll meet at the church for Sunday Mass," said Pedro. "And then afterwards come to my place for lunch. It'll be fun."

"That's great, Pedro. I can't wait to meet Goans and hear their stories about living here."

When we were back in our room, John told us that Kumar never showed up. He left about half an hour after we did and walked on the streets. He too had spoken with some fellows about living in Kenya. I thought to myself that this was good. We could share our stories, but for now, I needed to speak with Pedro and get his side of the story.

Pedro, in a friendly way, shoved me around, delighted to hear news about his family in Goa. He missed them very much. Paulo raised his eyes when Pedro talked about the segregation that we would have to adjust to while living in British East Africa. John nodded his head in agreement, but this time he was quiet—not the same fellow on the dhow who was always eager to create a funny story on any issue while the rest of us felt uncomfortable in the rowdy and tense situations on the dhow. Instead, he walked over to the wardrobe, opened his section and pulled out a bottle of Feni, Goan cashew liquor.

"What's that you got there?" asked Pedro. "My God, that looks like Feni. We can't find it here."

John smiled and handed the bottle to Pedro who held it like it was wrought of gold.

"I've been saving it for a special occasion," said John. "It's time to drink to our new African lives, don't you think Sabby and Paulo? Segregation or not, we'll make a go of it."

"Oh no!" I said. "There are no glasses. Never mind, let's drink from the bottle."

We each took turns at the bottle, talking about Goa and asking Pedro many questions about life in this country. He told us about his work and how he would never have had those opportunities in Goa. He loved what he did as a trainee engineer. His foreman was a Hindu fellow, Arun, born in Mombasa.

"Arun told me almost immediately when I met him, that as long as one keeps to the rules and doesn't make trouble there is a good life to be had here," Pedro said. "And that's what I do. That's my advice to you as well."

We quietly nodded in shocking silence. He left, telling us that we could talk some more on Sunday.

We arrived at the church in our suits for Sunday Mass. We noticed a mixed crowd of Europeans and Goans walking into the church. *This is unusual,* I thought after what we heard about segregation. Pedro arrived with his friends. Mass was in progress when we walked inside and we stood at the back. After Mass, we gathered on the grounds under the shade of a tree and were introduced to Pedro's friends and other Goans. We talked for a while, each one of them inviting us to drop by their homes. We left with Pedro, and it seemed like an endless walk in the blistering sun. I asked Pedro about the Europeans at Mass.

"Ahh, but did you notice that we Goans were towards the back of the church while the Europeans were in the front, and each one of them had seats and it was only the Goans who were standing. You see we have to stand to give the European a seat, and that's the way it is." Pedro said this as if it was natural and he accepted it without question.

"And they left after Mass," I said, "while we Goans stayed behind talking to each other. And everyone looks happy just like in Goa."

"Yes, it's a good life here. You will hear more when you meet some of our Goans at my home." said Pedro somewhat irritated that I wanted to know more about the Europeans; I was trying to figure out segregation and its practices.

We arrived at a street with rows of small houses on either side. Pedro pointed to his home somewhere in the middle of a long row of houses. He explained that these homes were for the workers of the Uganda Railway.

We made ourselves comfortable in his home. We drank African beer, which was bitter but good to quench the thirst. Then came the food that Pedro brought in from a Goan neighbour. She cooked for him on a daily basis. Other Goan neighbours joined in. We met some of them at Mass. It felt like I was back in Goa. Everyone gathered closer giving us advice—where to go and who to visit in Nairobi. They repeated the bit about segregation. It seemed that the rule was to stay low and not do anything that would cause trouble. I noticed that everyone was happy. We were talking, laughing and joking in this familiar crowd.

When I was alone with Pedro, he wanted to know more about his family. He had that distant look in his eyes as I talked about Goa. He was sad that his parents weren't there with him. Paulo and John joined our conversation. Paulo hadn't found work in

Mombasa and was informed to contact the railway depot in Nairobi. John was still trying to figure out what he wanted to do and decided to come to Nairobi with us.

Pedro seemed to think that we would be better off taking the passenger train and promised to help us get on one of these trains. But we wanted to get to Nairobi as soon as possible and were willing to take the freight train. The three of us looked at each other and almost together we said something that sounded: "A night on a freight train can't be any worse than a month on a dhow."

"All right, then. Be ready. It can happen within the next couple of days," Pedro said with a smile on his face as if he understood the sea voyage we went through.

We were about the last to leave Pedro's. Quite drunk, we felt on top of the world as we unsteadily made our way towards our lodging. We weren't paying attention to where we were going. It was a moonlit night. There were a few people walking on the street. We slowed down when we passed the people and then we continued our drunken conversation. Suddenly, out of nowhere, in front of us, were two fellows. They were tall and bulky. We could barely make out their shapes in the darkness. They were saying something to us. We could not understand what they said. They sounded aggressive and threatening. We gestured and tried to walk past them, but they moved from side to side. They stopped us from moving forward. One of them pushed me back, and I tried to duck the blows coming at me. I was hit and fell to the ground. John was also pushed around and went down. These fellows dug into our pockets, took our money and ran away. My head was spinning as I tried to sit up. John slowly did the same too. Paulo ran to us from behind a tree.

"Are you okay?" asked Paulo sounding somewhat timid. "As soon as I saw them attack you, Sabby, I ran for it, there behind that tree near the shop. Then I saw them push John down. This is bad."

"I'm in pain," John said. "They took our money, Paulo. Did you see that? Look at Sabby, he looks like he's been hit very hard in the face."

We stopped for a while to recover from this attack. No one was around except the three of us. It seemed strange. We were sure there would be a few people on the street, but there was no one to be seen. It felt scary. We stood up as quickly as we could and painfully and cautiously continued to walk towards our lodging, looking around to make sure no one else came for us. My face hurt, and John felt some pain in his right elbow. I didn't have much money on me, and neither did John. We had decided to go out with little money on us and hid the rest of our money in different pockets in our clothing in our wardrobe.

Once inside our room, Paulo became the nurse. He put a cold damp cloth on my face and helped John by gently tying his elbow with a piece of cloth to keep it from hurting anymore. We had a restless night. John jumped up twice, shouting, while I tossed and turned trying to fight off the blows coming at me. Paulo sat up with us and listened as we talked ourselves back to sleep.

As promised, at the end of the week, Pedro arrived at our place with good news. By that time, we were back to our normal selves and recovered from the shock and pain of being robbed. Pedro gave us each a piece of paper indicating that we had permission to board the overnight freight train in the dry goods carriage. We were to meet Pedro at around six in the evening at the station on Thursday. We looked at Pedro with gratitude whilst we made our way to our familiar small Indian restaurant nearby. We told Pedro our tale of robbery. He looked down at his sandalled feet, shifting them from side to side.

"I'm very sorry that it happened to you. Being as drunk as we were that night, I completely forgot to tell you to be aware of your surroundings." Pedro was solemn. "It's a horrible experience. You said you couldn't understand what they were saying; they were probably speaking Swahili. That's the African language we speak here. But these robberies happen now and again. Be careful when you're out at night."

"Someday, we'll probably look back and make a joke about it, especially with Paulo escaping the whole incident. Smart fellow to run away," I said, jostling Paulo.

"The language we cannot understand, it's Swahili, is it?" asked John.

"Yes, John. You said it right. You will be speaking it by the time I next see you in Nairobi." Pedro said, smiling at us. "Another adjustment, but this is an easy one, compared to that segregation."

That's for sure, I thought to myself as Pedro continued telling us about our train journey.

"Your train journey is a long one. It stops at a few depots to unload. Be very, very careful because fellows come in and out of the carriages. I've arranged for you to be in the carriage that will only unload in Nairobi and not before that. I'm sure you'll be fine. But be careful anyway. Oh yes, another thing, Sabby, there's a fellow going on holiday to our village in Goa. If you want to send anything home, bring it over on Thursday, and I'll make sure it gets to your parents."

"Thanks Pedro. I'll have letters for my parents and for my friends, Menino and Anton," I said.

When I turned to Paulo and John, I could tell that they were eager and maybe even nervous about this train journey.

Pedro stood up to leave. We could not thank him enough. We walked to our room, slowly and a bit heavy-hearted. We were uneasy about this train trip and hoped it would be safe and that we wouldn't meet any trouble. I was worried, and Pedro had reminded me of home in Goa. Tears filled my eyes. I avoided Paulo and John while in our room. I closed my eyes and fell asleep, to stop the feeling of loneliness that was taking hold of me. I missed Goa very much.

In the morning, I wrote several long letters.

On Thursday March 2, we were caught up in the commotion at the train station. There were many workers loading the carriages of the train. Pedro introduced us to the engineer, Arun, who would be taking us to our carriage. Before Pedro left, I handed over my letters. He put his hand on my shoulder and comforted me.

"You're in good hands with Arun. We've been working together since I arrived in Mombasa a few years ago. He will make sure you're safe," Pedro said, handing over this large box. With curiosity and hesitantly I accepted the package.

"It's nourishment for your train trip. Remember, that food you ate at my place on Sunday prepared by my neighbour? Well, she made some snacks for you, and I put in some water bottles for each of you."

"Pedro, this is wonderful. You not only get us on the train, but you provide us with snacks. I owe you a suit, and a few shirts. I'll not forget what you have done. The next time you are in Nairobi, huh?"

Pedro smiled as he walked closer to me.

"Sabby, it's wonderful to see someone from our village, and it is natural to help out when I can. That's all this is. By the way, I look forward to that suit anyway. Paulo and John, good luck in Nairobi and stay safe."

We bade farewell to Pedro and followed Arun to the front of the train. Our carriage was next to the caboose.

"This is where you will rest for your journey," he said. "Nothing special. Make yourselves comfortable among these bags and boxes of goods. I may drop by through the night when we make some stops on the way. If not, I'll see you when we arrive in Nairobi. One more thing, the train will pull out of the station at around seven o'clock and will arrive in Nairobi at ten o'clock the next morning." He slid shut the door, it was dark. We continued talking for a while.

I was emotionally and physically exhausted. Our time in Mombasa caught up with me. We had stayed there for two weeks. On February 29, I had spent a whole day at The Tailors' Club and was given good advice from some of the tailors. We celebrated the leap year and they wished me luck during this leap year. My thoughts were interrupted with the movement of the train. As soon as the train began chugging out of the station, I laid down on a layer of large bags that felt like a good mattress. I fell asleep to the gentle swaying from side to side. Paulo and John continued their conversation.

I woke up to the morning sun finding its way through the slits of the freight carriage. It was daylight and we still had a few hours before arriving Nairobi. Paulo and John were awake and once again we talked about our time in Mombasa and ate what snacks were left in the box that Pedro gave us. It seemed we weren't disturbed during the night. Finally, the train was pulling into the station. Arun let us out and recommended that we make our way towards the Indian bazaar where we would find accommodation—he suggested Mrs. Sequeira's Lodging.

It felt quieter and less hectic than Mombasa. The streets were wider, and it wasn't humid but pleasantly warm. We walked towards the Indian bazaar. We took our time looking at our new surroundings. It was very different from Mombasa. This was a city with businessmen walking around with purposeful strides. There was a calm sense of everyone going about their own way without much loud talking but polite conversations with each other. We found the Sequeira Lodging. We were once again in a room together. Mrs. Sequeira, we were told, provided meals and that made us happy that we would be eating Goan meals. We settled down, refreshed ourselves and were soon back on the streets to find our way around.

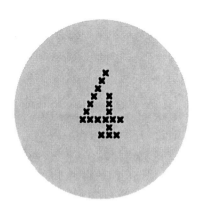

NAIROBI

Each day in the capital brought in new experiences, worry, and tension. Paulo, John and I went our separate ways to look for work. It was the rainy season, but Nairobi saw nothing like the monsoon rains of Goa. I walked into each of the tailoring shops and talked with the owners to find employment as a tailor. It was May before I started tailoring at the men's cloth shop, Ali Bux Ltd., on Bazaar Street. I was his only tailor. I had to visit him many times before he agreed to rent space at the back of the shop. He didn't pay me a regular wage. I had to earn my own wages from tailoring. But we agreed that he would send customers to me when they bought suit lengths from him, and I liked that arrangement.

Paulo and John had similar difficulties finding work. Paulo, within three months of continually visiting the railway company, was working as a mechanic. John, in early August, started work as a bartender at the Norfolk Hotel—for Whites only. In the evenings we would talk about our new life in Nairobi. It was different all right, much more different for John than for Paulo or I. John was learning to become a bartender and only served Europeans, for no one else was allowed in the Norfolk Hotel.

Every morning, I left early for work. I walked on a pavement wide enough for people to move in both directions. I sometimes stopped to look at the buildings. They had awnings jutting out onto the pavement that provided shade from the sun and protection from the rain—though, so far there had been remarkably little rain. The buildings were of different designs from those in Goa, British as opposed to Portuguese. On Government Road, some of the buildings rose taller than others, but most were painted white and looked brighter in the sun. By lunchtime, the sun settled on these buildings, and I felt the glare of the whiteness coming from these structures. It was a relief to walk under the shade of the awnings. The pavements weren't crowded, and there were a few cars, more bicycles and some carts on the roads.

I noticed the people walking on the pavement: some men were dressed in suits—a few with hats while others were dressed in shirts and trousers. The European women wore beautifully designed straw hats that matched their long dresses while the Indian women wore colourful saris. The people were confident and walked boldly. I saw Europeans and Indians but not many Africans. There was little interaction. Everyone silently walked to wherever they were going. It was different on Bazaar Street. We looked at each other with a smile and a greeting. The wide street was lined with low, one-story buildings with awnings.

Every day there was something different to notice and get used to. I liked tailoring in Ali's shop. I knew I belonged in such a place. I would walk in the shop, and on either side were glass cabinets with suit lengths. There were different shades of grey, blue, black, and beige, neatly piled one on top of the other. A perfect men's suit cloth shop.

One day in November, I arrived at eight o'clock in the morning, and Ali was already attending to customers. I saw him showing suit lengths that he had partially spread out on the delicately carved polished wooden table in front of the cabinet. I heard him explaining the quality of the cloth and encouraging the customers to touch and feel the suit length to enable them to make a choice. They looked like a father and son, probably there to purchase the son's first suit. When Ali saw me, he introduced us.

"Meet Sabby, he's a very good tailor. You may want to talk to him about making the suit."

"Hello," I said. "I see Ali is helping you choose a suit length. When you're ready, come see me at the back there. I will be happy to make the suit." Then I shook their hands and walked towards my sewing room.

My sewing room. Each time I thought of it, it made me feel good—my own sewing room in Nairobi. I had a good arrangement with Ali. It worked well for both of us. I walked to the wardrobe at the back wall and brought out a suit jacket, placing it on the long worktable in the middle of this small room. I reached out for the measuring tape from the box on the worktable and put it around my neck with the ends dangling in the front. Now I was ready to begin sewing. The suit jacket needed adjustments at the shoulders. With the needle still in the shoulder part, I continued hand stitching the shoulder area.

This suit jacket was for one of my regular and favoured customers, Nathoo Ram. Ali brought him to me during my first month at his shop. I'll never forget that day. My thoughts were interrupted with a knock on the glass cabinet counter top that separated the front area from the sewing room. I looked up and there were the customers I had met a few minutes ago.

"We bought this suit length," said the older gentleman introducing himself as Sylvester Dias. He placed the suit length on the counter top. "I'd like you to make it into a suit for my son."

"Happy to meet you Mr. Dias. I recently came from Goa. We can talk later about that. But let's see what I can do for your son."

His son was a young adult, average height, with light brown eyes, a walnut skin complexion and a slight frame. He looked shy and uneasy, and as soon as he caught my eye he put his head down.

"Hello, young man. What's your name, and tell me, is this your first suit?"

"I'm Robert, and yes it's my first suit," he said in a soft voice.

"Robert, come here, and let me explain how this is done." I brought him from around the counter cabinet closer to my worktable. His father stood back while his son moved with me. I explained the process of taking measurements and that he would have to come in for two fittings before the suit was ready for pick up.

"Will this suit look good on me, and is it the right colour for me?" Robert asked in a hesitant voice and with his back to his father.

I unravelled some of the suit length and asked him to stand closer to the light in front of the mirror. I draped the cloth over his shoulder and near his face.

"I think the navy blue highlights your skin tone and brings out the colour of your eyes. You'll look handsome. What do you think?"

He looked uneasily at himself, shyly smiled in agreement and quickly added that he liked the colour while glancing at his father. He admitted that his father chose the colour. He wasn't sure it was the right one for him. His father, in the background, stood firm and proudly looked at his son. I proceeded with the taking of the measurements, writing each measurement carefully in my new customer notebook. We made an appointment for the first fitting in two weeks.

Mr. Dias and I talked a bit about Goa. He was pleased with how I attended to his son. He said that he would come the next time to be measured for a suit. They left happier and more relaxed.

I finished the hand stitching on Nathoo's suit jacket, wrapped it around the hanger, and placed it in the wardrobe. To my surprise and in perfect timing, in walked Nathoo.

"Hello Sabby. I'm here for my fitting."

"Ahh, Mr. Ram. The jacket is ready for you to try on. The shoulders may need adjustments. Here, put it on."

"Call me Nathoo. I like the way you make my suits. You're a good tailor."

"Thank you, Mister... I mean Nathoo. This is my work. When I see the suit fits perfectly on my customer, then I know I made a good suit and the customer is happy."

"That's why I come to you for my suits. Now have you thought about what I said to you last week? You know about opening up your *own* tailoring shop."

"Yes. I've made enquiries, and I've added the costs. It'll be difficult. I have been doing tailoring for a short while. I need more customers."

"Look," he said. "We can't talk details here. Meet me tomorrow evening at the Indian Palace restaurant on River Road."

"Yes all right." I held the jacket for him and he slipped his arms in. It fitted perfectly. "How does the jacket fit? It's good at the shoulders. What about the length?"

"Yes, the jacket feels comfortable. Maybe the length could be shorter. The styles keep changing. Let's keep up with the current style. The trousers fit well, no?" I nodded and he took off the jacket. "When will the suit be ready? I don't have much time now. I have to rush to my office. See you tomorrow?"

He was halfway to the front door before I had an answer for him.

"It'll be ready for pick up next week. Yes, see you tomorrow." I said loudly as I watched him walk out of the shop.

I was in a state of anxiety, and with some uncertainty I thought it crazy to *consider* opening my own tailoring shop after such a short time in Nairobi. Ever since Nathoo put the idea to me, I had been working on a plan, and the costs increased each time I looked at it. I would need another sewing machine and space for a fitting room with a door. The shop, I thought, would look like Ali's only with slight differences. The rent would, of course, be much higher than what I was currently paying. And I knew that my earnings and savings wouldn't cover the initial costs. *Maybe*, I thought, *I should wait till next year. Let's see what Nathoo has in mind for me.*

The next day, I left early for home. I freshened up and changed into a dark blue suit, a white shirt and a navy blue tie. I regarded at myself in the mirror and decided I looked like a businessman. I headed out towards the Indian Palace restaurant. Within half an hour, I was walking towards the back of the restaurant to join Nathoo at a round table draped with a maroon linen tablecloth. The aromas of the different spiced meals filled the air, making me hungry. I was ready for a meal. It wasn't crowded. There were a few groups of people deep in their conversations, but it wasn't too loud as to drown out what we wished to discuss. Nathoo stood waiting for me with a broad smile. He had a butter-skinned complexion, and brandy brown eyes that meant business. He gripped my hand firmly and then we sat down. As I took a sip of water, the server brought chicken biryani and two vegetable dishes to our table. I followed Nathoo and spooned out portions onto my plate. He wasted no time. By my second mouthful he started talking about opening my own shop.

"I know you won't be able to cover all the costs until business picks up," he said. "This is where I can help you. I can refer people to you. Already, my friends and family come to you. We'll come to you no matter where you go. Why not have your own shop instead of renting the back of someone *else's* shop?"

I swallowed a spoonful of chicken biryani—it tasted good. I stopped to drink some more water, while Nathoo continued eating the vegetables on his plate, waiting for my response.

"Yes, I *want* to do that. You say you can help me. I'll have to go to the bank to get a loan. Can you tell me which bank will give me a business loan?" I felt nervous asking this, for it made me feel young and inexperienced.

Nathoo had a puzzled expression. He put down his spoon, and took a large gulp of water.

"Now, it'll be difficult for you to get a loan from the bank with its requirements and references. You're new here, and you don't know many established people. And besides, preference is *always* given to the Europeans. Your application will be at the bottom of the pile. The banks are out of the question." He sounded firm as though there was no doubt at all to what he said.

That was when I finally figured out what he was proposing.

"Are you saying that *you* can lend me the money?"

Nathoo gave me a nod and smiled, letting me absorb his proposal. I was uncomfortable not knowing what to say next. We both continued eating.

Eventually I said, "I've heard about your connections to the business community and that you own a few businesses. You're well off, why would you want to help me?"

"I like you, Sabby. You work hard. My friends and family praise your tailoring. There aren't many tailors like you. Yes, I can lend you money."

He explained that he ran his family business, which bought and sold properties in Nairobi. He had been running it for a few years. The Indians, he told me, had difficulties in securing loans from the banks. Hence Nathoo expanded the business to give loans to purchase property. By now they had started lending money to prospective businesses. He talked with Ali, and he found out that I increased my customers quite substantially since I started tailoring there.

"I think a loan to your tailoring shop is a good investment for our company. Also, I believe you want your own shop. I can see it in your eyes. You have the determination to make your tailoring business a success."

I was taken aback, and we looked at each other in silence. I saw his calculating business mind and an earnest look in his eyes. I was trying to make sense of what he said to me. Ali knew Nathoo Ram and had nothing but praise for him. I had a gut feeling of trust for Nathoo. We finished eating and put aside our plates.

"Figure out the total costs," he said. "What you can put in and how much you would need to borrow? We can make a financial agreement of monthly payments. What do you think?"

"This will take me some time. You know, finding a suitable place to rent that will be an attractive tailoring shop." I likely sounded hesitant because I felt I was rushing into this arrangement. I wanted to slow down and carefully think through this proposal.

"Don't wait too long," he said, tapping my hand. "It's the weekend. Think about what I've offered you. Another thing, take a walk along Gulzaar Street. I can see you on Gulzaar Street; watch for vacant shops and put the word out that you are looking to rent a shop there. Talk to Ali."

I smiled as I imagined my tailoring shop with my own sign in the front. Nathoo looked satisfied, for he knew he had convinced me. We ordered chai and changed our conversation to living in Nairobi. This was the only place Nathoo knew. In between sips of chai, he told me about the restaurants, cafés and hotels that we were not allowed to go into—the ones reserved for Whites Only.

In the office and government buildings, I was told, there were separate washrooms for Whites and Non-Whites. On vacation, Nathoo would go to Mombasa and Malindi—a short ferry ride from Mombasa. He owned a couple of holiday guest-houses there. They were located in the Indian area with our own beaches, for we dared not set foot onto the beaches where the Europeans had *their* holidays in the lavish hotels overlooking their beaches.

I shook my head. "This is confusing, trying to figure out how to live by this kind of rule of law. And what about the Africans? It's their country after all."

"They're ignored and treated as savages," said Nathoo. "They're left to their reserve lands. The British have claimed this country as a Protectorate of Britain."

"But I do see *some* Africans in the city," I said.

"Ah yes, some work in the households or do other work in the city. I've two of them working for me in my home. It's important to treat them with respect and pay them a good wage. They're seeing their country being transformed without their involvement. You know, in time, that'll change." He had a distant look in his eyes when he said that.

Nathoo's expression told me that we should not continue along this line of conversation. Still, I thought about how I would adjust to this kind of living. The more I heard about segregation, the more alarmed I became. I curiously considered how long it would take me to become content and hardened to these disturbing realities.

Most of the people had left the restaurant. According to custom, Nathoo picked up the bill because he invited me. The night had descended, and I could see the moon shining its light on us through the window.

"I've given you a lot to think about," said Nathoo. "I noticed the look of concern and worry on your face when I explained the segregation we have to live with. You'll learn to put it aside. Concentrate on your business."

"I understand. Is this what all the non-Europeans do here?"

"Yes, yes. We work within our own areas, and in a strange way, we're helping the British change this place. Mind you there are Goans working in government. They're good at government work even if their bosses are Europeans. I'm sure you've already heard their stories."

"That's right. I'm getting to know them at our Sunday custom of going to Mass and then socializing at different Goan homes. They've become used to this kind of living. They're content, but they don't talk much about this segregation."

"Yes, it's difficult to talk about it, but in time you'll get used to it. Put your mind on your business. Continue being the good tailor you are, and you'll prosper."

We left with a promise to meet again in a couple of weeks to talk about his offer.

That night, I was more awake than asleep. By that time, I had my own room, for John and Paulo had moved out to their own places—Paulo near the railway company and John a couple of streets from me. The hardwood bed had a thin mattress that felt more uncomfortable that night than it had before. I couldn't sleep. I stood up and paced the room, catching glimpses of my worried self in the mirror hanging off the door. I opened the wardrobe and brought out my plan from the top shelf. They were scribbles on pieces of paper. I sat at the table and stared at them.

Once again I sorted out the figures in columns and put down estimates of the different costs in my notebook. It was a good plan, but I needed to make adjustments. I went to the window of my room. The street was empty and dark, but the gentle light of the moon made it feel peaceful. I went back to the table and worked with the numbers on my plan.

I can do it with Nathoo's help, I thought. I have to wait for a year. By then I hope to have enough customers to pay for the higher rent, sewing machines and two more tailors.

I closed my notebook and put it away in the wardrobe. I turned off the light and crawled onto the bed. I tossed and turned and then ended up staring at the ceiling. There was a small lizard moving hesitatingly along the top edge of the wall. I smiled and turned on my side with thoughts of Goa, thinking about Mai and Pai and how they would advise me. I thought too about Mr. Fernandes my tailoring teacher. He would have liked Nathoo Ram. Apart from being businesslike, Nathoo had a soft side to him. He appeared confident, yet friendly. I trusted him. He genuinely wanted to help me. In my mind I saw a sign—S. Mendes Ltd. Tailoring Establishment—in front of my own tailoring shop as my drowsy eyes closed and I finally fell asleep.

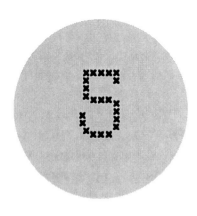

MOVING FORWARD
WITH MY DREAM

Between my November meeting with Nathoo and December, the time was entirely taken up with a rush of Christmas orders. Nathoo understood that my untried business plan had to be put on hold for the time being and besides there were no vacant shops on Gulzaar Street.

I was late for Sunday Mass on this warm February morning. I joined Paulo and John standing at the back of the church just inside the door. After Mass, we walked towards Paulo's place at the Railway Housing Complex for the day. Paulo shared a two-room house that had a small bathroom and kitchen at the side with an outside toilet room at the end of the small backyard. The living room had a small sofa near the window. Because it was Sunday, we rearranged the room with three tables put together in a row and a colourful tablecloth spread across that made it look like one long table.

A few of the neighbours gathered, bringing in dishes of food that were placed on this long table. There were beef rolls in a spicy curry sauce, *soropatel* [spiced pork meat, mixed with pork liver, heart and tongue], curried vegetables, meat cutlets and pilau rice. Tucked away at the end were pieces of mango and guava in a large bowl. There was beer, water, and coffee. I looked forward to this day among Goans. All was well. We ate, drank, talked, laughed, and felt and acted as if we were back in Goa. Once we had eaten, we re-arranged the tables in sections.

Some played cards while others played carom. John, Paulo and I moved to the backyard, drinking beer and taking turns in exchanging our news of the past week. John seemed impatient to share his news. In hushed tones he told us.

"The Europeans own this country, never mind the Africans. Europeans feel they are *entitled* to it. That's what they say. British East Africa will be white before too long. White Kenya they talk of. Anyone who is not white will live in their own areas with their social clubs. We'll live separately."

We glared at him.

"But John," Paulo said, "we're *already* doing that now. Tell us, how do they treat you? What it's like to be with the Europeans?"

"Look, I work for them," he said. "I serve them drinks, all kinds of liquor, beer and cocktails. I hear what they're saying. Some of what they say doesn't make sense to me."

What he told us was unsettling. Paulo and I were silent for a while.

"I don't like this making of a White Kenya. This country belongs to the Africans," I said. "This isn't right. Surely, some of them must think that, no?"

And I thought, *this is simply talk coming from me. We cannot do anything about this.*

"Who knows," said John. "For most of them, I'm just their bartender and that's it. No conversation with them, Sabby. There are a couple of fellows who sit at the bar, and we occasionally share jokes. I don't get into serious talk. These fellows are kind, but as for the others, I'm the bartender. I serve them their drinks." John waited expecting a response of some kind from either Paulo or I, but what was there to say?

John continued to tell us about the formal atmosphere. The wall behind the bar was stocked with different kinds of liquor and beer. The friendly fellows usually sat on plush barstools in front of the bar. The lounge area had richly designed leather chairs and long sofas with intricately carved tables in front of the sofas and beside the chairs. The drinks were served in the appropriate way, and no social conversation was permitted unless spoken to. In this way John was able to overhear their conversations. He was almost like a fly on the wall. They hardly noticed him.

Paulo looked at him in dismay. He told us about how different it was at the railway company—everyone picking and prodding at the machines yet talking and joking with each other.

"It's working with the different parts of the engine. Ah, but we're all Indians and a few Africans. I don't see any Europeans in the engine room. We're learning on the job. We're dressed in mechanic uniforms. I like the work. At lunch time we go outside, sit under the shade of a tree and we eat our lunch."

"Look at you, Paulo," I said. "You smile with enthusiasm when it comes to work. That's good. For me, it's the owner, Ali and I. He sells the suit lengths at the front of the shop and leaves me alone to do my tailoring at the back. I like it that way. I can concentrate and work on the suits without any interruptions. I'm busy. My customers are like us—no Europeans come into the shop. I don't have much time for conversation, except when the customers come in."

We were interrupted by a couple of fellows asking us to join them in a card game, while another group wanted us to play carom. I joined the carom group. John and Paulo played cards. Money was exchanged during the card game. But carom was my game. It was good fun. We shouted with joy over our wins and poked fun at our losses. I didn't pay attention to what John and Paulo were up to. Towards the end of the afternoon, when it was time to leave, I invited Paulo and John to my place on Wednesday. I needed their opinions, their advice and, in some strange way, their approval of my business plan. Paulo walked with John and I towards the end of his street.

"I like Nairobi, and I like the work at the railway company. John, I don't know how you work with the Europeans," Paulo said with his arms around us.

"Yeah, I don't think I'll get any European customers in my tailoring shop," I said, thinking to myself that I was glad I didn't have to deal with what John was going through.

"Fellows, it's a job," he said. "There's something else. I have to use the back door to get inside the hotel. Once inside, I quickly walk to the dressing room, change into my suit and then go to the Bar Lounge. It feels strange entering the hotel from the back door," John said standing back to look at us. We stopped and turned towards him with our faces flushed and angry.

"John! That would make me angry," I said, my voice raised. "But wait, I forget, you can't say anything to them. Follow the rules, and all will be well. Is this what we came here for?"

"What can we do, Sabby? We didn't know it would be like this, did we? We don't have the power; they do. Look, let's not talk about this anymore. It's getting late. I've got to go," John said as though he had given up hope of being treated equally.

I looked at him with some understanding. He needed the job.

"Okay, okay, but we must talk about this; we need to support each other. Let's not talk about it for now. See you both on Wednesday evening at my place. I need your advice and suggestions."

We waved to each other and went our separate ways.

I had much to think about. I kept to the rules as there was no other way to live in Kenya. John was right. There was nothing much we could do. I would see the Europeans on the streets, going into the cafés, or the buildings where they worked. We did not look at each other on the street. I looked straight ahead, and so did they. I lived and worked in the Indian area. I treasured Sundays because I was able to socialize with Paulo and John. We also met and became familiar with more Goans who were comfortably settled in Nairobi. Many of them had become my customers, which made me happy.

During the week, I thought about how Paulo and John would react to my plan. Before I shared my new business plan with Ali, I wanted my friends to know about it and hoped that they would be with me on my business plan. On Wednesday they arrived at the shop together, and I waved at them to come to the back.

"Give me a minute while I tidy up here. How are you fellows doing?" I asked while I put away the chalk, scissors and picked up the pieces of loose cloth on the floor.

"All's well with me. Oh, I have some letters for you, Sabby. Pedro sent them with Arun, the engineer from the freight train. Remember him?" Paulo was cheerful when he gave me the letters.

"How can I forget, Arun? I hope one is from Pedro. You remember I sent him a couple of shirts sometime ago. When he comes to visit us, I will take his measurements for a suit. Thanks for these letters. Great, I'll read them later." I put them away in my jacket pocket.

John was quiet. He didn't say much. I finished up, and we walked out on the street towards home. It was evening. I looked up at the sky and saw the traces of stars beginning to appear. As we came closer to my place, I told them that Mrs. Sequeira was preparing dinner for us. They smiled as they all too well remembered her delicious meals.

"Let's see what she has cooked for us today. John, are you up to a good Goan meal?" I hoped to cheer him because he looked sad.

"Anytime, Sabby. I'd love a Goan meal right now. I've brought some beer." He showed me the bag he was holding.

I knocked on Mrs. Sequeira's door. She handed me a large box wrapped with paper that I carefully carried to my room. Inside the box there were three dishes, pork vindaloo, saffron rice, and curried green peas. The room was filled with the aroma of the blend of spices coming from the opened box. Wrapped separately were mango pieces in a bowl. *Perfect.* I spread the dishes on the table while Paulo fetched plates and spoons from the small cupboard next to the wardrobe. We sat down to eat, and John handed over the beer. We were hungry and while enjoying the meal I broke the silence and told them about my conversation with Nathoo Ram. There was a tense silence. Paulo was fidgety while John was thoughtful.

"How can you trust this fellow?" asked Paulo. "He's only been your customer for a short while. We're new here." His forehead was crinkled with worry.

"You're rushing into this," said John. "I'm with Paulo on this one."

I became defensive. "Nathoo is one of my first customers. The shop owner, Ali Bux, brought him to me. Since that first time, I've made him suits and casual trousers. I sew for his friends and his family."

"Why do you need a bigger shop?" asked Paulo and stood up to pace the room.

"It's more that feeling of ownership. It'll be *my* shop with *my* sign."

Paulo sat down again, and we returned to the excellent flavours of the pork, rice and curried peas. I drank some beer, while Paulo and John were distressed.

"This Nathoo fellow, what's he like?" John wanted to know more.

"He's a business man. He's rich—I assume from his business dealings. He's tall, a kind face, smiles broadly when he's pleased or should I say when things go his way. He seems to want to help people like us to be successful in business." I could hear the admiration in my own voice.

"I don't know much about business dealings," John said. "Sometimes I hear the Europeans at the hotel talk about signing contracts, that the business deal is a good one or a bad one. It doesn't make sense to me. All I can say, Sabby, be careful. Make sure that you're not taken advantage of." John sensed that I had made up my mind and he could not stop me.

"Yes, John, I have to think about that. If he lends me money, then he owns that percentage of my business. I wanted to go to the bank, but he pointed out that I wouldn't get a loan from the banks. Europeans are given first choice while the rest of us will not be considered for a loan."

They were surprised at what I had shared with them.

We put the dishes aside and ate the mangoes, the pulp was sweet and the juice dissolved in our mouths. This was a sweet ending to a delicious meal. I took hold of their hands when we were done and looked directly into their eyes.

"This is my dream. I'm close to making it happen. I wanted to hear your opinions. I understand your concerns and worries. We're in a new country, working with people who are not Goans. I need you to stand by my decision."

I let go of their hands, and we silently sat on our chairs. John spoke first, his voice calm.

"Your face lights up when you talk about your dream. I can't help you make your decision, but I can listen and tell you how I feel about the risk you're taking." He folded his hands across his chest gazing deep into my eyes.

"Please, be careful, Sabby," said Paulo. "We're here to help each other."

With that the three of us formed a circle, embraced and promised to look out for each other as we adjusted to living in Nairobi. Once they left, I flopped down on my bed with various thoughts swirling in my mind. But soon I was on my feet, cleaned the dishes and put them away. I walked to the window and looked at the stars. They always brought peace to me and inspired me to carry on.

The next day, I jubilantly walked to work. It was a drizzly rainy day, but it did not dampen my spirits, and I almost ran to Ali's shop, brushing past the people on the street. I turned round the corner onto Bazaar Street and there was Ali unlocking the door to the shop. I slowed down to catch my breath. I wanted to appear calm and talk to him in a slow and appropriate way. He saw me, smiled and greeted me.

"Quick, Sabby, get out of the rain. Let's go in."

We walked in, smoothing the drizzle out of our clothes and at the same time watching the rain from the comfort of being indoors. Ali walked behind the counter while I hesitated and waited for him to turn around. He sensed I was still standing at the counter and turned around. We talked about nothing really important for a few moments. Then I informed him about my business plan with Nathoo. His dark brown eyes widened; he straightened his broad shoulders and listened carefully to what I had to say.

"Nathoo is a very good businessman. He's reliable and will not hassle you. He understands business. You know, the ups and downs? Remember that because you will have times when the business will not do well." Ali's respect for Nathoo was clear.

"You brought Nathoo to me," I said. "I'm grateful for that. He's a good customer, and he brings other customers to me.

Now he wants to help me open up my own shop. I should trust him, right?"

"Absolutely. He helps other people with their businesses. He's highly regarded and well liked in the community. I wouldn't hesitate to do business with him," said Ali.

"That makes me very comfortable. Now I've to follow through with my plan. First, I have to find a shop to rent. Do you know who owns any of the buildings on Gulzaar Street?"

"Yes, I know Mr. Desai who owns two buildings. I'll put a word out for you. I know the one renter who will be leaving next year. I can talk with Mr. Desai for you, right? I'll be sorry to see you go."

"Thanks Ali," I said. "You've been good to me. You allowed me to rent the space at the back and then some of your customers come to me. I'm very grateful for the business. I am a bit concerned and excited about being in my own shop."

He clapped me on the shoulder. "You're a good tailor. I know because you have made suits for me and I've heard nothing but praise for the way you make the suits. I'm not sure that I can find another tailor to take your place. If not, I'll send my customers to you."

"You're too kind." I could feel emotions thickening my voice. "I must get back to sewing. Let's talk at lunchtime."

I was worried that Ali would not be happy with my leaving. But then, I remembered when I first met him. I had to convince him that I would not be any trouble for him and that I would help his business. I know I did that, for more and more customers came to the shop, especially my Goan customers.

At lunchtime, Ali and I looked at the two shops. I was surprised to see the good condition they were in. They both had almost everything I needed, but I preferred 60 Gulzaar Street. It simply gave me a good feeling. Either of them would be good for a long-term rental.

"Well, what do you think?" Ali said. "You have two good shops to choose from."

"Number 60 is my choice. Can I talk to the owner?" I was overjoyed now.

"He'll be here at around closing time. He's showing some other people these shops."

"Let's keep our fingers crossed."

"You're moving fast. Don't show *too* much interest. He may raise the rent higher. Think carefully about how much you'll be able to pay. Negotiate with him. And another thing, you don't have to leave right away. Take it slow." That was good advice from Ali.

"You're right, of course. I mustn't appear too enthusiastic," I said as I returned to my sewing.

As I finished up at the back, Ali brought in the owner of the shops to meet me. His name was Barun Desai. We talked for a while, and then we walked to the shops on Gulzaar Street. Ali did not accompany us. This time I carefully looked at each shop. I still chose 60 in my mind.

We began negotiating the rental charge. It was becoming a tough conversation. I was tense because I wanted this one shop. I tried very hard not to show it. I talked about the differences in the shops. Soon, we began negotiating for my chosen shop. Each time I negotiated, Mr. Desai wrote in his notebook, making calculations and responding with a counter offer. I did the same. This back and forth continued for three different rental charges. Finally, we agreed on my offer. It was a bit higher than what was in my business plan, but I felt very good in this shop and was sure that I could make it work for me.

Through a gentleman's agreement, we shook hands on this deal. He left me alone in the shop while he attended to another fellow who had come to look at the other shop. I stood at the entrance giddily looking at my new place of work. It was almost the same as Ali's shop. It was perfect. Mr. Desai returned and told me that the shop would be available next June. We shook hands once again.

June 3, 1918. I thought. *By then I will have enough money for rent and sign and machines and two tailors.*

I left to go back to Ali's shop, hoping he was still there. I wanted to shout out the news or I would burst. I needed to tell someone immediately. I turned round the corner and saw Ali locking up the shop. I ran towards him, shouting his name. He stopped, saw me and waited for me. Breathless, I gave him the news.

"I got it. Thank you, Ali. I think you put in a good word for me. Didn't you?"

"Yes, I did. You are a good tailor, and I want nothing but the best for you. Are you happy with the arrangements?"

"I'm paying more than I wanted to. After haggling, I negotiated the rent closer to my plan. There's something special about that shop. I can feel it. Thank you, Ali."

"Now tell me my bad news," he said. "When will you move?"

"June 3, 1918. I will have a whole year to save money. In the meantime, I have to increase my orders."

I said that I was sorry to leave him and that he had been very good to me. Then I added that I wanted to take the risk of being on my own. The shop was big enough that would allow me to have two other tailors for the extra orders that have been coming in.

"You're a good tenant. Remember, I didn't have a tailor before. You convinced me to have you here. Who knows? I may decide not to have anyone else here and instead send the business to you. Gulzaar Street is only the next street. That may work out for me. We'll see."

"Ali," I said. "I would very much like your customers to come to me. Thank you."

He smiled at me. “I know the joy and thrill of having one’s own place. I wish you more ups than downs and all the best. It’s time to go home.”

The next morning, I visited Nathoo and informed him of my agreement with Mr. Desai. He was delighted. We sat down and discussed a loan agreement. It was a one-page agreement that showed the monthly payments including the interest amount on the loan. This agreement would begin in June of next year. I left to do a day of sewing.

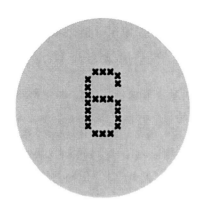

1918 – A LANDMARK YEAR

At home, I could not believe that, within two days, I had actually made two business deals. I, Sabby Mendes, had become a businessman. I rushed to get my notebook, flipped through the pages and reviewed my numbers again. My loan from Nathoo was larger than I had thought. I went to the window. It was just past twilight, and there were not many people on the street. I looked to the sky and there were a couple of stars clustered together blinking at me as though smiling in some distant approving way. A sense of joy overcame me.

I joined the people on the streets walking towards John's place, hoping that he would be home. When I knocked on his door and saw his smiling face, I almost jumped on him giving him my news. He pulled me in and told me to slow down. We went out for dinner, and John appeared happy for me, but I could see he was still troubled because he thought I was moving too fast.

Now, I thought, *everything is coming into place just like I want it to.*

Soon after the Christmas rush of orders, I was enjoying the quiet time and was actually preparing to go to Miguel's wedding in Goa. This would be my first visit to Goa. I booked a bunk in a steamer ship leaving on January 21 arriving Goa in time for the wedding on February 2. I was excited about this first visit back; I wanted to tell Mai and Pai about my business plans and visit Mr. Fernandes. 1918 became a landmark year for me.

But sometimes plans have twists and turns, and my business plan took a different turn. Nathoo sent a message to me requesting a visit to his office. It was January 10, and dressed in a suit, I sat on the chair across the desk from Nathoo. It took him a while to start the conversation while I impatiently wondered why I was here. Finally, he spoke up.

"Sabby, here is a revised agreement that I want you to look at and sign. Read it carefully, paragraph by paragraph."

I didn't know why he appeared aloof and not as friendly as before. I took my time reading the one-page agreement. In the second last paragraph, it clearly stated that I would have to pay a higher interest on the loan that was agreed upon earlier. My head was spinning trying to calculate the cost of this loan; it was a large cost for this loan. I couldn't believe it as the numbers were blurring on the paper.

"But Nathoo, this is a very high rate of interest. I can't pay you that much for a loan. This is too much."

"I am taking a risk on your business, and I need to get my money back and this is the way I can make my money. Look, think about it. Take the agreement with you, make your calculations, talk to other business people and then come back and let me know your decision."

I sat there for a good minute and then I responded. "I'm going to Goa for my brother's wedding, leaving in ten days. My mind cannot concentrate on this at the moment."

"I understand. When you come back, you can let me know your decision. Let me know by March 4, which gives you and I plenty of time. What do you think?"

"Yes. I will meet with you as soon as I come back from Goa." I stood up to leave as we both shook hands. I left his office.

I walked into Ali's shop and immediately asked Ali if I could talk with him. He curiously eyed me and walked to the back of the shop. We sat down. I informed him about the revised agreement and showed it to him. He read through it without any kind of reaction. He handed the agreement back to me and said that this was business. Now it was my turn to negotiate with Nathoo.

He advised that I had till March 4 to think about my negotiation plan and that on my return from Goa I should meet with Nathoo immediately and start the negotiation. I thanked Ali for his advice. A customer walked in; Ali went to the front to serve the customer while I returned to chalking the design on the cloth for a suit jacket.

For the next few days I prepared for my trip to Goa.

I was on the overnight train to Mombasa on January 20, 1918, just in time to board the steamer ship, *Ocean Breezes* on a ten-day journey to Goa. I had my business plans in my suitcase along with notes on Nathoo's agreement. While on deck, I met up with an Indian businessman from Mombasa. We talked about business, loans and rates of interest. He gave me enough information to help me negotiate with Nathoo. This eased my mind; I was confident that I could bring down the interest rate to suit my accounting for my shop. I relaxed for the remainder of the journey to Goa. This was a short trip to my homeland. I was to attend Miguel's wedding and to see Mai and Pai again after two years.

Mai and Pai were overjoyed to have me at home. Mai prepared a huge festive luncheon for me and invited the neighbours, friends and relatives. It was a wonderful welcome home party. Miguel was in a different world since he would soon be the groom. He told me that he was happy to marry Fatima. But that they would be going to Beira since she had relatives there and her parents wanted them to go to Beira. I told him to work hard in Beira and that he could be happy there as it was in Portuguese Mozambique. He, uncertainly, smiled at me. I clapped him on the shoulder with brotherly love. The wedding was another great party. I was very pleased that I came to the wedding. Secretly, I could tell that Miguel was happy too that I came back for his special occasion.

I had two free days; one I spent with Mr. Fernandes explaining my business plan and sharing with him my success. His face beamed with happiness for me. I tried to explain what it was like in Nairobi, but by the look on his face, I could see that he could not understand what I was saying about Nairobi. But he seemed genuinely happy for me and that was all that mattered to me.

After the wedding, I spent the day with Mai and Pai. I told them about my opening a tailor's shop in Nairobi. They listened and did not say much. I was surprised that Pai was very quiet and mostly nodded in agreement to what I said to them. He said I was to be cautious with my dealings with the people in Nairobi. Then he added that he wished me all the best in my business and that he and Mai would pray for me. I was grateful. They both asked me many questions about Nairobi and the Goan community. They were enthusiastically interested in my stories. Afterwards Mai looked at me and told me that I must consider getting married. I immediately said that as soon as my business brought me enough success, I would be ready to get married. They looked at me and quietly nodded.

It felt good being home for this short visit.

Back in Nairobi I was set to make my business plan workable. My parents now knew what I was doing and they approved as did Mr. Fernandes. I was ready to re-negotiate my loan with Nathoo. I dropped off a bottle of Feni for Nathoo and set up an appointment to see him on Monday February 25.

When I arrived at work, Ali greeted me enthusiastically. Unfortunately, I couldn't give Ali liquor as he didn't drink alcohol. Instead I brought him two shirts from Mr. Fernandes' shop. He gratefully accepted them. We talked for a bit about my visit to Goa. He announced that he referred a couple of customers to me and that they would be dropping by this week. I walked back to my sewing room and reviewed my customer book. It was time to work through my orders, some for pick up at the end of the week.

My meeting with Nathoo was a difficult one. It was a back and forth negotiation on the interest rate. Finally, we agreed on an interest rate that was closer to my accounting. I was cautiously happy with this agreement. While Nathoo claimed that I had a good business sense and that I was becoming an astute business man. This was a good compliment coming from Nathoo. We both waited for his secretary to bring in the revised agreement. In the meantime, he wanted to know how business was progressing.

"Business is good at the moment. In the new place, I'll have another two tailors to help me with the suit orders. I'm also getting some orders for women's clothing; I want to expand on this kind of tailoring as well," I said hiding my uneasiness. I knew my face lit up when I talked about tailoring, but inside of me, I was concerned and hoped for the best. I relied on my reputation to increase my clothing orders.

"So long as business picks up, you will be fine. I like your confidence and enthusiasm. Ah, here's the agreement with the adjustments. Let's go over the details." He gave me a copy, letting me read through it again. I made sure it showed the new amounts.

Once again Nathoo reviewed the details that would take effect on June 1, 1918. My main responsibility was to ensure that I repaid the loan in monthly payments over a period of two years with a further renewal of the loan if necessary. I signed the agreement, and then we shook hands. Nathoo insisted on taking me back to the Indian Palace restaurant for a celebratory meal.

At the restaurant, I met his two brothers and a couple of his friends. It was overwhelming. I seemed to become part of this business group. Yet, it was comforting to be with this crowd. For me, it ended as a great afternoon lunch of talk and laughter with business people. I couldn't wait for the weekend to share my news with Paulo and John at our Sunday gathering. That night I slept well.

At the first sign of daylight, I jumped out of bed, freshened up, dressed, sat at my table and reviewed the figures of my business plan. I was taking a risk, but I felt it was a good risk. I hadn't spent much on my business or myself since coming to Nairobi, but now the expenses would increase. The two extra sewing machines would be the biggest expense along with the increased rental cost. I was more than pleased about my own tailoring shop. I could see the sign on the top of my front door of my shop. *Oh yes, another expense for the sign.* I closed my notebook, put it away in my wardrobe, and bounced out to the street towards Ali's shop. It was time to put in a long day of sewing. Hopefully, I would get one or two new customers today. I did. The two men that Ali talked about came in, to be measured for their suits.

I met up with Paulo and John on Sunday. Paulo was not too thrilled with my news because he believed I was taking too great a risk too soon—I only half-heartedly listened to him. We walked into Cyprian's home for our gathering of lunch and activities. I moved with the crowd sharing my news of my tailoring shop.

Out of nowhere, Pedro appeared backslapping me. I shouted with joy, welcomed him with similar backslaps. He was visiting a relative and would be in Nairobi for two weeks. We exchanged news about Goa and our families.

"I have news for you," he said. "I'll be going to Goa to get married. My parents have found this lovely woman who they think is a perfect match for me. You know how it is."

"Yes, you've been in Mombasa for a while, and you're quite settled here. It's time to take the next step. I'm happy for you. When is all this happening, Pedro?"

"I'll spend Christmas there and then the second week of January will be my wedding. While my parents are making the arrangements in Goa, I applied for a married quarters' home at the Railway Housing Complex. This takes time. I'm excited but a bit anxious about bringing my bride to settle here. It'll be an adjustment for her and for me." He winked at me with a broad smile.

"Yes. It'll change your life I expect. When I'm ready, I'll do that. But it'll be a while before I get married. I will open my own tailoring shop in June. I can't wait for that day."

"Yes, I heard you tell these fellows here. I wish you all the very best. Will I get to see it before I go back to Mombasa?"

"Yes, come by Ali's shop tomorrow. I will take you to see it, and I'll also take your measurements to make a suit for you. I haven't forgotten my gift to you."

"That's kind of you Sabby. I'll drop by tomorrow."

He turned around, and there were Paulo and John softly punching him on the arm, delighted to see him. We ate and drank. Then the card games began. I left early. Pedro decided to come home with me instead of waiting for the next day. He too was not the card-playing type. We walked to my place at the Sequeira Lodging. We sat at my small table, and I described my business plan. He didn't interrupt me, not once. Instead he listened with interest and some curiosity.

When I stopped, he smiled and said that I was ambitious, which in his mind was a good thing. He added that such ambition would help me get over any difficulties I would have over time. We talked late into the night, mostly about my visit to Goa. He stayed over at my place.

The next morning, I showed him my new tailoring shop, and then we walked to Ali's shop. Ali helped him choose a suit length before we went back to my sewing room to measure him for his suit. It was good to have Pedro visit. I was very comfortable with him. We were interrupted by a customer who came in for his fitting. Pedro wandered up front to chat with Ali while I attended to my customer. I was with the customer longer than usual. We didn't have any more time with each other. Pedro left, telling me he would see me at the end of the week for his fitting. Later the next week he picked up his suit.

It was Sunday and there was Pedro wearing the suit I made for him. I was proud that he looked very smart in it. I could see other fellows gathering around him. When I approached them, two of the fellows told me that they would come to me for their suits. Pedro smiled at me and said he might wear it on his wedding day in Goa, especially after the praise for the suit. I was delighted.

We moved around the crowd that seemed to be getting bigger and bigger each Sunday. I met Luis and Manuel who had recently arrived from Goa. They had tailoring skills and were looking for work. I took them aside and told them to visit me at Ali's shop. They were gratified as they didn't know how to go about looking for tailoring work. This was not the place to talk about employment.

Instead we took a bottle of beer and spoke about Goa. Over in the far corner was a group of folks singing, accompanied by a young fellow with a guitar. There were children gathered around the singers. They clapped their hands to the rhythm of the music and the encouragement of the singers. While in the opposite corner there was a rowdy bunch playing carom. I liked this group. They played for fun. I bumped into Paulo and John. They invited me to join them in the card game in the backyard, but I turned them down. Paulo shook his head and walked off to play cards, and John followed him. I was annoyed that they played for money—and on Sunday too. It didn't feel right. Mai and Pai would have definitely disapproved of this kind of activity on a Sunday, a day of prayer, rest and relaxation with family and friends. Anyway, I didn't like playing for money and had never been tempted thus far. Instead I left early and walked towards home.

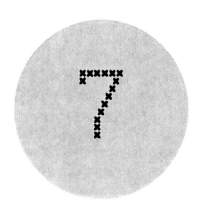

BUSINESS OPENING

On the morning of Monday, June 3, 1918, I stood on the opposite side of the street to look at the sign prominently displayed on the top of my shop:

S. Mendes Ltd. Tailoring Establishment.

It was perfect. This was my place. I crossed the street, walked to the front door, unlocked it and stepped inside. In a thoughtful mood, I walked behind the counter and ran my left hand over the countertop, looking at the samples of shirts and ties displayed in the glass cabinet below. I opened one of the wall glass cabinets behind me. My hands touched and flattened the different suit lengths arranged in rows according to the shades of blue, black, and grey, neatly piled one on top of the other. In the next wall cabinet there were the pin stripe suit lengths in the same colours.

I walked to my worktable towards the back of the shop. I re-arranged the pieces of the triangular chalk together in a pile and then rolled up the measuring tapes, positioning them next to the chalk in a large wooden box. The scissors were laid out in a straight line at the horizontal edge of the table next to the iron. I fingered the design magazines and placed them on a shelf behind the worktable. The wardrobe was almost full with suits in their different stages of completion—a couple of them were ready for pick up. The office desk was in the middle of the shop, separating the sewing room from the front of the shop.

I sat at the desk. I found myself thinking, *this is my dream come true*. And thus another day of sewing began for me. At the end of day, I walked home becoming more aware of my surroundings. I stopped at Jeevanjee Gardens off Government Road. It was a good place to walk around in peaceful contemplation—just as Mr. A. M. Jeevanjee had wanted it. He was a prominent businessman in Kenya and had this garden developed in 1906. He donated it for the use of the people of Nairobi. I walked out of the garden and headed for home. There were a few cars on the road, but there were more bicycles and some carts being pulled by young African men. I wondered if someday I would own a car.

The next morning, I walked briskly towards my shop. I saw a crowd of people gathered further up the road. When I reached the corner, I saw that there was an African on the ground with his damaged bicycle next to him. A European man was shouting obscenities at him, kicking him, yelling at him to get up and get off the road. I shoved my way through the crowd and approached the African. I helped him to his feet as another Indian came forward, and we both helped the man to the pavement. He was not too badly injured even though there was blood around his mouth and his face.

MARIA LYNCH

The European came to us and continued shouting that this savage couldn't stay here and had to move away. Slowly we walked him to Ali's shop that was a short distance away. Inside, we made him sit down on the chair. I gently dampened his face with a wet cloth. Ali let him sit there for a while and brought him some water to drink. After about ten minutes, the African stood up, and said he had to leave for work. We tried to keep him down, but he left, walking slowly in the other direction. Ali and I watched in silence. Ali reminded me that some of our Indians treated the Africans badly. They followed the ways of the British. It was not right. I did not respond and left.

I was agitated on my way to my shop. That was no way to treat another human being. Yes, he looked and even acted differently, but that did not mean the European had to treat him like that. After all, it was the European who *caused* the accident. The African was injured. Instead of assisting him, the European kicked him and expected him to get up. This was very upsetting. I hoped there were *some* Europeans here who were more caring. And now Ali said that there were some Indians and possibly some Goans that ill treated the Africans. We should not follow the ways of the British.

There must be people that care. Otherwise, I have to wonder what kind of a country I have come to live in.

This was a bad start to my day. I flipped through my customer book looking for today's fittings. Accordingly, I picked up a suit and worked on it. The more I sewed, the easier it was to put aside what just happened on the street. Two suits had to be ready for a fitting in the afternoon. I was interrupted by voices in the front of the shop. I looked up and saw familiar faces.

"Hello, Sabby. Remember, we met you many Sundays ago? I'm Manuel, and this is Luis. We met with you at the other tailoring shop."

"Yes, of course," I said. "At that time I couldn't do anything for you, but now I have my own shop, and I need tailors. Come, sit and let's talk about what you can do for me."

I was very glad they had come back to see me. They described the tailoring skills they gained from their apprenticeships in Goa. Their experience was very similar to my own.

"Tell me," I said, "after your apprenticeship, how long did you work at the tailoring shop?"

"I worked at a tailoring shop in Varca for two years after my apprenticeship." said Manuel.

"What about you?" I asked Luis.

"I was with Manuel too. Sometimes, I did dresses, mainly for my younger sisters. I like doing dresses. But I did fewer suits than Manuel."

"Then Manuel has more experience than you, Luis, which makes me think that Manuel is older than you, yes?"

"Yes, I started work at the tailoring shop a year after Manuel. He has more experience." Luis glanced at Manuel.

After a while, I told them they could work for me. Initially, they would be paid on a piece-work basis, and then as they proved themselves, they would be on a regular salary. They wanted to start immediately. I took them to the wardrobe and showed them the two suits that required minor sewing for fittings that afternoon. I explained the customer book that I had on the office desk.

"I will supervise your tailoring until I'm satisfied," I said and turned around to check their responses.

They were in agreement and listened carefully to my instructions. I would design and cut the cloth while they would use the sewing machine to stitch the pieces of the suit. We worked on the suits for the fitting that afternoon. It turned out to be a good working morning. With their help, the two fittings were ready quicker than I would have managed on my own.

At lunchtime, we stopped for a break. Manuel brought in some snacks from the snack shop at the end of the street. I brought out water. We sat around the office desk. Luis was tall and slim with closely cropped black hair with tinges of brown. He had a broad smile and was quiet by nature. Manuel was shorter, bulky in appearance and had a domineering personality that came through with his hearty laughter and loud voice. We talked about Goa again. After an hour, we were back at the sewing machines. I liked the company in the shop, and it was good to see the suits being sewed without that pressure on me to finish them in a hurry. We shared the sewing duties. Sometimes, they worked on the hand stitching while I worked on the sewing machine. It was a good working arrangement for the three of us.

Later that afternoon, the two customers came in for their fittings, one after the other. Their timing was perfect. Luis and Manuel observed as I wove in the pins on the sections that needed adjustments for one of the customers. The second customer was a regular with no adjustments necessary. An hour later we continued working on the next orders.

At the end of the day, Luis and Manuel left, but I stayed behind to review the customer book and my accounts book that had my business plan in it. I kept checking the figures in the accounts book—this was new to me, and I wanted to be careful with the money. There were no outstanding payments from the customers. I now had a few orders for women's clothing. I wanted to do more of this kind of creative tailoring. I flipped through the magazines. I knew I could make these dresses for my women customers. I closed shop and walked to the post office to get my letters from box #2215.

Sitting comfortably in my chair at home, I opened a letter from Mai and Pai. It was a short letter. They wrote that they were doing well and shared bits and pieces about neighbours and relatives. There were more hints about my coming back to Goa to get married. I ignored that part.

It'll happen when I'm ready to bring a wife to Nairobi, I thought, *but not now.*

Then I opened Miguel's letter. His was longer. He and Fatima were settled in Beira—more so Fatima than him. He worked at a tailoring shop in Beira on a piece-work basis. Even though they had been there a short time, he wrote that he wanted to come to Nairobi. That, he said, would make Mai and Pai very happy, but he could not convince Fatima. She wanted to be with her cousins in Beira.

It would be wonderful to have family here. I miss them very much.

The letters from Anton and Menino were amusing. Anton was happily married to Tina. She was beautiful and looked after him very well. He wrote that he couldn't wait to get home after a long day in the carpenter's shop. He still wondered if they should come to Nairobi. I remembered this conversation when I visited him while in Goa. He had heard of and seen more and more people leaving Goa. He and Tina wanted to come to Nairobi, but her parents still didn't approve of her being that far away.

Menino was on a ship, working as a steward. He was assigned to cater and serve the senior officers in their dining room. I could see him, sorting out the details of creating a menu and then supervising the staff in the galley. His quick witty comments spoken with a serious look on his face would serve him well. Though I was not sure he would say too much in the dining room among mainly British officers. I brought his happy personality to the top of my mind and thought about our times in Goa where my heart still remained. I put away the letters. I had to adjust to being in Nairobi. I had to make my business a success.

There was a knock on the door. It was Mrs. Sequeira who came to invite me to dinner at their place. This was unusual; I was surprised. She smiled and said that her eldest son was home and she would like me to meet him and his wife, Tom and Mary.

"Well then," I said. "How I can I turn down this invitation?"

It was my first time inside the Sequeira flat. I walked in the living room. There were people seated in the chairs placed against the wall of the living room. In the centre was a long table with a variety of delicious dishes of food upon it. I was uncomfortable. I didn't know anyone in this crowd. A couple introduced themselves as Mrs. Sequeira's son and daughter-in-law, Tom and Mary. We shook hands and before I knew it there were a few fellows around me talking and asking questions. They had heard about my shop. That was when they told me, in no uncertain terms, that I had to have the priest come by and bless my shop—and then of course, have a party in celebration.

"You *must* do a special opening," one of them said.

"Yes, in that way your shop will be blessed, and all good things will happen there. It will take away any of the bad spirits that may have been there before."

"Oh I agree," said another. "You *must* clean it out with a priest's blessing. It is important."

"We can help you."

I stood back as these voices came at me. They were friendly, truthful and were advising me on something that had slipped my mind. I concentrated on setting up my business and didn't think of anything else. Mrs. Sequeira came forward.

"I want them to know about your shop, Sabby. And make sure that you follow our Goan traditions. We can do it on Sunday. What do you think?"

I was genuinely embarrassed.

"You're right. I've waited too long. Honestly, I've forgotten about our traditions, and thank you for reminding me."

Then we ate, drank and planned the blessing of my shop. Two of them would inform Father O'Brien and bring him over on the Sunday afternoon. Mrs. Sequeira would prepare the snacks for the party, and I would purchase some snacks from the Indian snack shop and ask John to bring in some beer. I was embarrassed to think how I could have missed this part of our Goan traditions. This was when I truly missed Mai and Pai. They would have had it done on the Sunday afternoon before my shop opening. Anyway, it was now organized and thanks to Mrs. Sequeira. Back in my room, I picked up pen and paper and wrote a long letter to Mai and Pai, then to Miguel, Menino and Anton.

It was the second Sunday June 16, 1918, the day of the blessing of S. Mendes Ltd., Tailoring Establishment. It was crowded. Father O'Brien arrived and moved towards the centre of the shop, and when everyone was quiet, he began the prayer. I liked him as he was one of the few priests who treated us kindly and with respect. When the prayer was said, he sprinkled us with holy water, and we made the sign of the cross. Then Father O'Brien proceeded to sprinkle holy water on the furniture, walls and doors. At the end of the blessing, I thanked Father O'Brien. Paulo and John said a few words. To my surprise, from the back of the shop, Nathoo spoke up and proposed prosperity for S. Mendes Ltd. My face flushed with emotion. I tried to keep the tears away. John noticed and approached me with a beer and put his arm around me

"It's time to drink to your happiness and success."

"Thank you all," I said "Now let's enjoy the snacks that Mrs. Sequeira has laid out for us."

At that moment, I felt shy being the centre of attention in this crowd. I really missed Mai, Pai and Miguel. Paulo made sure everyone had a drink in hand while John stood behind the counter serving the drinks.

Father O'Brien stayed awhile, talked with everyone and then excused himself. I walked him to the door. He shook my hand and, with a broad smile—and in a thick Irish voice—wished me well. I looked into his deep blue eyes. I could barely understand what he said. I nodded and thanked him for being there, and before he left, I asked him to bless the crucifix I held in my hand. I told him that I would hang it somewhere in the shop. He blessed it, smiled and disappeared into the sun on the street.

I turned back to my guests and was amazed at the crowd that had gathered for my opening. Some of them I knew, while others I would become familiar with later, as customers. Nathoo and Ali grabbed my hand and congratulated me.

The celebration was memorable and pleasant though my thoughts were on those absent, back in Goa. Mai and Pai would have happily moved around the crowd. Miguel would have lurked in the background, for he would not have been comfortable with this kind of celebration. Though I missed sharing this celebration with him. He was quieter and slightly envious of me, but I would have been by his side reassuring him. As a brother I loved him, of course, but I didn't like it when we disagreed sometimes. I was brought back to the celebration by people wishing me well as they left.

"Hey Sabby," John yelled from behind the counter. "Give me a hand clearing out these bottles. It's time to tidy up."

"Yes, yes. I wasn't expecting this crowd." I walked to the counter to help him.

He nudged my arm and put the bottles away in the boxes on the floor. "It's good advertising for you. Don't grumble about it."

He was right and I certainly wasn't grumbling. It had been a good party. I helped pick up the scraps, while Mrs. Sequeira piled up the dishes and put them away in a box. She was a short, slim woman with curly black hair and hazelnut brown eyes that showed kindness and gentleness. I embraced her with gratitude, and she moved backwards from my embrace and graciously said that I could count on her to remind me of our Goan traditions. Once again, I talked with Tom and Mary, her son and daughter-in-law as they stood next to her. Mrs. Sequeira in a motherly voice, told me to be mindful of what I did. I shied away from her words, but with a grateful smile and wink I thanked her again for making this celebration happen. With Tom, Mary and the box of dishes, they left, as did the remaining crowd.

I joined John at my office desk. Paulo had left to meet up with his buddies at home to join them in the game of cards.

"Paulo loves his card game on Sundays," said John. "He has to play every Sunday."

"You don't have to tell me," I said. "I worry about the money that he puts down. You play the game. Does he win or lose?"

"He mostly loses. But he keeps thinking he's going to win the next time."

I shook my head. "That's a problem. He has a good job with a good salary, and it seems he spends most of it on the card game. I hope his parents are arranging a marriage match for him. That may change him, huh, John?"

"I doubt it. He will continue playing. It's in his blood. I'm not *that* into the game. I can walk away. I do it to be with the boys. But I can stand up and leave the table when I'm losing. But not Paulo."

Poor Paulo. "He needs help. I don't know what. Sounds like he's playing his salary away and that's not good."

"The danger will be when he comes to us to borrow money once he runs out of it. Then we have to decide if we loan him the money or not."

John, I noticed, had used the words *when* and *once* rather than *if.* I felt a tightening in my stomach.

"You know my thoughts on that. I will not. Money is not for playing cards. It's for improving your life, for buying a house and then looking after it. He needs a wife to help him see that," I said in a harsh tone that surprised John.

He shook his head. "Sabby, you know a wife wouldn't be able to convince him of that. She would have to be someone very, very special. Even with that, there will be arguments between them. It's not a good situation when someone is into playing cards and does not do anything else. That's our Paulo now."

John stood to leave. There was nothing more to say about Paulo's bad habit. I closed up the shop, and we stepped out onto the street. It was peaceful in the darkness. There was no one around. When we spoke it felt like an echo in the night. We went our separate ways at the end of the street, and I walked home feeling blessed.

The next morning, I saw Luis and Manuel waiting for me to open up the shop. I unlocked the door to the smell of some of the leftovers from the night before. I kept the front door open to let the morning air in. With a damp cloth, I wiped the counter tops again to clear off any bits and pieces of dried food. Luis and Manuel helped out. They used a damp cloth wrapped around the broom to wipe out the floor. They scrubbed some ground in stains that looked like spills from beer and curry.

"It was a good party. There were many people." Manuel said with a smile on his face.

"Manuel, there were people that I didn't even know," I said. "Let's hope we will see them again here."

"It feels different, different in a good way," Luis said looking around the shop.

I thought that too. "The blessing was the most important part of yesterday. It was a weight off my shoulders that I didn't know I was carrying. Thank goodness, Mrs. Sequeira put me up to it."

"I feel the difference too," said Manuel. "It's like there's quietness in the air. Peaceful. I cannot describe this feeling. What are you doing, Sabby?"

"When Father O'Brien was leaving yesterday, I took out this wooden cross with the image of Jesus on it and asked him to bless it for me. I want to hang it up somewhere, but I don't know where."

"I don't think it should be seen in the front of the shop," said Manuel. "Maybe in the sewing room at the back"

"Yes," said Luis. "Besides, it would make us work harder and concentrate on our sewing." He smiled.

"I'll put it in the sewing room on the rim of the ceiling facing us while we work. In this way, each morning, I can say a little prayer for a good working day without any troubles."

Once the shop looked tidy, clean and fresh smelling, we worked on the suits that needed completion. There were no fittings due until the next day.

John dropped by during lunchtime. He was grim looking, the kind of look that meant trouble. Luis and Manuel had gone out for lunch. I closed up shop and walked with John to a nearby snack shop. We got some samosas and a pitcher of water and sat down at a table.

"What's wrong, John?"

"Paulo was in a fight last night. He lost the card game. He was frustrated and took it out on the fellow who won the game. It was bad. He did not go to work today. He's home."

"He has a bad temper and tends to blow up unnecessarily. I don't want to know the details. Today is your day off. Let's visit him this evening."

"I don't think he wants to see us, especially you, Sabby. He's embarrassed. He knows what you think about playing cards. We have to leave him for now. We'll see him on Sunday."

Some played cards for fun, while others, like Paulo, played for money. They usually played in his backyard or a neighbour's backyard. No one else went there unless they wanted to play the money card game, as I called it. They played in the hope of winning, but on any given hand there can be only one winner. They were quiet and serious during the game. At the start of the game, money was put down. Each player looked at others seriously. If there was any talking it was about the next move in the game. For me, it was not the type of activity for a Sunday. I liked to meet different people, talk and laugh. That was *my* idea of Sundays.

John was still bartending at the Norfolk Hotel. More of the Europeans were friendlier to him. They were usually the ones that sat at the bar. It alarmed him to see how differently we were treated and that we could not do much about it. The hotel paid him a good wage, and he could not think of anything else he would do. He said that he had to act perfectly always and was expected to do the right and proper thing at all times. He had seen how mistakes, no matter how small, would mean no work. It worried him. He wondered if he would ever get used to our new life in Nairobi.

"We're here now," I said. "Can't go back home. We have to create our home here."

"How do we do that, Sabby?"

I didn't know what to say. It was harder for John because of where he worked. My shop was in the Indian section of Nairobi, and my customers were Goans and Indians. They were the people I would have served back in Goa, only I served them here. John, unquestionably, had to serve the European patrons who considered him culturally inferior to themselves.

After a moment John said, "I love our Sundays. They are special to me. It's very good being among Goans. I feel free during that time. I don't have to watch what I do or say."

"Yes, I'm glad we have our Sundays too," I said.

We were quiet as John walked with me back to the shop. Within minutes Luis and Manuel were back and busy at the sewing machines. I embraced John and sadly I saw him leave. I went back to designing a dress for Mrs. Coelho.

At the end of the day, I visited Ali. I noticed he still didn't have a tailor at the back. He continued to send some of his customers to me. He told me that he gave up looking for a tailor and that, since I was within a short walking distance, it was just as easy to send his customers to me. Of course, I was very happy and grateful. So far business had been good.

"Is Omondi around?" I asked. He was the young African fellow, who regularly came to sweep, dust and clean Ali's shop at the end of the day.

Ali smiled. "In the back. He's begun cleaning up. I suppose you're going to want to ask him to clean your place as well."

"Well, I thought about it. If that's okay with you."

"Yes, of course," he said then called. "Omondi, can you come in the front?"

"Hello Sir," he said when he appeared from the back. "Nice to see you. How's your shop?"

"It needs cleaning," I said. "Can you come to do it after you finish here?"

"Yes, I'll do it. You'll pay me good, no?"

We settled on the same amount that Ali paid him. I walked back to my shop to wait for Omondi. While I waited, for the second time that day, John walked in. He looked troubled. Before we had a chance to say hello, Omondi walked in and went about cleaning the shop while I spoke with John.

My friend had been very troubled about his job at the Norfolk Hotel since lunch. This time I listened and nodded caringly between sentences. I could not imagine half of what he was going through at his workplace. This went on for a good hour.

When Omondi finished I thanked him and saw him out. I turned to John.

"Let's go to the Indian Palace restaurant. If Nathoo is there, he may have some advice for you."

"I briefly talked with him at your opening party on Sunday. He seems a nice fellow, but I don't see what advice he could give me."

"If you knew the advice he would give, you wouldn't need it, would you?" I punched John in the shoulder. "He may not even be there. Look, Nathoo was born here and has lived here all his life. And it is important for us to learn from him."

"Yes I suppose you're right. And if nothing else we can have a good meal."

In the restaurant we did not see Nathoo. We sat down at a round table near the window and ordered dinner. The server recognized me and said he would bring in a special order for us. He smiled and said that he expected Nathoo that night. John observed the crowd and sipped his water. His face was calm, the lines of anxiety disappeared.

When the server brought in the dishes of food, Nathoo was right behind him. I rose to my feet and greeted him.

"Hello Sabby. It's very nice to see you here. You have your friend here. Your name is?"

"I'm John Fernandes. I spoke with you at Sabby's opening party."

"There were many Goans there. It was a good celebration. May I join you until my friend comes? He's late."

"Yes," I said. "I was hoping to see you here."

He pulled a chair forward and began talking about my tailoring business. I quickly changed the conversation to John's situation at the Norfolk Hotel. Nathoo raised his eyebrows and told John that he was fortunate to work at the Norfolk Hotel. John was taken aback but cautiously listened as Nathoo continued.

"I'm sure you meet the best of them and the worst of them. Learn from that experience. The important thing is to put your attention on those who respect you and treat you fairly. They are the ones who appreciate your service to them."

After a moment or two, John nodded. "I never thought of it in that way. I only think of those horrible experiences and those who are nasty and demanding. There are quite a few good fellows and ladies who are very grateful for my service. Sometimes they even bring me small gifts that say thank you. I like that."

"Among all of us there are nasty people and good people," said Nathoo. "We have to learn to work with them. It's always difficult to work with nasty people and very easy to work with the people who are kind and pleasant."

I too listened carefully to what Nathoo had to say. He talked about people and how to work with them and their different personalities. It was the same for me. I had customers that were like that. Nasty or nice, my work was to make suits and clothing that made the people look good and feel good. Nathoo's friend arrived, which cut our conversation short and Nathoo stood. He firmly shook both our hands and advised us to continue doing the best we could and that we would soon adjust to living in Nairobi.

We watched them sit at another table and we continued sipping our chai. Nathoo said: segregation is the law of the land and nothing can be done about that, but we could still do our best and survive, even be successful, in British East Africa. Still, it was difficult to ignore segregation; it would be a new way of living. John and I both agreed that it had been good to hear Nathoo's positive talk on the situation.

While walking home, John said that he had spoken to our Goans who worked in the government offices with European bosses. It was different there. The boss assigned the work and let them do it with little talking between them. There were some Indian bosses as well. There was no socializing with the Europeans. Whereas, being a bartender at the Norfolk Hotel, it was all about socializing. He could not have conversations with the Europeans—they did the ordering while he served their orders. He was the server and had to perform exactly as they wanted.

It was a particularly warm night, but we carried on walking for a while, past where we lived, and onto Government Road. There was no one around. We could hear our footsteps on the moonlit pavement. I told John I was ready to find my own place to live in.

"I was wondering when you would do that. You are more than satisfied with your work and your shop. I'm very happy for you. I wish I could say the same for myself. I seem to be stuck with this European crowd I work for. I'm not sure what the future holds for me." John said with sadness. He slowed down his walking.

I wasn't expecting this response. He was stuck all right. He didn't have any other skills or desire to do anything else. I could see him being at the Norfolk Hotel for a long time.

"Look, John, they pay you well, and you're learning to be with people who are very different from us. Maybe—"

"What good is that?" he asked. "Yeah, I know how to serve different kinds of drinks and there are those friendly fellows who sit at the bar. Whenever they are there, I feel happy and love my work for that little while, but if they are not there, then it is the job of serving nasty people."

"I don't know what to say, John. Except that you are working and earning a good wage. Remember what Nathoo said. Think of it as learning to work with different kinds of people. That is really what your job is about."

"It's also about making and serving the drinks in the right way. Make sure that the cherry is perched on the mound of creamy fluff or don't forget the olive in the martini drink. Then it's about presentation of the drink to the customer. Place it on the table just in front of the customer. Oooo… and so it goes on."

"You love it, that part of the job anyway. If you could see yourself as you describe your work, you would think, *that fellow likes what he does*. And you know what, I think you like your work."

We both looked at each other and then I took hold of John's arm and locked it in mine and almost ran down the street laughing and breaking out into what sounded like a song. We were horrible at singing. Thank goodness no one was around to tell us to stop. We needed that moment of absolute nonsense and madness to get over our troubles of trying to live in the dark shadow of life under British rule. We came to the street where John lived and and we parted ways.

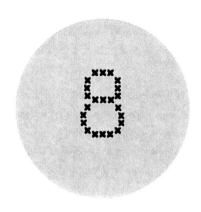

REALITIES OF SETTLING IN NAIROBI

John left the Norfolk Hotel in September of 1919.

I remember the night I found out. None of us had seen him for a while, and he hadn't attended the last few Sunday gatherings. One evening I decided to visit him to make sure that he was all right. I was worried about him and felt a little guilty for not checking in earlier. I was doing well and, with the support and advice of Nathoo, was living through the normal ups and downs of running a business. The Goan community in Nairobi continued to grow; our Sunday groups were smaller as most of the Goans went to the Goan clubs for recreation and socialization.

But John had been very unhappy with his work situation the last couple times I had seen him.

I knocked on John's door, and when he opened it, he looked puzzled and distracted, but then he recognized me and jovially welcomed me inside. We both needed a walk. I could tell there was something on his mind—I was glad I came.

On the street, it was quiet with few people around. We walked at a steady pace feeling the cool night air, and before I had a chance to speak, he spilled his news.

"I have a new job. I'll be the butler for Mr. and Mrs. Glover who own the Limuru Farm. They've asked me to move in their farmhouse, where I'll have my own flat in the far end of their residence."

That stopped me dead in my tracks. I stared at him in shock.

"What? You are going to move in with a British family? I can't believe it. Who are these people?"

"It's true," he said. "Mr. Glover is one of the friendly fellows at the Norfolk Hotel. A bar patron, who always treated me well and took the time to speak with me. Over time he introduced me to his wife—"

"But when did this happen?" I asked.

"Over the last couple of months. The Glovers became friendlier with me and then last week they asked me if I would consider leaving the Norfolk."

"That's certainly big news, isn't it? I am happy for you. You disliked many of the patrons at the Norfolk. But how do you feel about this change?" I was very surprised over the news, but I wanted to hear more about how John made this decision without even a hint to Paulo or I.

"I've entered a different world. I can't turn back, Sabby. Mrs. Glover organized one part of the house for me. It's like a flat with my own bedroom and a small bathroom nearby. I can't believe it myself." His voice was kind of flat, neither happy nor sad, as though he was still struggling with the decision. He started walking again.

"What choice do I have?" he said. "I was unhappy at the Norfolk from the start, and the Glovers seem like decent people."

I walked after him. This was troubling news. How could he live with a British family? What was going on here? John turned to look back at me but didn't say anything.

"John," I said. "I don't know what to say. It looks like you have made up your mind. When do you move in?"

"Next Monday. Mrs. Glover will send her driver to take me to their farm in Limuru."

"Does this mean that you work for them all day and all night?"

"Yes, it's too far to go there daily. I have to live there as I will be their butler. They have many parties; they want me for these different parties at different times of the day and night." He spoke in a low voice that didn't sound like the confident John I knew.

"Oh John, your life will be changed. We won't see each other as often as we do now. I'll miss you."

"Not so fast," he said. "I *will* get days off during the week. Could I stay with you then?"

"Of course!"

I was concerned by what was happening in John's world and avoided asking too many questions. As a friend I supported him, but this was unusual. It seemed that we aimlessly walked towards Paulo's place.

Now it was my turn to talk about what had been happening in my shop. I believed that there was something going on with Manuel; he didn't seem as content as he had been at the beginning. I described the lunch discussion with Manuel; I wanted to find out what was wrong. It turned out that he didn't like it when I worked with Luis on the dresses and that he wanted to do dresses as well. But he never showed any interest in making dresses; he was very good at making suits, and that's what I assigned to him. But he complained about what seemed like a lack of attention to him. John and I agreed that there was nothing I could do because Manuel was very good at making the suits and some customers always asked for him to do their suits.

"Nothing you can do until he lets you down," said John. "You may be imagining things that are not there. But I think he's the suit type as well. I picked up on that each time I visited you. He gets to it fast. He doesn't have the patience to be imaginative to make dresses."

"Funny you noticed that too. At the beginning he mentioned that he liked doing the suits and doesn't have the time to work around the frills or slits of the dresses on the sewing machine. But now he wants to makes dresses; he won't be good at it. There is something else bothering him. I suppose eventually, I'll find out."

John shrugged in agreement. I had to sort this one out myself, of course. We knocked on Paulo's door, but there was no answer; we walked back home in the dark. We quickened our pace, for after our Mombasa experience, we were extra careful at night; we spoke less and were more aware of our surroundings. We didn't speak any more about John's new job, for he didn't bring it up again, and I didn't want to be nosey. It was late when we parted company and headed to our homes.

It was early November, and during one of our usual Sunday gatherings, we caught up with Paulo, long enough for him to tell us that he was going to Goa to get married. The railway company was providing him with a house in the married quarters' section of the Railway Housing Complex. Of course, we were really happy for him.

Let's hope he won't play as many card games and go into debt, I thought.

At that moment, I had a big back slap. I turned around and there, in front of me, was a face from the past.

"Anton!" I yelled. "When did you come here? Couldn't you write to let me know you were coming? When we met in Goa last year, you did talk about coming to Nairobi, but you seemed uncertain. Now you are here. Good. Good!"

He smiled. "Yes, I remember that conversation with you in Goa. Everything was uncertain at that time. But here I am and I wanted to surprise you. Tina's parents finally approved of our coming here. They wrote to her cousin who lives here. Come, let's go over there to talk with her."

We greeted each other, talked for a while, and then left her alone with her cousin. Tina was very beautiful, and Anton was happy. Tina's cousin had arranged for Anton to get a job doing carpentry. He had arrived on Wednesday and would start work on Monday. They were living with the cousin until they found a suitable place to rent. This was good news.

I could not stop talking about my tailoring shop. He stopped me to tell Tina that he had to go with me to see it. I introduced him to John and Paulo before they went out back to play cards, while Anton and I walked in the direction of my shop. We spoke endlessly about Goa and Menino and his work at sea. So far Anton liked Nairobi and what he saw around him. He said it was the right decision to leave Goa. When we arrived at the shop, he stopped, stretched his arms out in front of him, and admiringly came to me.

"You finally did it. You have your own tailoring business. Look at you!"

"Isn't it amazing Anton? I cannot believe it myself. I had help in getting started and now it seems everything is going smoothly. Yes, it's only been a bit more than a year." I looked to Anton for his approval, and he nodded.

As I unlocked the door and let him in, he was impressed and happy for me. He walked in, looked at everything with wide open eyes and a big smile on his face.

"This is wonderful, Sabby. I always knew you had the determination to do it. Congratulations, my friend. Now I can come and have my suits made by you. Wonderful, wonderful!"

We sat down for a while and talked some more about Goa. Anton was very grateful for being in Nairobi. He had heard about the segregation and the different way of living here, but he seemed to accept it. We walked back to our Sunday gathering. Most people were settled in their groups, quietly having lunch while others had disappeared to play cards. Anton and I joined the carom game. Though it was fun, there were some serious conversations going on in the groups.

Emilio called me over and told me about these conversations. He was a tailor as well; he worked for a large tailoring company. He loved to socialize and was always at these Sunday gatherings—never missed a Sunday and stayed quite late in the night. There were grumblings among our community, and they happened after I left. They gossiped about who belonged and who didn't—the caste system had followed us to Nairobi. It was getting late, and I didn't want to get into a heated argument about this at a Sunday gathering. I invited them to my place next Saturday night. This time I included Anton among the group.

He may as well hear what is happening within our own community, I thought. *Never mind the segregation outside, it is happening inside our own community.*

Saturday came around and I prepared for my guests. I now lived in a flat on the second floor. It had a separate bedroom. I had a comfortable bed with a side table, a small wardrobe and a long stand up mirror near the wardrobe. A small window looked out onto the street. The living room was big enough for a sofa and two upright chairs on either side of it. To the far side near the kitchen was a dining table with four chairs. I shared a common bathroom in the hallway on the same floor. I liked it, for it was my own home. Kamau, my African housekeeper and cook, cleaned the flat and cooked my meals—having been taught Goan cooking by none other than Mrs. Sequeira. He came in everyday.

As evening drew near, Kamau arranged the food on the dining table, making sure everything was set for my friends. There were seven of us. As usual John brought the beer, lots of it this time. Our conversation was loud. We told jokes and laughed at each other's acting out of stories. Then the talk changed, as it usually did after a few drinks.

"Sabby, you know I have joined the Railway Goan Club," Paulo said in an uncomfortable voice knowing that it was only for the Goan employees of the railway company.

"That's good, Paulo. I suppose, you too, Cyprian are a member." I expected him to be part of this club since he too worked for the railway company.

"Is this the club that will not allow us tailors to join?" Emilio asked in a harsh voice.

Paulo shrugged but looked a little ashamed. "The caste system lives on here. What can I say? We have to live with the prejudice from the Europeans and now we get it from our own people. But I heard that this Railway Goan Club was set up for the Goans who worked there and yes they don't allow non railway employees to join."

John, who had been quiet decided to speak up. "As with everything, some of them do it in a cruel way, while others are good to us, even among the Europeans. I can tell you many stories. I was a bartender, and now I'm a butler, but I'm proud of the work I do because I do it well. The Glovers treat me very well, and I'm happy. Now, as for the Goans...." He rolled his eyes and noisily blew out a puff of air.

There was laughter.

"The funny thing is that *all* of us face prejudice from the Europeans," said Cyprian. "We are all Indians to them, right Paulo?"

"Yes, that is it," said Paulo.

"I don't like the caste system," said Cyprian. "You will never find me treating any of us differently. We're Goans in Nairobi, and we don't have to bring that nonsense from Goa here. Look at you, Sabby. You have a tailoring shop. You're a businessman. I admire you. I couldn't do that." Cyprian glanced at the rest of us. Everyone was surprised at what he declared.

"I love what I do, Cyprian, and John loves what he does. We are both earning a very good living. It doesn't matter what the Goans think or do. Mind you, John is right. There are the good and the bad. Being a tailor is rewarding if you love the work, but it can also be challenging if—"

"We should build a clubhouse, like the one in Mombasa," said Emilio.

Nairobi had a Tailors' Society. It was formed in 1916, and both Emilio and I were members. It did not have a clubhouse. Activities were held in church halls, but that would change with the building of a clubhouse. Emilio liked the idea, and it was not the first time he had brought it up. The alcohol, as much as anything, else made the conversation loud and angrily noisy.

"Yes, it's a nice clubhouse in Mombasa," I said. "I visited that club when I first arrived there a few years ago. It is very good. They not only socialize together as tailors with their families. They have regular activities and people go the clubhouse almost daily. But they also help newcomers to find tailoring work, and they—"

"Hmmm. Now who is being exclusive?" John said (mostly to Emilio). "I don't suppose a butler could join the Nairobi Tailors' Club. See, we are segregating within ourselves. I don't like it. It is too easy to break off into little groups, and the problem is that there are always people on the outside looking in."

John's point was not easy to talk about. Emilio was persistent and determined to set up a clubhouse. Anton looked on without saying much. Paulo, Cyprian and John were silent and only listened. Emilio started making grand plans for a clubhouse.

Monte, a newly arrived tailor and who worked with Emilio at the tailoring company joined Emilio in this plan. I listened with great interest and was determined not to let it affect my friendship with John, Paulo or Anton.

I'll invite them to our activities. I thought. *We want to socialize, to be together in Nairobi and share our Goan traditions no matter what work we do.*

For some of our Goans it was always about what you did rather than who you were. Tradespeople were not accepted by some. It was ridiculous. We worked hard and earned a good living. In many ways we, in the trades, took more risks. Many of the supposed high-level Goans who snubbed us were government workers, the clerks. To me clerical work was boring.

As a tailor I made suits and was creative in designing and sewing beautiful dresses. I thought my work was much more satisfying than checking through papers and more papers. The British Protectorate Government had nothing but praise for its Goan clerks. They said that Goans stood apart from the Indian community in that we were Christians, Catholics to be exact, and that we could relate to the European way of life.

Discussions of segregation—both within and without the Goan community—continued into the night without a proper resolution because what resolution could there be? It was clear that Emilio and Monte were determined to have a clubhouse built for the Tailors' Society in Nairobi.

xxx

The World War had ended in August 1920, having barely touched Nairobi. At the Paris Peace Conference of 1919, German East Africa—which lay directly to the south of the British Protectorate—had been divided between Britain and Belgium.

In 1920, I witnessed Kenya going through the change from being a Protectorate to a British Colony. Through the complications of British laws these changes became clear in Kenya. Sir Edward Northey became the first Governor of Kenya. Before 1920 there were Commissioners and Administrators of the British East Africa Protectorate. And thus began the time of colonization. The British confiscated property from the Africans who moved from being farmers to working on the plantations owned by the British settlers.

During the 1920s I concentrated solely on developing my business. I had an increased number of customers, and I found it quite remarkable that I had European customers—especially European ladies in need of dresses for the various parties they hosted in their homes. I had John to thank for this new growth in business. He had referred Mrs. Glover to me, who then referred her friends and people she knew. I had never thought I would make clothing for the European women of Nairobi or make suits for the European men, but I was. I had orders for specially designed shirts with special markings on them, long trousers and shorts with stripes along the sides. I liked these different kinds of orders. It kept the business growing, and we continued to become better at doing a variety of tailoring. I paid off Nathoo's loan. We celebrated in his usual manner at the Indian Palace restaurant on River Road. Of course, he said that if ever I needed any more help he would be glad to assist. I thanked him.

My Goan friends continued to argue about who belonged and who did not and barred the tailors and their families from joining the two Goan Clubs—The Railway Goan Institute and the Goan Institute. Even though the Tailors' Society did not have a clubhouse, we continued to celebrate and had our functions in the church halls. John and Anton were always welcomed at our functions.

Apart from Nathoo Ram and other Indian business customers, there was the famous Goan pioneer who was my regular customer. He was Dr. Rosendo Ayres Ribeiro, a medical doctor who travelled on a zebra to care for the needs of his patients. He was the first medical doctor to diagnose bubonic plague in Kenya. I was grateful for the many customers he brought to me including his family and their friends. Here was a shining example of a Goan brahmin who treated everyone with great kindness and respect. It was the middle of August of 1929; business was steady. In walked Dr. Ribeiro.

"Good morning, Sabby. I stopped by to tell you to expect Mr. Murray to come in sometime this week. He is from the Health Office and a good friend of mine."

"Mr. Murray, why will he come to see me? I hope I'm not in any trouble."

Dr. Ribeiro laughed.

"You in trouble? That's not possible! No, Mr. Murray wants some clothing made for his staff. He wants them designed in a special way, and I told him that you are the person for this kind of work."

"That's good, Doctor. I like work that is different, and especially if it means working with designs on the clothing. Thank you. You're very kind."

"Now, my wife, has she come to see you yet? She wanted some dresses made for herself and her friend."

"No, Doctor. I'm afraid I haven't seen… oh wait! Here they come."

With the arrival of his wife and her friend, Dr. Ribeiro left the shop. I attended to them. Seated at the office desk, they looked through the Women's Clothing magazine to pick out the style of dress they each wanted. They would flip through the pages, stop at a page or two, say something to each other and then move onto the next page. After about, what seemed like half an hour of looking through the magazine, they chose a style.

"This is the one I'd like, at the top right corner on this page," said Mrs. Ribeiro. "And Janet, my friend, would like this one on the bottom part of this same page. Here we have the two different kinds of cloth for these dresses. Is it the right kind for the style of dress we each have chosen?"

I looked at the styles and then I examined the two different pieces of cloth they had brought in. Mrs. Ribeiro had an organza cloth of pale orange, while Janet was holding a soft sunflower yellow cotton cloth. It felt more like fine Egyptian cotton.

"These are excellent for the styles you have chosen. A formal style for a formal occasion, I'm guessing. Once I have created them, they will look very beautiful on you. Come, let me measure you."

"Thank you, Sabby. It's for an evening wedding party in the middle of October. It is now the beginning of September; will you be able to have it ready by then?"

"Yes, of course. Come at the end of next week for fittings, and by the end of the last week of September, you can pick them up."

Once I had finished the measurements and seen the ladies out of the shop, I asked Manuel to complete the suit I was sewing while I worked on the dresses. I received more orders for dresses than I had in the past though suit orders were still the lion's share of the business.

A week later, just as Dr. Ribeiro said, in walked Mr. Murray—a short man with a flashing and friendly smile greeted me. Pleasantly surprised I welcomed him and inquired how I could serve him. He had four young chaps waiting in the car. He wanted two pairs of trousers and two shirts for each chap. He brought in the stripes and badges that were to be sewed on each pair of trousers and shirts. I was delighted and asked him to send them in. It was on a late Friday morning and after about two hours I was done with the measurements. Later within the next two weeks they came for their fittings and eventually picked up their clothing. Mr. Murray was delighted and promised to return at a future date with more orders. He also said that he would come in himself to be measured for a suit.

Business is getting better and better, I thought.

When I looked back at what I had accomplished since I opened my shop, especially within the 1920s, and all that was happening around me in my new home of Kenya, I felt blessed. As I had told Anton on a few occasions, it was time to get married. I needed to share my life with someone else. I wanted to have children and spoil them. Marriage and a family would be a big change, but I knew then that I was ready.

That evening I wrote to my parents telling them that I was ready to be married. I knew that they would be very happy to receive this letter. Ever since Miguel had married, they had been writing letters telling me that I should do the same. I mostly ignored those letters.

I mailed the letter the next morning, and within a month, I received a response from them. I wasn't surprised that they wrote back quickly; they were happy. They began organizing the match for me. I trusted them to find someone who would be able to adjust to life in Africa. From my letters and my visit to Goa, they had my stories of my life in Kenya.

The last letter from Miguel had said that he and Fatima were still not quite settled in Beira, and that he had not found regular tailoring work. He was called upon to do suits whenever needed by a couple of tailoring shops, but he seemed unhappy. I thought this was unusual; they had been in Beira since 1918, and it was now a little over ten years and they were still not settled. I wrote him a loving letter and told him to be patient even though I did not know what it was like to be living in Beira. He was now with his wife, and I could not interfere in that relationship.

As for myself, my future was in the hands of Mai and Pai.

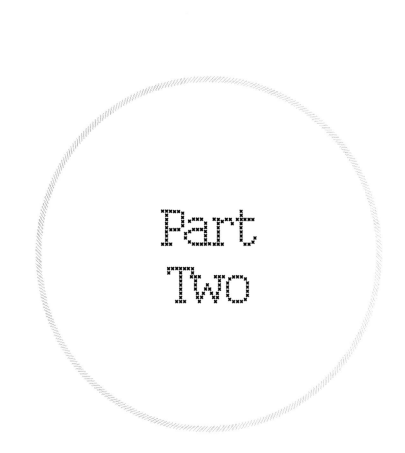

Part
Two

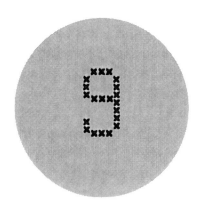

MY MARRIAGE IN GOA

I returned to Goa the second week of January 1932. This return was special as I was to be married. My parents hoped that, this time, their search for a suitable wife would be acceptable to me. Mai was no doubt thinking that I would not consent to marry and was even questioning my determination to do so. But she need not have worried. I *wanted* to get married—many of my friends and people I knew in Nairobi had married, and their lives were better for it. No, I had wanted to be sure my business was a success and sure of the woman I was to marry, both for my sake and for hers. Kenya was a different world, and I knew what an adjustment it would be for a Goan.

I sat in the front room of the family home of the woman I was to marry. Mai and Pai were with me. In my jacket pocket I carried the photo Mai had sent me six months earlier. I wanted to look at it for the hundredth time, but I didn't. I would be seeing her, face to face, for the first time in a matter of minutes. Trinia. I would see her and make my final decision.

I sat nervously on the edge of my chair, almost sick with anticipation, while our parents happily ate and talked about the snacks and sipped tea. Then Trinia walked in. We looked at each other. I saw her beautiful face, her smooth, creamy complexion. Her long black hair fell loosely over her shoulders. Her light brown eyes were sparklingly kind looking. She did not appear shy. She boldly looked at me. Both our parents left the room, leaving the two of us alone. The moment was electric. I walked to her and sat on the chair next to hers. She took my hand and we looked into each other's eyes, but we did not say anything to each other for a few seconds.

"I feel wonderful, do you?" I said in a whisper.

She squeezed my hand. "Before you came here, I didn't know what I'd feel. I was worried. Then I saw you. Yes, it feels good."

"You are beautiful, Trinia." She was only twenty-one, much younger than I was.

For the first time, I saw her smile in a reserved way. She was embarrassed I think.

"I like the way you are dressed in this fine white shirt and navy blue trousers. You look good. I like you, especially your smile."

She came closer to me. We embraced, but had to let go abruptly when our parents walked in. They saw it as a sign of my approval.

The parents discussed the details of the wedding plans and the dowry. Trinia and I kept looking at each other, not hearing anything in the room. Our silent exchanges were interrupted when Mai and Pai stood up to leave. On our way home they told me that the wedding festivities would begin shortly and would last for a week before the church ceremony.

"Sabby," said Mai. "You're not listening to us, are you?"

"No, what do I have to do? I'm happy with Trinia. Thank you, Mai and Pai. I have good feelings for Trinia. But I have one request—please arrange the wedding day for January 24. That is the day I left Goa sixteen years ago. Will it be possible?"

"That's good that you approve of Trinia. We will arrange your wedding date with the priest tomorrow," said Pai while Mai smiled at me. They carried on talking about the details of the wedding festivities. I drifted off again, hoping that I had made the right decision. But, I felt very excited about Trinia; it had to be the right decision.

I left Mai and Pai and went to visit our village chapel. The priest was delighted to see me after that many years. I gave him a large donation, telling him that I was doing well in Nairobi. He was very grateful and said that my name would be on the list of donors, etched on a marble slate and placed on the wall at the back of the chapel. I thanked him and left to look for Menino.

He was on holiday from his ship's duties, which meant that he would be at my wedding festivities. We went to the beach for old times' sake and exchanged stories of our very different lives—mine in Nairobi, his on the ship. I told him about John and Paulo; John was very much like Menino himself and Paulo was a different person altogether. It felt strange being back in Goa as a grown man in his thirties who ran a business in Nairobi. Menino recognized how I had become a different person.

In Menino, I saw an air of confidence that hadn't been there when we were teenagers. He was happy and more sociable than ever. His quick answers were even funnier than before. He loved his work on the ship and proudly told me about his duties as a steward. He hinted that his ship might soon be doing longer journeys and that he might see me in Kenya. We dodged some crashing waves as we walked along the beach; then the surf grew more gentle. We continued to relive our memories of our teenage years on this beach. As we prepared to leave, he promised to see me at my wedding.

Miguel, Fatima and their sons, Albert and Joe came back to Goa for my wedding; I was very happy. I managed to spend some time alone with Miguel. He was tense and anxious. He didn't like it in Beira, but Fatima did and was determined to stay there. Miguel still wanted to come to Nairobi. I told him it was difficult for me to advise him other than to say that, should the day arrive, I would welcome him in Nairobi. The rest he would have to sort out with Fatima.

Since the wedding was taking place on a short notice, we had to rush to complete the traditional rituals before the church ceremony during the week of January 17. There were daily activities with luncheons and dinners that included a special luncheon for our deceased relatives. We went to the civil registrar's office to register our marriage. The banns of marriage were announced on the Sunday before the ceremony. It was a busy week, as Trinia and I moved from one activity to the next.

The Ros (Roce) ritual held the day before the church ceremony was especially memorable. Mai prepared and laid out a variety of delicious dishes of food and drink for our family, friends and neighbours. We ate, drank, shared jokes and laughed. By the late evening, the people gathered for the ritual. This was held in the front yard of our home. Menino, my best friend, and I sat on the chairs positioned in the centre of the front yard. Each person lined up to pour coconut juice over us. Some mixed the coconut juice with beer or milk and even eggs. They delighted in pouring this liquid over my head or rubbing it on my face, arms, legs and letting this mess soak in from head to toe. I played up as well. I would shake out my head to let the juice spray onto the fellows near me. It was happily noisy with the crowd laughing and shouting. Lastly, water was poured over me and Menino. It cleansed me and signified the end of being a bachelor. Trinia went through the same ritual at her home.

Then, on January 24, came the church ceremony where Trinia and I stood side by side. My heart was warm and elevated throughout the ceremony. She looked beautiful in her wedding gown. Everyone was fussing around us. The party after the church service was about constant music and dancing—and lots of both. The food was delicious—I especially liked the soropatel. And there was plenty to drink. The speeches were long, but I enjoyed meeting and speaking with everyone at the party.

We danced the night away. I was very happy while I looked adoringly at Trinia; we held hands and squeezed them tightly. I had a good sense that there were happy times ahead of us. At the end of the night, I brought Trinia to my home, according to our custom. Mai prepared the back room for us. We were there by ourselves as a married couple and would be there for the rest of the week before we left Goa for Kenya. I couldn't be happier that I was married on January 24; Trinia smiled and agreed that it would now become a special day for her as well.

During the days, I took Trinia to a quiet spot on Benaulim beach where we were able to get to know each other on our own without curious neighbours around. I explained to Trinia about life in Nairobi. She had many questions about the different people there, for she understood that it was not like Goa. Then came questions about food items, spices, clothing, and climate. Her questions told me that she had thought about this move to Kenya. She seemed to know that it would be different there—she had a clearer sense of it than I had when I left for Africa sixteen years earlier.

I looked at her with much fondness and respect. Her light brown eyes showed warmth as her face glistened in the sun. I was already falling in love with her. She had an inquiring mind. Sometimes she looked puzzled at my answers while at other times she was excited. She could not imagine living very far away without her parents, sisters, brothers and friends. I comforted her by telling her that together we would make many friends and that there was an established Goan community in Nairobi that would make her feel at home.

We became distracted with the crowds that gathered on the beach; the fishermen were pulling in the fishing nets. We stood up and watched them as they pulled and pulled the rope to haul in the fish loaded in the net. Trinia looked at me and asked if she would see that in Kenya. I shook my head and told her Nairobi was quite far away from the sea. She reminded me that fishing was the main occupation of the people in Goa. I smiled back at her in recognition of this part of life in Goa.

We departed on January 30, 1932, on what would be a ten-day voyage via steamship to Mombasa. Trinia was distraught and quite inconsolable. Family and friends hugged us and wished us well. It was two days on the ship before Trinia was calm and more like herself. We occupied a very small private cabin. I continually spoke about Nairobi, my adventures in Mombasa, and how we would travel there for holidays as time went by. She listened to everything I said and did not have many questions. There were times when we were quiet and did not say anything to each other. When the waters were calm, we would go out on deck to look at the horizon over the sea, while the crew were busily working on the ship. This time around, it seemed that the sea waters were calmer, or maybe I was preoccupied with Trinia that I didn't notice the roughness of the sea voyage.

We talked with a family in the cabin next to ours. They had visited their relatives in Goa and were returning to Mombasa. I let them talk with Trinia about life in Kenya. We shared the differences between living in Mombasa and Nairobi. They informed Trinia that she would like Nairobi and that they sometimes spent time there with friends. Trinia smiled and said she would miss her family and friends in Goa—then she turned around to me, grabbed my hand and said she hoped to have a good life with me. I put my arm around her shoulder and told her that she would be happy in Nairobi.

We spent three days in Mombasa with Pedro who welcomed us, especially Trinia. He showed us the sights of Mombasa;

Fort Jesus and the beautiful beaches. I could see her becoming relaxed as we walked on the streets in Mombasa and strolled on the beach.

She's happy, I thought.

The best part of our time in Mombasa was dinner with Pedro's family. Trinia talked about *her* first experience of being on a ship, about feeling nausea, having to hold onto the handrails while climbing up and down, and the constant feeling of unsteadiness. She proudly talked about her sea legs and being able to move around the ship. They laughed with her. She quietly listened to everything they said about living in Mombasa.

Yes, it was very different from Goa, but it was a good life. There were different kinds of people to know and different places to visit in the big city of Nairobi. Pedro moved closer to Trinia, pointed to me and advised her that I was doing well in business and that she would have many joys in Nairobi. Trinia turned to me and gave me an irresistible smile. I gently put my arm around her, in full agreement with Pedro.

Trinia and Pedro's wife, Anna continued to exchange stories while Pedro and I talked about Goa. He assured me that, in time, Trinia would adjust and, yes, she looked happy with me. I watched her moving around, and she was at ease.

After three days, we set off on our train journey to Nairobi—a passenger train this time. We were in a private second-class cabin. I told Trinia about our new home that I had rented a couple of months ago. It was a small home with two bedrooms, a bathroom, a kitchen and a toilet room at the very end of the backyard. There was a small garden with a little fence around the home. I told her about Kamau; he cleaned the place and even cooked meals for me, and how Mrs. Sequeira had taught him how to cook Goan meals.

Trinia looked at me quite puzzled.

"Who is Kamau? I will look after the house and cook the meals. There's no need for Kamau." She sounded defensive and almost annoyed.

"Kamau is African. He left his shamba in the countryside for a life in the city. Shambas are African owned plots of land. They grow vegetables and fruit for their food and some of them sell these varieties to us in our neighbourhood. Many of the Africans from the countryside come to the city looking for work. Kamau is one of them. He's a reliable and trustworthy housekeeper. He'll show you around. Take you to the market. You'll find him very helpful. Let us continue to keep him. Later, if you do not want him around, that is okay."

I spoke cautiously because I knew this would be one of the many adjustments she would have to make.

Hesitatingly, Trinia looked at me and shrugged her shoulders. She was quiet and probably wondering about Nairobi. It would not be anything like she was used to in Goa. I had a strong desire to be protective of her while she adjusted to life in Nairobi. She was a gentle person, and I was in love.

NEW ADJUSTMENT
IN NAIROBI

Upon our arrival at the railway station in Nairobi, we took a taxi home. It was late afternoon. Kamau was standing outside and rushed to us to help with the luggage. I introduced Trinia. She stood back, unsure how to respond. She smiled at him.

"Welcome, welcome," he said.

We settled down in the living room, he brought tea and some biscuits. We quietly sipped on our tea. I picked up a biscuit while Trinia looked towards the kitchen. When I finished my tea, I noticed that she had only taken a couple of sips of hers. I took her hand and showed her around our place. She stopped in both of the bedrooms and, from the windows, looked out into the garden.

We walked to the kitchen where Kamau was preparing dinner. He stood back and let her walk around. She was quiet. Shortly thereafter, we had dinner. Trinia watched Kamau serving us, unprepared for this kind of treatment. She shifted about in her chair, not eating much of her dinner. I comforted her by sharing news about my tailoring shop. On our way to church, on Sunday, I said to her, we would stop by the shop. She looked at me shyly, and I shared with her the household routines. Kamau arrived at around six every morning and left after serving dinner.

"I don't know how I'll get used to this. It's different, and now I see that we have Kamau to help around the home." She was distressed and looked in my direction.

"I understand your confusion." I moved closer to her on the sofa.

There was knock at the door, and when I opened it, there were Luis, Manuel and their wives. After introductions, we sat down and talked for a while. The women sat together and were deep in conversation while we enjoyed our drinks at the other side of the living room. John and Paulo dropped by as well. It was getting late into the night when our guests left, and it was with an invitation from Luis to come to Sunday lunch at their place. Trinia's first day in Nairobi had been unusual. We settled down for a lovely night together alone in our home.

I now have a wife to share my life in Nairobi.

On Sunday, on our way to church, I took Trinia to my shop. We stopped on the street. I proudly pointed out my sign, S. Mendes Ltd. Tailoring Establishment. I then took her hand and we walked across the street. I unlocked the door, stepped back and held her hands as we entered the shop together. I could feel her pulse racing when we stepped inside. She let go of my hand

and slowly walked through the shop. She smiled at me and stopped near the desk.

"You own this?"

"I own everything *inside*. I pay rent for the shop. What do you think?"

"It's nothing like I imagined. I don't remember seeing anything like this where we lived in Goa. Maybe there are shops like this in Panjim. You know, I always wanted to visit Panjim."

"Yes, probably in Panjim, but in Margao there are shops like this. Remember, I trained in Margao. Maybe when we next go to Goa, we can take a trip to Panjim."

"Yes," she said. "Next time we go back."

"I'm not sure Panjim compares to Nairobi. You'll see. This is a big city, bigger than Panjim. The British do things differently from the Portuguese, you'll see."

Trinia cuddled up to me. I locked the shop, and we walked to church. After Mass, I introduced Trinia to my regular group of friends. Anton and Tina came over. We stood under the shade of a tree talking awhile. Trinia looked comfortable with this crowd. We soon left and walked to Luis' place for Sunday lunch. Anton and Tina joined us. It was a noisy luncheon. I noticed Trinia in conversation with the women, and I was thrilled she was with me. When we came home that night, Trinia became very talkative.

"You know, at church, I noticed that the priest is European. When Mass began, he looked around and asked some of our Goans to stand up to give their seats to the Europeans who were late for Mass. I found that strange. Why did he do that?"

"Because we are under British rule, the Europeans get special treatment. They show prejudice against anyone who is not European. And some, not all of the priests, practise it in church as well."

"Does that sound right? We are in church to pray and say the prayers of the Mass."

"No, it's not right. I heard that, in the early days, the British were quite surprised that Goans were Catholics. I heard many stories of the struggles of the Goans to attend church services in the same church as the Europeans. It makes me feel annoyed. We live in a segregated society."

Trinia continually asked me questions about segregation and how it would affect our life in Kenya. I told her everything I had seen and thought about it. She looked sad and found it difficult to understand. She said some of the women had talked about this segregation in hushed voices, and said that we could not do anything except to live with it.

"It was only in church that I saw the Europeans," she said. "They live separately from us and we don't mix with them at all? You know this is something I'll have to adjust to as the women said to me. It was not very good what the priest did in the church, calling out the Goans to stand up and give their seats to the Europeans."

"Yes, I know. In Goa, on village feast days there are reserved seats for the brahmins and none of us would take those seats in the church. I remember that. But that is different. Here the priests embarrass us by telling us to move in front of everyone in church."

"It's different here all right," she said. "What else do I have to know? Tell me Sabby."

"We keep to ourselves, and so long as we don't go to their restaurants or clubs, it will be all right. We must constantly be aware of that all the time. We're not allowed in certain places. In time, you will know where to go and where *not* to go."

"This worries me. How do I know where to go and where not to go? Are there signs that tell us that?"

"Yes, certain places have the signs, especially in the buildings on the main streets in the city. But there are places outside the city where the Europeans live in their own areas and have their own clubs. We do not even *think* of going there. Anyway, it is too far away for us to get there."

She sighed. "Too much to adjust to. I don't believe this segregation is right. But when we are with the Goans, everyone seems happy and doing well here in Nairobi. They seem to ignore this segregation and only a couple of women spoke about it."

"It is an unspoken code that we live by. We cannot do anything about it. We are under British rule; they make the laws and we have to follow them. Come Trinia," I said. "It's late, let us go to bed. We can talk some more about this tomorrow and the days after. I have my own opinions which I will share with you as the days go by."

As she stood up, a question occurred to her.

"Do you have any European customers?"

"At first I didn't, but yes, now I do, and they add to the success of the shop each year. When it comes to serving their needs, they will come to our shops. My European customers appear to be kind and accepting. But I'm never sure. I don't ask many questions. It is business. Come come, let's go to bed. It's getting late, and I have a busy day tomorrow," I said. "My first day back after our lovely time in Goa."

The next morning Luis' wife, Josie, and Anton's wife, Tina, came to be with Trinia for the day. I left for the shop and found myself walking on air, very happy to have Trinia with me in Nairobi. It was time to get back to work. I stopped by Ali's shop to get the spare keys. He grabbed hold of my hands and congratulated me on my marriage. He told me that everything went well at the shop while I was away. Every day he would check in on Manuel and Luis.

Before I left for Goa, we had gone through a busy Christmas season with orders for suits and dresses. There had been no outstanding orders by the time I left for Goa. While I was away, Luis said he worked on dresses for his relatives. Manuel talked about making a suit for one of his friends. That was good—they kept themselves busy. Everything looked exactly as I left it.

That first day back turned out to be a social day and not a usual working day. My regular customers dropped by to congratulate me on my marriage, including Nathoo. He invited Trinia and I to dinner at his place to meet his family. Mr. Desai, who owned the building, stopped by, and by the end of the day, as I was closing shop, Mr. Rana another one of my regular and favoured customers came in. We sat and talked by my office desk. He advised me that it was time to buy a house of my own, now that I had a wife and with children to come.

"I like this advice," I said. "I'll talk to Trinia."

"When you are ready, let me know. I can help you with purchasing the land and building your home. It's now time for you to plant your roots in Nairobi, you know."

"Yes, I understand, it's time to do that. As soon as we're ready, I will talk to you. Business is doing well. I think I can do it. But let me talk to Trinia. Everything is very new to her now. She needs time to adjust to Nairobi. She's only been here for a few days. She needs time to adjust."

"I understand. But don't wait *too* long."

We both left the shop. I locked the door and hurriedly made my way home. I couldn't wait to see Trinia. I wanted to surprise her by dropping by for lunch, but that hadn't been possible. I hoped she had a good day with Josie and Tina. When I approached home, I could see her in the garden. She was bending down picking the flowers, I assumed. I called her name. She looked up and came to the street. She grabbed my hand and we walked inside. Once inside we hugged each other—she cried without stopping.

I did not let go of her. She missed her family and friends in Goa. She felt lonely. We sat down in the living room, and Kamau brought us tea. She looked at me and told me how helpful Josie and Tina had been.

"We talked and laughed. We sat in the garden. Kamau pre-pared lunch for us. Then Josie left soon after lunch. But Tina stayed and we went for a walk outside. She left around three o'clock to get dinner ready for her family. Suddenly I felt alone and strange."

"I'm very sorry you're feeling this way. I know you miss your family. We have to get used to each other and being in Nairobi. We're going to create a good life for ourselves with children around us. I promise you it will get better for both of us."

She wiped her eyes with the back of her hand.

"After Tina left, Kamau told me that he was preparing dinner. I went to the kitchen with him, and he showed me what he was preparing. You know, he is good at cooking our food. It was strange seeing him cook, but I thought I better leave him to his usual duties. I went in the garden again, and your neigh-bour Naseem came over and talked with me. That made me feel happy. Then we walked around her house. She told me about the flowers and plants she had in her garden. She gave me some seedlings to plant in our garden. I was trying to decide where to plant them when I heard you calling my name."

"When I saw you in the garden," I said, "I began smiling and came even more quickly towards you. When I see you, I feel very happy."

"Yes, I feel the same way, especially when you called out to me. It was this wonderful feeling of warmth all over me."

"We must use this happiness to create a beautiful life for our-selves and the children we will have in Nairobi."

Kamau interrupted us. He wanted to know when to serve dinner and if Trinia wished to check out the dinner he prepared for us. Trinia left with Kamau for the kitchen. I stayed in the living room. It struck me again how in love I felt; she would be a loving wife and a wonderful mother to our children.

Unconsciously I picked up my pipe, cleared it of any left-over ash and filled it loosely with tobacco, compressing it gently until the pipe was tightly packed. I lit the tobacco with a wooden match, moving the flame carefully on the surface, while drawing in gently and rhythmically, until the tobacco was evenly lit. I relit it again and again and eventually began puffing, taking in the aroma of the tobacco that filled the air. This relaxed me.

Trinia walked in and was surprised to see me smoking my pipe. I quickly told her that this was my routine when I came home. She gave me a slightly disapproving look and said that dinner would be ready soon. We spoke about my day at the shop, and she listened curiously about the people that had come to visit me to offer good wishes for our marriage.

All through dinner Trinia was talkative. She liked her time in the market, and repeated some of her conversation with Josie and Tina and her visit with Naseem. She was grateful for Kamau and that he had been very good in the kitchen and cleaned up the house very well. She seemed to approve of him. This was good. I could sense her slowly adjusting to my routines that would eventually change to suit her style, I assumed.

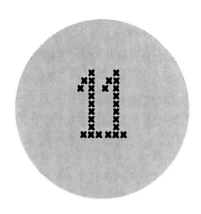

THE 1930s – A DECADE OF SIGNIFICANT EVENTS

We were happy together. Trinia was pregnant with our first child. Peter was born on November 14, 1932. We were filled with joy with a child in our life. During the days, Tina and Josie would visit, and that made Trinia very happy and settled in.

Trinia contentedly cared for our son Peter. She showed him off to anyone who visited us, and even on the street when people stopped to look at little Peter in the pram, she beamed with pride and joy. She was almost a different person when she became a mother.

She began making the variety of Christmas Goan snacks in preparation for our Christmas celebrations. Josie and Tina came by to help with making these Christmas snacks and at the same time Trinia cared for baby Peter. It was a busy time at home. During the week before and after Christmas Trinia prepared trays of her Christmas snacks to give to our friends and relatives. They would drop by for a Christmas visit with a tray of Christmas snacks and then Trinia would give the visitor her tray of Christmas snacks. This was a traditional Goan custom. On Christmas Eve there was Midnight Mass but we didn't attend as Peter was only a baby this first Christmas of ours as a family. Instead we stayed home, Trinia and Kamau cooked a feast for Christmas Day. Friends came and went during this festive season.

She pleaded with me to take her to Goa to show our son to our families. It was in February of 1934 that we sailed to Goa with our fifteen-month-old baby. We stayed with Trinia's family; there were many celebrations. Mai and Pai were jubilant to see their grandson. I felt ignored as everyone was fussing over Trinia and baby Peter. Actually I felt fulfilled to see such happiness around. It was a wonderful trip. But I did notice that Pai was not his usual self; he looked tired and older.

On our return from Goa, there was a letter from Miguel. He was desperate to come to Nairobi. Even Fatima had come around to his way of thinking, for they did not have a good life in Beira. My letters to him were always welcoming, and I let him know that Trinia and I would support them in whatever way we could, should they decide to come to Kenya.

Over the months we wrote letters to each other; mainly about their move to Kenya. They decided they had to save enough money to make the journey for the five of them—including their sons, Albert and Joe. But Fatima wanted to spend Christmas in Beira with her family. That meant that they would not be in Nairobi until January or February of 1936. But in the meantime, Miguel wanted us to find a place for them to live. He asked me if he could work at my shop, which would be difficult as I had enough tailors. Miguel, my brother, would be coming to live in Nairobi. Trinia was glad to have family in Nairobi—but told me that the business side of things she would leave to me to sort out. Miguel would need to start work immediately upon arrival in Nairobi.

Trinia announced more good news. She was pregnant with our second child. We were both grateful for our growing family. There was no question that Trinia had adjusted to Nairobi, and little Peter kept her busy, then there was a second child on the way.

We were active in the St. Francis Xavier Goan Tailors' Society Club and went to all the social functions—the most popular was on December 3, the feast of St. Francis Xavier, the patron Saint of Goa. The society continued to have our functions in the church hall because we still didn't have a clubhouse (and the attempts to get one built in the twenties had led to disagreements and bitterness). Paulo, Cyprian and their wives came to our society celebrations. Anton and Tina, attended as well. Of course, John was always there and stayed over at our place for the weekend before he returned to Limuru on Sunday evenings. John was dropped off and picked up by the driver of the Glover family. They treated him fairly, for they knew how important it was for him to socialize with our Goan community. Tina and Josie had become good friends with Trinia. They often visited each other during the day and sometimes they went to the market together.

In the meantime, we had our own routine. I left early morning for the shop while Trinia looked after Peter. On October 20, 1935, Matthew was born. Peter was three years old and could not quite make out baby Matthew. Trinia was very affectionate to both of them and played all kinds of games with them. When I came home, it was always a noisy time with a baby and a toddler. I would spend time with Peter while Trinia fed, cleaned and clothed baby Matthew.

On this one evening with the children asleep and when we settled down to our quiet time in the living room, I showed Trinia the letter from Mai. It was a sad letter telling us that Pai had passed away. I was filled with sorrow, thinking of my Pai in Goa. Trinia came up to me and we quietly said the rosary for his soul. She said that the next day she would go to the church to request a Mass for Pai. I nodded in thankful agreement. I wrote a long letter to Mai. As our custom I would wear a black arm band for the one-year mourning period. Miguel and I wrote letters to each other in remembrance of Pai.

The hot season came in November as did the Christmas time rush orders. I had many orders for suits and many more orders for dresses. Most of my Goan male customers had three suits made in a year—one at Christmas, one at Easter and one at their birthdays. The women, in addition to these special occasions had dresses made for parties, dances and sporting events. This kept me and my tailors busy with a growing business. In between this busy time, I thought about Pai and wondering how Mai was coping alone in our home. I wrote her another letter.

Soon after the Christmas season, we settled down to some quiet family time at home and taking stock in the shop. Miguel's next letter informed us that they would be arriving on February 1, 1936. After a week of searching and with the help of a couple of people at the Tailors' Society we found a suitable flat for them close to the city. I sent off a letter giving him this news and indicating that he could work with me in my shop to start with even though I had my tailors. When he was settled, we could talk about his future plans in Nairobi.

Miguel and his family arrived in Nairobi on Wednesday February 5 and settled in their flat. We visited them and talked about Pai. We were both still sad that he was no longer there with Mai. We had another Mass in memory of Pai; then we gathered at our place for lunch on the Saturday. Miguel said that he would come to my shop on Monday.

When Miguel came to the shop. I showed him around, introduced him to Luis and Manuel, and explained how I ran the business and how Luis and Manuel worked on the orders that came in.

That's when Miguel told me that he wanted to become a *partner* of my business.

I was taken aback. After all I did to develop this business on my own, this would not happen almost immediately; I took a deep breath and explained to him that, for now, he should work *for* the business, and later, once he had adjusted to working and living in Nairobi, he could decide what he wanted to do. Perhaps he would want to set up his own business. I advised him that I would put him in touch with people who would help him.

"But Sabby, I want to do what you are doing. I want to be part of the business," Miguel said defiantly looking around the shop and at Luis and Manuel working at the sewing machines.

My anger was rising like a tide. *Leave it to Miguel to expect something handed to him.* If I remembered correctly, he simply did not have that same passion that I had for tailoring. He always considered it a job and was not enthusiastic about being a tailor. I knew he would be a decent employee, diligent at least if not as disciplined as Luis and Manuel.

"Miguel," I said as evenly as possible. "I have spent *years* taking risks, negotiating business loans, and carefully developing and growing this business. I have been sole owner with help from other business owners. I now have special working relationships with them. I cannot simply take you on as a partner the day you show up."

He listened with his head down, shifting his feet about.

I took a deep breath. "I don't know what it's like working in Beira. But I know for certain that working in Nairobi is entirely different from working in Goa. Give it some time, and let's talk about your future in a few months. Not now."

"You know, Sabby, while we were in Beira there was not much work. I was doing odd jobs here and there, and that caused anxiety and uncertainty, especially with the money. It seemed we were constantly running out of money. Then I received letters from you, saying that you were well established in your business and that Trinia had adjusted nicely to being in Nairobi. Fatima and I want that too."

"I worked very hard to *become* established, Miguel. That is *why* my life looks the way it does," I said. "Let's not talk about it anymore today. I want to help you become settled in Nairobi; earn money and get your feet firmly planted here. That is the first step. You can't stitch something that has not been cut, and you can't cut something that has not been chalked out, and you cannot make chalk marks until you take measurements. One step at a time, right?"

He was quiet for a moment.

"You're right, Sabby," he said. Then he looked me in the eye. "I would like to start work right away if you'll have me."

"Of course," I said and walked him to the back of the shop.

When I informed Luis and Manuel that Miguel would be working with us, I could see that Manuel was not pleased. I saw what I thought might be a look of disappointment in his eyes. I explained to them that we had quite a few suit orders and that Miguel would be a good addition going into the Easter period—but neither of my tailors looked convinced. I showed the wardrobe of incomplete suits to Miguel and assigned him one to complete.

We resumed our work with very little conversation. At lunchtime, Luis and Manuel left while I had lunch with Miguel. At the end of the day, Miguel left early saying he wanted to talk to Fatima about working for my business. When he was gone I brought in Luis and Manuel.

"Look, I know you are not too pleased with this new arrangement, but he is my brother, newly arrived in the city with his family. Know that I consider you both a big part of the success of this shop, and I will not forget that."

Manuel nodded, and I could tell that he was not in complete agreement.

"Family," said Luis. "We understand, Sabby. You're right."

"I want to see him get his feet on the ground here. Besides there is enough work at the moment." I responded with some uncertainty.

That night after the children had been put to bed, and with Kamau cleaning the kitchen before leaving for the day, Trinia and I were comfortably seated in the living room. I had my pipe and Trinia, her coffee.

"Miguel was at the shop this morning. We spoke for a while. He wants to become a partner in the business. I discouraged him and offered him work at the shop. I think he and Fatima need more time to settle in. Besides, I am not sure I *want* him to become a partner. If he wants to be in business, he can start his own business. For the last few years, I went through many ups and downs to be where I am now in my business. What do you think?"

"Yes and, while Miguel was at the shop, Fatima was here," said Trinia both hands around her cup. "She kept talking about Miguel becoming a partner in your business. I listened and told her that I don't know much about the business and that it would be up to you to decide. She looked angry and said that she wanted me to support her and that I should *tell* you to make Miguel a partner. I said I couldn't do that. It was very uncomfortable. Remember Sabby, I don't know Fatima very well."

I sighed. "I am sorry that happened."

"You don't need to be sorry. They are family and we need to help each other. I understand that."

"At least I employed him much to the disappointment of Manuel. You know he and Luis have been with me from the beginning. I think I may lose Manuel. He appears unhappy and

I certainly hope he will not leave. They are getting regular salaries. But I had to give Miguel the opportunity of regular tailoring work."

On Sunday after Mass, we had Miguel, Fatima and their sons, Albert and Joe over for lunch to meet our friends. This was a good introduction to the Goan community in Nairobi; they moved around the crowd, and talked with our friends. When our friends left, and alone with Miguel and family we spent some more time talking about Pai. I kept thinking of him. Later they left and we thought it was a good afternoon with family and friends.

In the evening, Trinia and I continued discussing our obligations to our extended family. She did not want to get involved in the business side, and I understood that. I had to sort that part out with Miguel. I had to give him time to get used to working *for* the business. In the meantime, Trinia suggested, we could spend more family time with them. We were two different families and we would not interfere with each other's lives. But we had to love each other as a larger family and celebrate each other's joys and help each other out when necessary. These thoughts kept going through my mind as I lay awake till later that night. I did eventually fall asleep, only to be woken up before dawn by Matthew crying out to be fed.

This is my life, I thought. *This is family life and I like it.*

Back at the shop, Miguel appeared to understand that he would continue working for me, at least for a while. He wasn't happy about it, but he accepted it. He said that Fatima was not at all happy, but he managed to convince her that they were new to Nairobi and they needed time to adjust. I hoped it would work out in time.

But that wasn't to be. After the Easter rush Miguel again started pressuring me for a partnership.

In July, I met up with Nathoo and asked his advice. He knew my situation with Miguel and had given it some thought. He shook his head and said he didn't want to be involved in a family matter… but that looking at it in terms of a *business* matter, it was a bad situation.

"Don't enter into a business relationship with someone you aren't free to cooperate on a business basis. He is your brother, and with some families, you cannot have a professional relationship. He wants some form of partnership now, maybe later he will want an *equal* partnership. What happens when he wants to make decisions that you don't agree with?"

"You're right," I said.

"You need to ask yourself what he brings to a partnership. That is what you would do if he wasn't your brother. Is he as good a tailor as you?"

"He's not as dedicated as I am. He considers it a job. At the moment I assign the orders to the tailors. I give him the orders mostly from our Goan community. Therefore, when he opens his own shop, which I hope he will do, he can take these customers with him. I also want him to adjust to living in Nairobi."

"You have bills to pay and loans to take care of. Does he know this?" Nathoo said in a defiant voice that surprised me.

"I explained the situation to him but did not give him details because he would not understand it. I think he has to adjust to living here like I did."

"Sabby, you need to think like a business man. Don't be affected by emotional ties to your brother, not in this situation. When it comes to business it must be treated as a business. I sense that Miguel's not very business minded. He's more interested in earning a living than creating a business. Is that right?"

"Yes, I always wanted to own a tailoring shop, whereas he is happy with working as a tailor. I'll have to find a way of explaining that to him without offending him even more."

"That'll be a difficult conversation. I don't envy you, but I do wish you luck with it. Family can be tricky at the best of times."

This had become a bigger mess than I had expected. Trinia said that her relationship with Fatima became difficult. Our families were drifting apart. As the weeks became months, the tension could be felt in the shop itself. The atmosphere in the shop had changed. We quietly worked on the orders that came in. Since there was tension between Miguel and I, we only visited them once over the Christmas holidays.

Then in late January 1937 it became worse. It had been almost a year since Miguel started working for me, and I could tell that he felt it was time for a change. One day after lunch, I could see Miguel and Manuel in deep conversation and not sewing the suits. I was very uncomfortable. At the end of the day I asked Miguel to wait because I wanted to speak with him. As soon as we were alone together, it was Miguel who spoke.

"I want ownership in the business, and I want to earn more money." He had raised his voice and was quite upset. "I'm not happy with our arrangement."

I glared at him, guarding my tongue as I did not want to say anything I would not be able to *unsay*. Miguel stood and paced back and forth in front of the office desk.

"We've been over this before, Miguel. Owning a business is not as simple as you make it—"

"You take care of the accounting, and I'll be partner of the business."

He was determined not to listen. I had, of course, explained it before.

"No, that is not how it works," I said (and not for the first time). "You'll have to share the expenses and bring in more orders from customers. You haven't been here long. You need more customers to ask for you to do their suits. At the moment, they're not doing that."

"I have a few Goan customers."

"Yes, you do, because I *assign* their orders to you. I don't see customers coming in *asking* for you to do their suits. You have heard them come in asking for Manuel or I to do their suits. That's when you know you're a good tailor."

That stung him, but I took no pleasure in it. Miguel was unhappy and had been for a long time. And his unhappiness in the shop had changed the atmosphere. There was tension and that took away much of my joy at work. He had to go out on his own.

After a long silence, that he seemed either unable or unwilling to break himself, I spoke.

"Miguel, I cannot do any more for you. You need to make a decision as to what you are going to do next. You are my brother, and you always will be, but you need to stand on your own two feet and take a step."

He stood then.

"I will not be back tomorrow. And what's more neither will Manuel. I have found a place where the two of us can set up our own business. I would have stayed here as a partner and you are forcing me to leave."

I didn't bother to point out that it was he who was being unreasonable; he was hurt and had always wanted what was mine. Perhaps that was the way with younger brothers. I was surprised about Manuel, and was sad to see him go. But if I had to lose Manuel to see Miguel go out on his own, I wouldn't complain.

I opened my desk drawer, picked out my chequebook, and wrote out a cheque to him for the work he had done.

"Miguel," I said, handing it to him, "I wish you the best. I truly do. I am glad you came to Nairobi, and I hope you and Manuel will succeed in your business. No hard feelings follow you from my shop."

He took the cheque, nodded, and left. I could tell that he wanted to say more, but couldn't. That was fine. Miguel was still in Nairobi, and he was still my brother. There was time for us to settle our differences yet.

Still, it was with a heavy heart that I began putting my sewing away and tidying up my worktable ready for the next day. As I was finishing, Manuel walked in. He appeared awkward but decisive.

"Sabby, I want to tell you myself that I will be going with Miguel. We'll be doing tailoring together."

"Yes, Miguel told me. I'm pleased you came to tell me yourself even though I'm disappointed that you are leaving me. But it's your choice. Let me see, I owe you some money for the month."

I went to the desk and once again wrote out a cheque. He was uneasy, and our combined silence was clearly felt. I handed over the cheque and shook his hands.

"You're a good tailor. You'll do well. Look after Miguel for me. He needs support and guidance. You know what needs to be done. Good luck."

"Thank you, Sabby," he said. "Thank you for the tailoring experience; I will remember it always. You know I too wanted to go out on my own, and now I can do it with Miguel. I could not do it on my own."

I wasn't sure if that was true but I didn't say any more.

"We have said enough. I'll come to visit you now and again, and if I'm too busy I'll send some customers to both of you."

"Thank you," he said and left.

I breathed a sigh of relief. I looked around and the shop felt as it once had. The tensions had just departed. It was time to go home.

After dinner, once the children were put to bed, I shared with Trinia everything that had happened in the shop. She took my hands, looked in my eyes and whispered to me that she supported me.

"Our families might not be in a good relationship for a while, and Fatima won't make it any easier. But remember, what happened in the shop was for the best. I am relieved. I hope you are too."

"Yes, I suppose I am. I will have to replace Manuel though. He was a good tailor, but I am glad that Miguel has him, it will improve his chances. I'll put the word out for a tailor at the next Tailors' Club meeting."

The next day, I spoke with Luis and my other regular tailor—a young man who had been working part time for me for six months—and explained the situation to them. They listened carefully and then Luis declared that he was pleased that they had left; it was very unpleasant the last few months. I agreed with him and apologized for my part in it and assured them both that I would replace Manuel soon. They went back to sewing.

Now I have to explain it to Mai, I thought. That would be a difficult letter to write.

It did not take much time to replace Manuel. My shop had a good reputation, and there were a few willing unemployed tailors. Joseph was our new tailor. He worked well with Luis, and during busy times, he was able to work with little supervision.

Unfortunately, our relationship with Miguel and Fatima was not so quick to heal, which made me sad. After Sunday Mass, Trinia and I would always make an effort to speak with them and invite them for lunch, but each time they had an excuse for not coming over. Whether it was bitterness or pride that kept them distant was hard to tell.

It was July of 1938 before I started making any progress with my younger brother. During the week, I visited him at his place of work. It was on the second floor of a building not far from my shop. He had one large room with a couple of sewing machines. He seemed to be content, and both he and Manuel were busy. Miguel would not tell me much about the business, but he said they had enough orders that paid the bills and kept his family happy. He admitted that he didn't get as many orders as I did—I informed him that it would take time to increase the number of customers. The more I visited Miguel, the more he—slowly—came around to a closer brotherly relationship. Trinia and I decided to visit them at home and did what we could to become closer to them. In time we continued to invite them to our home. They would visit sometimes but not often.

It was around late September 1938 that Dr. Ribeiro came to the shop for a new suit and, asking after my growing family, suggested that our Peter should be attending the private Goan school. Though the school was named for him—for he donated the land on which it was built in 1931—his suggestion had nothing to do with ego. He simply felt that all Goan children deserved the best education available. I said that I would discuss it with Trinia but that we would probably follow his advice. By that time Trinia was pregnant with our third child.

In January we did enrol Peter at the Goan school. Trinia was happy to take him to his first year at primary school. Peter turned six in November 1938. The school year commenced in January and the children had to be six years to enrol in school, and since Peter was born in November, he was one of the older children starting school on Monday, January 9, 1939. Trinia was kept busy as she had our four-year-old Matthew to look after while Peter was at school. A few months later Theresa was born on May 8, 1939. Trinia thought that we were blessed as Theresa, a girl was born in May, the month devoted to Our Lady.

As each year had passed, I thought of how my dreams came true. It was July of 1939, the shop was running well, my tailors were happy and productive, and the strain of Miguel had been healed and forgotten. It was while these thoughts were going my mind that Mr. Rana walked in to pick up a suit and a couple of pairs of casual trousers.

"Sabby, it's been a few years now since I suggested you buy a house. You now have three children. It is time for a place of your own."

"Mr. Rana, I had too many distractions. First Trinia's adjustment to Nairobi, then the children came quite quickly, and lastly I had to sort out my problems with my brother. That was a difficult time the short period he was here with me. Now he has gone. I'll definitely talk with Trinia soon."

"Trinia settled in now? When I see you, I think all is going well at home. You look happy and eager to get home at the end of the day. That's a good sign, you know?"

"Yes, yes, Trinia is well settled in Nairobi. We visited Goa twice already and that made her very happy. But she has decided that Kenya is now her home. She is a Kenyan like the rest of us."

He smiled, a broad genuine smile.

"Good. That's good, Sabby. Maybe now is the time for a house. Who knows? There is talk of war on the news. How will it affect us here? No one can say. You may even have to postpone building your house. Still that should not stop you from moving forward. No plan can wait for the *perfect* time," Mr. Rana said with a more serious tone to his voice.

"Yes, I heard about the war too. But I'll talk with Trinia, and we can always make plans now and then see what happens."

I thought I felt anxiety in Mr. Rana as he shook my hand and then walked towards the door, wishing me well. On my way home, I went to the post office to check for letters in my post office box; there was an envelope with a black edging. This only meant a death. I put it in my jacket pocket and went home.

That evening after dinner, Trinia and I sat in the living room while the children were asleep, including baby Theresa. I sipped my cognac while Trinia sipped her coffee. It was a good time to talk about buying our own home but I had to open the letter first. I looked at Trinia and asked her to open the letter. She read it and with tears in her eyes she said that Mai had passed away. I cried and Trinia cried with me. After several moments we recited the rosary for Mai's soul. The next day Trinia would go to the church to request for a Mass for Mai's soul. We sat quietly for a long time. It was no time to talk about building our home.

Together with Miguel and his family, we attended Mass for Mai's soul. Then we gathered at our home for a quiet Sunday luncheon to remember Mai. We were deeply saddened. Miguel was quiet and didn't say much. I had many memories of Mai flash through my mind. We would mourn her passing for a year.

A month later I sat with Trinia in the living room during our usual quiet time when the children were asleep. She looked at me and knew that I wanted to talk about something different even though my thoughts were in Goa and that my parents were no longer there. I straightened up and in an almost different tone I said.

"The business is doing well, Miguel is on his own, and I want to talk with you about something special. We can afford to buy a house. We can be more comfortable in a place of our own, maybe even a bigger place. What do you think?"

"But houses are expensive here, are you sure we can afford to buy a house?"

"Well, I was talking with Mr. Rana. You know, my regular customer. A long time ago he suggested we buy our own house, but I didn't talk about it because we were busy with the children and then there was Miguel. And, of course, I wanted you to be well adjusted to Nairobi. Now let's talk about it."

"You know, Sabby, it's good to see you cheerful again. I know how your Mai's death affected you; but you will always have memories of both your Mai and Pai." I agreed and we were silent for a few minutes.

She broke the silence, "the house, I will be very happy to have a home of our own. Where would we buy a house?"

"We have to buy land and then have it built. Mr. Rana said that it has to be in the area designated for Indians. There are many Goans settled in Pangani and there is a church there that is attended by Goans. There are no Europeans there."

"Yes, I would prefer to live among our own people. Not that we have a choice, no?"

　　　　　　　　　　　　　　　　　　　　　　　　　MARIA LYNCH

"No indeed. The British claim what they desire and push everyone else to the side. I have been here many years and that doesn't seem likely to change. You are beginning to understand life here. The British have used their power to suppress the Africans in their own country so that Kenya can become a White Kenya. It's not right."

"Sabby, you are getting political again. What can we do? You chose to come here, and now I am married to you, and we have children, and we promised ourselves that we would make our lives here."

I drifted into my own thoughts for a few moments. I thought about the injustice of it all. The ugliness of segregation and the shape of the world in which we had chosen to raise our children.

"Sabby, did you hear what I said? Tell me what Mr. Rana said and how do we get our own place."

"Sorry, Trinia. I was distracted with other thoughts about living here in Nairobi. Mr. Rana is willing to lend us the money to purchase the land and build a house. He would draw up a set of payments that we would have to pay on a monthly basis. It is called a mortgage. It's a good plan. I would like to do it. But I want to put the house in your name. In that way we can keep it separate from the business. What do you think?"

"My name? Oh Sabby, I don't know. You are the husband. It seems strange that I should own anything like a house. What would people say?"

I smiled at her as she continued talking about our traditions. She was beautiful when she spoke in that serious tone. She continually surprised me.

"Trinia, you're right, of course, about our traditions. But we can keep it to ourselves. No one has to know, except, of course, when our children get older. They will have to be told, when we are getting closer to our retirement stage of our lives. We'll make a will for you; our home will be in your name."

"Sabby, this is getting very complicated. Did Mr. Rana give you this advice? When you talk about a will, this means we will have to go to the lawyers."

"Yes. I have checked this out, not only with Mr. Rana, but also with Nathoo who knows this sort of thing. It is important to keep personal wealth separate from the business, he said. Don't worry, we'll get a lawyer to draw up the will."

"I will leave it in your hands," said Trinia coming closer to me on the sofa.

We cuddled together. Then we talked some more about my memories of my parents in Goa. I would feel sad now and again thinking about them and Goa. She grabbed my arm and continued to console me and changed our conversation to our children; our future she said. How wonderful it was to have children around with their noises and laughter in our lives. Then she reminded me that she would in her thirties within a couple of years and maybe we wouldn't have any more children. But she quickly said, "It's all in the hands of God."

"I want to say one more thing about building our house. There is something that may stop our plans. Mr. Rana said the news is about war in Europe. You remember, we were listening to the radio last night, but I didn't think it was serious. Maybe it is more serious that I thought."

We turned on the radio, and once again, the news talked of war. I whispered to Trinia that we might have to let our plans sit for a while until we knew for certain how the news of the war might affect us in Kenya.

It was late when we went to bed. We brought with us cautious thoughts of owning a home of our own, one that would have enough rooms for our family. I fell asleep thinking of the life I left behind in Goa, my parents and the shape of my further dreams to come. I wondered if a war would take my dreams away. I hoped not.

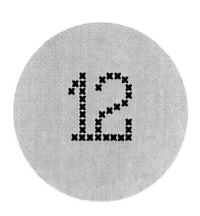

WORLD WAR TWO

In September 1939, war surrounded Europe. Our plans for building a house had to be delayed because Kenya was a British colony and would certainly be affected in some way—though how and to what extent was not clear. Fighting had not started, but the armies were getting ready for war. I could not understand it. But I knew that this would be a difficult time for us.

I soon had fewer orders. My customers from the Highlands did not come into the city as often as they used to. They would get disturbing news from friends and relatives in England; sometimes quicker than we would hear on the radio. They spoke in grave tones about what was happening in England when they picked up small orders from my shop. There was talk that Germany and Italy would try to divide up all of Africa. There were many rumours, and the news changed rapidly. We would have to wait and see. My tailors were anxious, but I told them to keep coming to finish the few orders we had. We would take it day by day.

We would wait and see.

As residents of a British colony of Kenya, the Goan community was worried. Some Goans were told to stay at home, while others went to work anyway and waited to be told what to do.

Even though I had very few orders, I was at the shop daily. My Goan customers would come in to talk. Paulo came in regularly, but we didn't see John for he did not take his days off anymore. A few times, he came in with Mrs. Glover, but he went back the same day with her. Nairobi felt different, for there was a hushed silence on the streets, and people walked hurriedly from one building to the next.

On the radio, it was suggested that there may be bombings. We heard air raid warnings, and when this happened, we would rush to the underground shelter. It was very quiet in there. All of us were squeezed in together while we waited and waited for the all-clear signal.

One day, a little more than a year into the war, Mr. Brown was in the shop talking about the London bombings. It sounded unbelievable to me. I could not imagine destruction and death on such a scale. He warned me that I should not keep the shop open and that I should stay at home. I visited Ali and we tried to decide what to do. He was unsure as well. He thought that whether at home or at the shop, it would be the same. It would be better to come to the shop—at least then we could do some work, even if it was only to take stock or keep up with the customer books and accounts. When Nathoo next came in to pick up his casual trousers, he thought it was better to come in. I continued to open the shop and some of my tailors came in when they wanted to find out what was happening. We spent the time sharing what news we knew about the war. Whenever there was an air raid warning, I closed the shop and—after the all-clear signal—I went home for the day.

At night, I listened to the radio for the news. The British had recruited many Kenyans to join the army. They were called the King's African Rifles Regiment. They would be rewarded after the war was over. I wondered what that meant. I did not believe that bit of the news. They treated the Africans poorly and without cause. Would that really change after the war? I doubted it.

There was a very large Army base in the far end of Eastleigh. When I took the bus to and from work, there were many British soldiers on the same bus. This was a horrible time. We prayed to God to end the war because we could do nothing else. We prayed and hoped we would not be affected and that Kenya would not be bombed.

It was December of 1943, and the war was still raging in Europe. In Kenya that meant uncertainty more than anything else. The air raid warnings were terrifying for us. Trinia was frightened and often talked about the times she had to rush to the underground shelter with little Theresa. I tried to comfort her as much as I could because I was just as frightened. Peter, Matthew and Theresa were young children. Peter and Matthew still attending primary school told stories of how they had to run to the shelter with their teachers. At ages eleven and eight they thought it was a great game of hiding in a dark place underground. While Theresa only four years old stayed close to Trinia. We were scared and hoped this War would end soon.

On Sundays we continued going to church, and it was the one place we felt peace because the sirens had never sounded while we were there. On this one Sunday, after Mass Anton and Tina had come home with us for lunch.

"Sabby," said Anton. "I heard on the news about the Italians fighting in Ethiopia. Will they come towards Kenya?" He looked quite fearful while we thought about that.

"I heard that too," I said. "And there is fighting in Somalia."

It was difficult for us as we didn't understand the details of what we heard on the news. Tina and Trinia were solemn, while the children sat quietly eating lunch unaware of our conversation. We finished lunch and moved into the living room while the children went to their bedrooms. It wasn't safe to be outside.

After half an hour or so, Trinia and Tina were deep in conversation, and it seemed to be a happy one for they were both laughing at different times.

"...and it's been weeks since I heard anything from Goa," Anton said.

"Yes, who knows what is happening in India?" I said. "The letters have stopped coming from Goa. I heard from a customer that—"

The air raid siren sounded.

Conversation stopped. Trinia gathered the children, and we rushed out to the underground shelter at the end of the street. Once again, we were silent in the underground space, and it almost seemed that I could hear my heart beating in my chest. We were huddled together in this dark place. Trinia was holding Theresa close to her with Tina standing next to them. Peter and Matthew were standing close to Anton and I. After what seemed like hours, we heard the all-clear signal. Anton and Tina hurried to their home while we went back to ours.

As the war carried on, we heard that the Italians were now in northern Kenya even though Italy surrendered and pulled out from Kenya. There were some Italian soldiers who would not give up and continued fighting—this was frightening. We also heard that Germany was losing and that Britain and her allies were winning the war in Europe.

Thus far, there had been no bombs dropped on Kenya, and we thanked God for that. Instead we heard, on the news, about the destruction that had been clearly visible in different parts of Europe. I could not understand it. Many lives lost and many buildings destroyed. As a Goan community, we felt set apart from it though we lived in Kenya under British rule. The colonial government had decided who in Kenya would be part of their fighting men—they chose the Africans. We were left alone and were to keep out of the way. It felt strange to me.

I missed the peaceful and joyful times we had enjoyed before the war.

During the war time I would take Peter and Matthew to the shop whenever they were sent home from school. They liked being in the shop. They had many questions about the tailoring I did. One day while at the shop, I showed them my customer book. There was one order of casual trousers for Mr. Glover. I picked out the cloth for this pair of trousers and unravelled it onto the worktable. I then chalked the cloth according to the measurements for Mr. Glover. They stood at one end of the table looking at what I was doing. I took the scissors and cut along the chalk lines, telling them what I was doing. They silently watched. After the cutting was done, Peter saw me gather the trouser pieces together while he came around to pick up the left over pieces from the floor.

"Pai, what do you do with these pieces? Do you throw them out?" He asked with a puzzled look on his face.

"Yes, they are very little pieces. But look how carefully I cut the cloth towards the edge, making sure that I do not waste too much of the cloth."

"Pai, this looks difficult," Matthew said, as he helped Peter pick up the pieces.

When I went to the sewing machine, they sat around and watched me sew the legs of the trousers together. Matthew stood closer to get a better look at how I did this.

"Pai, this is complicated work you do," Matthew said, turning to look at Peter.

"Yes, when I first started tailoring, it was complicated," I said. "But now I do it easily, and remember, Mr. Glover is a regular customer. I know his measurements, and you saw me chalk the cloth quite quickly, and now I'm sewing the trousers just as quickly. This is good work I do." I was proud to see them closely observing me while I sewed the trousers. We were interrupted by Nathoo.

"Sabby!" he called, walking into the shop. "I came to tell you that the war is coming to an end. The fighting has stopped. This is good news, no?"

I looked up at him coming forward to shake hands with my children. He had met them before when they were much younger, but they didn't remember him. Then Ali and Mr. Desai came in with the same news. We shook hands and looked at each other feeling relieved; we escaped the horrors that Europe experienced. Thank goodness, we thought. We continued talking while the children stood back near the sewing machine listening to our talk in the front of the shop.

"Now we can get back to doing business, right?" shouted Nathoo. He strode out of the shop followed by Ali and Mr. Desai. This was good news.

I enthusiastically walked back towards my sewing room, hugged my children and told them how great it was that the war was nearly over and we were lucky that we were unharmed. They smiled and didn't say anything. I returned to my sewing machine as I had to finish the trousers before we could go home with the good news. Matthew walked towards the front of the shop while Peter continued watching me sew the trousers. It was late afternoon by the time I finished the trousers, locked up the shop and caught the bus with my children.

By the time we arrived home, Trinia had heard the news about the war coming to an end; the neighbours had come over to tell her. Tina and Josie were there. Everyone was happy.

It was August of 1945 when World War Two ended. My European customers talked about nothing but peace. The city returned to normal. Britain and her allies had won the war, and the British were more determined than ever to stay in Kenya forever.

The Italians who had continued fighting in the north part of Kenya had been captured and made prisoners of war. They had been made to build the roadway from the Rift Valley to Nairobi along the escarpment. It had been dangerous work, but they built that road from Nakuru in the Rift Valley to Nairobi. I heard from my European customers that this road made a great difference to them, for they could now easily travel back and forth. With admiration they spoke about a significant landmark the Italians had left behind. They not only built the road, but at the end of the road, they erected a remarkable Catholic chapel in honour of the Italians who died working on the road.

It was peaceful once again. Everyone was happy. I was particularly delighted because my customers had come back on a more regular basis. People were spending money again. It was time to rebuild—more so in England and Europe. In Kenya, people on the streets wore smiles on their faces and were walking with confidence and not fear.

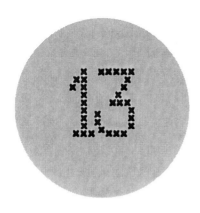

OUR SHIFTING LIFESTYLE

The War was over, and we renewed our plans for building our house. It was January 1946 when Trinia once again announced that she was pregnant and that the baby was due in July. I looked at her, smiled, and thought we left it in the hands of God.

After the lawyer work was completed, and with help from Mr. Rana, our house construction began. This was going to take some time, and both Trinia and I were impatiently waiting for our house to be built and ready to move in. But on the weekends, we went to the site and saw the different stages of it being built. We stood there looking at the half-built walls of the different rooms. Peter, Matthew, and Theresa would curiously walk around the construction site—after being told to be careful. At dinnertime the children would want to know when we would move into our new house. We would always tell them the same thing.

"As soon as it is ready."

Trinia gave birth to our Mina on July 14, 1946, at Dr. Haq's hospital, not far from where we lived. She was our first child born in a hospital, the other three had been born at home with the help of our doctor. It was unusual to see Trinia and Mina together in the hospital bed. All went well and, thank goodness, there were no complications as Trinia was older and the doctor reminded us that there *could* be complications. I thanked God for giving us another healthy baby girl.

In the meantime, our house was ready for us to move in. We waited until Trinia was back to normal again. In October of 1946, we were in our home, an Indian-designed house. The entrance way had two tall pillars with a rounded concrete awning that connected the pillars from left to right. The five cement steps to the front door were curved from end to end and painted red which was Trinia's choice. Inside a small hallway led to a living room on the right and on the left were the bedrooms, dining room and kitchen, with the bathroom next to the kitchen and toilet rooms in the back compound. The left side of the house was narrow and looked out onto our neighbour's home, whereas the right side of the house was a large area for gardening and a play area for the children. Towards the back, there was the stone fence, and inside the fence, was a small guest room with kitchen facilities—on the other side was the housekeeper's room for Kamau. Now he didn't have to leave in the evenings.

For the first few months, Trinia walked around looking very happy and kept saying how blessed she was to be in this new home with enough rooms for the family and a place for Kamau. She loved the outside area, a place where she would watch the children cheerfully play in the sun. Our dinnertime conversations were about flower gardening to the right of the house. There was to be a banana tree, a papaya tree and a guava tree planted within the year in the narrow part on the left side. Trinia was determined to entertain our friends. I had to tell her to slow down and to wait until the furniture was made for the living room and dining room. Anton and his friends made our furniture.

Anton seemed to have stopped doing other orders and concentrated on making our furniture. In the meantime, Trinia agreed with me and said that we would do our house blessing soon after the feast of St. Francis Xavier in December. Once we agreed on a date, she visited the church and reserved that date for our house blessing. The furniture had to be in place. Anton had to work hard to meet her deadlines, and Trinia visited Anton regularly to see how the work was progressing. I could see her characteristics quite clearly.

The day of the blessing finally arrived: Saturday December 7. Our home was fully furnished, and Trinia had a feast laid out on the dining table. She invited everyone we knew including Miguel and his family. The children were extremely happy; Peter was fourteen, Matthew eleven, Theresa seven and Mina a little baby. Father Doyle arrived, and I welcomed him in. He began the prayers at the front entrance and then slowly moved inside, blessing each room, stopping at each door with more prayers, blessings, and holy water. We joined in the prayers as Father Doyle walked through our home.

When he finished, we invited him to stay for the party. He smiled and stayed for a while. It was noisy and crowded, and Trinia and I spent time with our guests. Then John began singing and everyone started clapping in time to his singing while Anton accompanied on guitar. Trinia and I could not have been happier. Our new life was truly rooted in Nairobi.

As the days and weeks progressed, and the months passed away, 1947 slowly came forward. Back across the Arabian Sea, Indian Independence became a reality, and there was tension between India and the newly partitioned nation of

Pakistan—Hindus, Sikhs and Muslims spilled blood in violent clashes. Goa, however, remained in Portuguese hands. It was a very difficult time in newly independent India.

In Kenya, however, we found ourselves comfortably settled in our new home. Trinia planted her garden with flowers in the front area and some fruit trees at the side of the house; the fruit garden. Soon we had two dogs: a great dane named Rover and a golden retriever named Simba. Trinia had a soft spot for cats, and it seemed that every stray in Nairobi found its way to our home to be fed and cared for alongside our dogs. Trinia was happy at home, raising the family and being with her friends, while I was busy with my tailoring business. On a daily basis, Kamau would bring a lunch to the shop for me. I could hardly believe how my dreams had come true.

If only we could freeze time, I thought, *and keep things as they are now.*

But amidst the richest joy there was always something to worry about. For Trinia and I, there were two constant problems that cast long shadows over our life together. We were living in a rigidly segregated society where the Europeans lived separately from us and we lived separately from the Africans—socially we were kept within our own designated areas. The second problem existed within our own community, for our family was shunned by many in the Goan community because I was a tailor.

Unfortunately, I could no more change this second issue than I could change the first. I concentrated on running a successful tailoring business and I took pride in my work. Though I had many happy Goan customers, the children were often teased and bullied at the Dr. Ribeiro Goan School. This affected them and, I believed, their future. I valued our many Goan friends and ignored those who snubbed us.

These were thoughts that often occupied my mind, and while I was working on a cocktail dress for Mrs. Glover. Luis interrupted my thoughts, reminding me that it was time to go home. I had been worrying, and there was a heavy feeling in my heart.

"Oh yes, yes, Luis. It's time to close up. See you tomorrow. I see the others have already left."

I put away my bits and pieces of sewing, for Omondi was already cleaning the shop, moving around quietly.

At home, Trinia and the children eagerly greeted me, for I was later than usual for dinner. Before I knew it, I was seated at the dinner table. Everyone took their favourite seat, and dishes of curry, vegetables and a jug of water were placed on the table. I led the family in saying the Grace Before Meals, and they joined in the prayer. Trinia passed each dish around, and I watched the children make their selections. Trinia, as always, took a little bit of everything to experience the differences in the dishes; she encouraged the children to do the same.

As we ate, I told the children what was on my mind because I knew how much it affected them. I let them know how important my work was to me. Tailoring, I told them, was a creative type of work. For me it was about designing, about rolling out cloth, drawing out the design, cutting it in its designed shape to make a beautiful dress for a woman or a classic suit for a man. That was the only way I knew how to earn a living. And business was doing well. It was the reason we lived in our own home and no longer had to rent from somebody else.

"I know you are being teased and treated very badly at school. It's not right. But there is nothing your Mai or I can do because it is about the work I do."

Matthew swallowed a mouthful of curried chicken and then asked. "Why is it that the Goans do not like what you do, Pai?"

"Well," I said, taking a deep breath. "It's about the caste system. Tailors are in the trades' class, which the Goans consider to be a lower caste."

"But why?" Peter sounded uncertain. "Whenever I come to the shop, I see you busy making suits or dresses. You like doing this kind of work, no?"

"Oh Peter, I like it very much. You have seen me work at the shop. When I unravel that piece of cloth, I take the chalk and draw out the outline of the suit jacket, then I make sure it is correct according to the measurements. Then comes the cutting of the cloth and the—"

"Pai loves his work," said Trinia "and I have to stop him or else we'll be here all night listening to how he works. The more you visit him in the shop, the more you'll see how he works. Remember he likes his work very much. He makes people look good."

"Mai is right," I said with a slight smile. "I love my work, and it does not matter what some Goans think."

"But Pai, it is difficult for us. We don't know what to say to those fellows who are always saying that we don't belong to the school because we are tailor's children. Sometimes we get into fights." Matthew's voice was thick with anxiety, he glanced at Peter as he spoke.

Trinia was silent, and I knew she was hurting inside. I looked at Theresa—she was only eight and did not seem as affected as her brothers. Perhaps there was change in the air, I thought.

"Here's what I know," I said, trying to gather my thoughts as best I could. "I'm not ashamed of the work I do. Like Mai says, I make people look good. I'm very proud I'm a tailor. I have my own tailoring business. But I'm truly sorry that you are being treated badly because of what I do. It doesn't make sense. Without tailors the upper castes would be wrapped in rags."

There was more silence, for no one knew what to say next. The children quietly returned to their meals. Trinia broke the silence.

"Look, Pai was able to buy our home. We own this home. We no longer pay rent, and there are many clerks in the colonial government who can't say that, though they look down their noses at us. I am proud of your Pai, proud beyond any doubt, and you should be proud too. Let's raise a cheer to that!" she said. "To Pai and his tailoring work."

"To Pai and his tailoring work."

I smiled, though it almost broke my heart to hear them, for I knew what they were going through.

"This is very nice," I said. "And remember that Mai and I love you very much. Your school reports make us very proud. You're doing well at our Goan school. Keep that up. And remember no one can take that away from you."

"I like doing school work," said Matthew. "I share my notes with my friend Robert who sits next to me in the class and we talk about what we learn in the class. Not *everyone* treats me badly."

"That's good, Matthew. And what about you Peter? Do you have friends?"

Matthew looked nervously at Peter.

"Yes Pai, I have friends, many of them. They come to help me when some of the fellows are constantly teasing me. I was in a fight with two or three of them. My friends come to help me out and pull us apart. I have my friends all right," he said defiantly.

Trinia put down her glass and looked at him. "You get into fights, Peter? That's not right."

"You have to defend yourself," I said. "But be careful. It's not always the right thing to do."

"But Mai and Pai, when the teasing becomes unbearable, I become very angry, and before I know it, I'm in a fight. I know you don't like it," Peter said, all defiance gone from his voice. "But *they* start it, and my friends are there to help me."

"Learn to walk away and keep your head up," I said. "I know it's difficult, but you'll be a better man for it. Always remember that."

Even as I said it, I knew it would be difficult advice to follow.

"Yes Pai, I'll try," Peter said with his head down.

"I don't like fights," Theresa said. "It makes me sad to hear Peter say he fights. Do you get hurt with blood on your face or nose? Tell me, Peter."

"Don't worry about it, little sister. I am fine. It's like Pai says, we have to defend ourselves." Peter responded in a loving tone.

"Here in Nairobi, we face prejudice from the Europeans and also from our own community. There will always be prejudice from one person or a group. Always try to do your best. You can't fight your way out of prejudice. Instead, show you're capable, be smart and make solid decisions, and then nobody can deny you the opportunity to work and make a living for yourselves." They seemed to accept my advice; there was nothing more to say.

Dinner came to an end. The plates and dishes were cleared. I stood up, and they followed me. We individually and silently said our Grace After Meals prayer. Feeling thoughtful, I went to the living room, poured a shot of cognac, put the glass on the coffee table, and sat down. I lit my pipe. Trinia checked in on baby Mina, fed her, and then later walked in and made herself comfortable beside me on the sofa as the first puffs of smoke rose into the air.

"I liked your advice to our children. It's very difficult to hear their stories when they come home from school. I know, I do not hear all the stories, but they're hurting, and I do my best to make them feel good about themselves."

"You're wonderful with them," I said. "Who knows what the future will hold for us and for them? Whatever it is, we have to be there for them while they grow older."

We sat quietly. I sipped my cognac, and Trinia enjoyed her coffee. When my pipe was out of tobacco, it was nearly time for bed as I finished my last sip of cognac.

"We could send them to school in Bombay," I said.

"What?"

It had come out the blue and caught her off guard.

"The boys. When we were in Goa, your brother Frank talked about the Don Bosco boarding school for boys. We could send them there and get them out of this closed little community for a while," I said. "It would broaden their horizons."

We heard that the Don Bosco School was an excellent school. The priests who taught there were said to be very good. Strict, perhaps, but excellent educators.

She looked at me still shocked at my suggestion. "Sabby, I never thought of that. At least they wouldn't be teased about being tailor's children. This is a great idea, but I have to think about it more. I'll miss them. They are still too young. Are you sure we can do it?"

"We can do it all right. Business is doing well, and what is more important than educating our children? In fact, the more I think about it, the more I want to do it. As for them being young, Peter's fifteen and Matthew's twelve; they only *seem* young to us. Write to your brother tomorrow morning, will you?"

"Yes, I'll write to Frank. I feel the excitement in your voice. But I'm frightened for the boys being that far away from us."

"I understand, I do, but it is for their education. I think it will be good for them."

We went to the children's bedrooms, hugged them and reminded them to say their night prayers before going to sleep. In our bedroom, we continued whispering about the possibility of sending Peter and Matthew to Don Bosco School, and did so until we fell asleep.

The next morning, it was busy and noisy as Trinia organized the children for school. I waved goodbye to them, making my way to the city. I unlocked the door of the shop and let my tailors in. They went to their workspaces in the sewing room at the back, while I slowly walked in and stood in the front section. I stood silent for a while and looked very closely inside the shop. *What a wonderful set up*, I thought, walking to my worktable and picking up the cloth to create a dress for Mrs. Button.

Mrs. Button was a regular customer. She lived in the White Highlands and had frequent tea parties and insisted on having a new dress every month. November brought in the hot season. The dress would have a cool appearance with a plain low neckline and it would be sleeveless. I worked at it diligently, but I would let Trinia do the hemming.

She would be coming in with Kamau at lunch. I always loved it when Trinia came to the shop. She did this about once a week. It gave us extra time to talk without the children interrupting us. We had good conversations about our life in Nairobi even though, after years of living in Kenya, Trinia continued to miss her family.

I hoped she had written the letter to Frank and would bring it for me to post it today. But before lunch, I still had time to start on the next outfit for Mrs. Pereira—she was celebrating her fiftieth birthday and having a party. She told me her dress had to look and feel special. I smiled looking at the design she had chosen for her dress. It would look good on her. She would stand out in the crowd. But that dress was not due for another month, towards the end of December.

Instead, I moved to the front of the shop to pick up a suit length to work on Dr. Carvalho's suit. He would arrive for his fitting in a couple of weeks. I had two other fittings for the next week. With the suit length tucked under my arm, I walked to my worktable and checked out Dr. Carvalho's measurements. I laid out the suit length on the table in preparation for the cutting. With chalk in hand, I proceeded to draw the lines for the different parts of the jacket: two fronts, the back, the sleeves and the collar leading to the lapel in the two fronts. With precision and skillful use of the scissors, I cut the suit length. I placed the pieces together and told Joseph to work on the sewing. I looked up to see Trinia walking in with Kamau and lunch.

"Ahh! It's lunchtime already! I have some jobs for you to do."

"Good," Trinia said. "First let's take a break, enjoy our lunch, and then I'll work at the jobs you have for me. Here is the letter to Frank. Now you can post it. I told him to write back quickly."

I smiled and took the letter from her. Later when they would go home, I would post it.

She reminded me that she couldn't stay for long because she had left Mina with Connie, our neighbour, who needed to go out later that afternoon. We sat to enjoy lunch. Before we had time to finish our conversation, in walked Anton, and he joined us for lunch. As always, he gossiped about the different people in our community. But his main reason for visiting was to let us know that a couple of fellows had arrived from Goa and were looking for work. I looked at Anton.

"Do they have any tailoring skills?" I asked.

"A little, I think. But they do not have a place to stay."

I looked at Trinia, thinking aloud if we could have these fellows stay at our place until they were settled. Trinia smiled and was quiet for a while. Then she nodded and was willing to take them in for a short stay and not a long stay like some other fellows did some months ago.

"Trinia, you are wonderful. See, Anton, you have to thank her," I said.

Anton softly said something that sounded like a thank you. I looked at Trinia gratefully as she walked towards the back of the shop, and Kamau put the dishes away in the bag. I continued my conversation with Anton while I saw Trinia working on the dresses that I left for her to complete.

When Anton left, Trinia asked, "Do we know when these fellows will be coming over to stay at our place?"

"The weekend. It's only Tuesday, we'll have enough time to get ready for them."

"That's good. Sabby, these are lovely dresses. I like this design."

"Mrs. Button likes anything I make for her. She is not a fussy customer. But it seems that anything I make for her always looks beautiful on her."

At around two in the afternoon, Trinia left with Kamau, and I left with them to post the letter. Trinia decided to walk home even though I tried to convince her that it was safer and quicker to take the bus home. She was adamant, because she liked the walk.

"Besides I'll have Kamau to protect me if anything goes wrong."

We squeezed our hands before parting ways, and I told her to be careful on the walk home.

When I returned to the shop, a busy afternoon of sewing was underway. My tailors were at the machines and no one was talking or taking any breaks. It was that time of year when many orders came in. It was also the time of year when it became very hot in the sewing room. The fans helped, but not enough. I decided to close up shop at around four o'clock and requested everyone to come in an hour earlier the next morning. We left for home.

It was strange, when I arrived home. Kamau came up to me and told me a bit about what happened to Trinia on their way home. I was shocked and wanted to see Trinia right away and he let me go inside. I found Trinia in the bedroom and Mina asleep in the cot beside the bed. Trinia I could tell was not herself.

"What happened? I asked. "Kamau was trying to tell me, but I wanted to see you right away."

"I was robbed on the way home. You were right, we should have taken—"

"Are you all right? Where on earth was Kamau?"

"He was there. It's not his fault, Sabby. It happened very fast. We were walking in the field through the tall grass, and since the path was narrow, he walked in front of me. I was attacked from behind."

"My God, look at your neck!" I said noticing the bruise for the first time. "Are you all right?"

"I am fine, just shaken up. I have been crying. It was very frightening."

"What happened?"

"It was the gold chain from my dowry. I was to keep it as a family heirloom and hand it down to our eldest daughter but now it has gone. The robber ran up grabbed it… or he came out of the grass, I'm not sure. I put my hands to my neck and was dragged off balance and fell backwards. The chain broke and the robber looked down at me for a moment. He was a tall African with smooth black skin and wide eyes. He looked a little frightened himself. Then he came at me again because he saw my bracelet as my hand was still at my throat. Of course, Kamau had heard my grunts and jumped the man, knocking him back. They both went down but the robber was on his feet first and ran off."

"My dear Trinia!"

"You know Kamau was very good. He let me sit on the ground until I was ready to stand up. It took me sometime to breathe normally again."

"Oh Trinia, this is horrible. Your neck is bruised. You could have been injured a lot more." I examined her throat and then looked at her wrist. It too was bruised but not as bad as her neck.

"I'm okay now," she said. "We walked home as fast as I could. I was more shocked than hurt, and I had to rest. Connie brought Mina in but was in a hurry and didn't notice anything. The bruise is probably darker now," she said brushing her fingers at her throat.

"Kamau made me some tea while I put Mina to sleep in the cot. I told Kamau to see to the children when they came home from school and he was to tell them I was resting. I think I may have fallen asleep waiting for you."

Trinia sat up on the bed, while I went to the cot to pick up Mina who had just woken up.

"I'm glad that you were not badly hurt. Do you want to come for dinner, or do you want to rest some more?" I brought Mina to her and we sat together with Mina between us.

"No, I will come down," she said then shook her head. "There is something else Kamau said to me, and I feel foolish for not realizing it. He said that gold shines in the sun like nothing else, and everyone can see it. Robbers can see it from a distance and come to steal it. He said that I mustn't wear these chains and bracelets."

Like many Goan women, Trinia wore her jewellery as part of her everyday outfits, and perhaps because of this, she was not as aware of it as she should be.

That has probably changed forever, I thought.

"I know, if I go out on those kinds of walks again, I will put a light scarf around my neck to cover my chain. What do you think?"

I gently laughed because I knew she would never stop using her jewellery, for it was part of her and our traditions. We walked to the dining room as dinner was ready to be served.

The children were in their chairs noisily talking among themselves. I looked at them and saw how each one was very different and yet magical in their own little ways. They talked about school—who said what and what they did. They discussed how they liked certain teachers and which ones they didn't like. They must have had a good day at school. Everyone was talking, eating, and saying out loud what was their favourite dish and not so favourite dish. I looked around the table and winked at Trinia because everyone was happy. It was during a lull in the conversations that Trinia decided to bring up what had happened.

"Listen children," she said. "I don't want to alarm you or make you sad, but I think it is important to tell you what happened to me today. It was bad and quite frightening, but I want you to know first that I am all right."

"What happened, Mai?" asked Theresa. "I was looking for you, but Kamau told me not to disturb you because you were asleep."

And thus Trinia told the same tale she had told me when I came home. Everyone was silent.

"But Mai, are you hurt?" Peter looked very concerned; staring at Trinia and noticing the bruise for the first time.

"Mai, did you scream? How did he go away?" Theresa had tears in her eyes.

"Kamau helped me, as I said. The robber only took my gold chain. I still have my bracelet, which is a special jewellery though he tried to pull it off my hand but he didn't get it."

"I can see some marks on your neck, Mai," said Matthew. "Does it hurt? Good that Kamau was there to help you."

"Yes it was good that Kamau was with me. I am fine. I am sad to have lost the gold chain that I had hoped to keep as a family heirloom. But I am not hurt."

"It is important," I said "that we learn to be aware of our surroundings. I have never told you this, but when I first came to Kenya I too was robbed. I was with my friends, John and Paulo. It was late at night and we weren't paying attention to our surroundings. This happened when we were in Mombasa. We were attacked but none of us were hurt badly. Since then we became more aware of our surroundings."

"Pai, why do they rob?" asked Matthew. "Mai was just walking home. She wasn't doing anything."

It took me a while to answer Matthew. *How do I explain it?*

"Some of the Africans come from outside the city for work. Sometimes, they cannot find work. They don't have money to live in the city, and out of desperation, they rob to have money to live."

"They don't have money?" said Peter. "That's why this man took Mai's chain, to sell it for money?" Peter looked confused.

"Yes, that's right. Always be careful when you are walking outside. It's more dangerous at night time. Always walk with friends and neighbours when you go to school or church. It is better in a group."

The children seemed to accept what I said to them. They were at an age where they were still carefree for the most part. But as I looked at them around the table I knew that they would change before too long as they would grow up to be adults.

Trinia left me to look after Mina while she went to the kitchen to make coffee. We quietly said our Grace After Meals prayer, and I took Mina to the living room. I put her on the floor near her toys and together we played with her toys. Trinia joined us, and we played for a while longer.

"Come let's sit on the sofa together. Do you feel back to your usual self now? That was a frightening experience, no?"

"I'm very happy I talked about it during dinner. I feel much better now. I didn't know how to let the children know. I don't want them to be scared of walking on the streets. You gave them a good explanation and good advice." She sipped her coffee.

"It is important for them to know how to be safe on the streets."

"But Sabby, it's like telling them not to trust people outside. You remember in Goa how we lived as children; carefree, noisy, trusting the neighbours, and anyone on the streets. Nothing happened to us."

"That's right, but this isn't Goa," I said. "And besides they aren't looking back, as we are, to that kind of life. They are growing up here. This is their country, and they have a good sense already of what to expect. We must help them understand the life here."

We sat quietly for a while, both of us thinking about what had happened. Mina was still happily playing with her toys when Trinia picked her up for a bath and left me to my thoughts.

As much as I was angry at what had happened to Trinia, I knew it was a cause of a much more serious problem. The British dream of a White Kenya was a sickness, and now that India had gained its independence, Britain would try even harder for a White Kenya. The Africans, though hidden from the eyes of society, were still here. They had been here since time began. It was *their* country, and I wondered how long they would be shut out of it before they pushed the doors open. The thought was troubling.

While it often seemed as though nothing could be done and that British rule was carved in stone, I wondered just how solid that stone was. Gandhi had left South Africa for India in 1915, a year before I left Goa for Africa. And as 1947 drew to a close, India was no longer a colony and was facing its future on its own terms.

Frank's letters about Don Bosco were very encouraging. We followed his instructions, applied for the boys to be in Bombay. It happened very quickly. School commenced in June with three separate terms during the year. The last week of May 1948, I took the boys to Mombasa and saw them sail away to Bombay. Trinia didn't want to see them off in Mombasa. She was anxious and worried for them, but relieved that Frank would meet them in Bombay. Their holidays were spent with Trinia's family in Goa. It was sad that my parents were not alive to see their grandsons spending time in Goa. My thoughts were on my parents again.

We regularly received letters from our sons. They especially enjoyed their holidays in Goa. They were spoiled and given more freedom than they had while at school. Their school reports were mailed directly to us in Nairobi. Peter was slightly above average in his marks, but Matthew was doing very well. Trinia was missing them very much. We decided to bring them back after three years. It was time well spent as they had a good education and learned about Goa and India.

It was May 1951. We were seated at our dining table with Peter who would turn nineteen in November and Matthew sixteen in October—two teenagers who looked confident and acted mature. This was a celebratory welcome home dinner. Theresa had just turned twelve and little Mina would turn four in July. Our children were together once again at home. Trinia was beaming with pride and joy. Normally our Goan children did not leave home until they were married, no matter what age. With some families, the eldest son when married brought the wife home to continue to live with the parents.

There was too much to talk about at the dinner table. We discussed India's independence; their lessons in school discussed the benefits of an independent India. Then we spoke about Kenya where we continued to experience the same tensions under British rule. Trinia, on the other hand, wanted to talk about her family and what each of her siblings were doing. Then Theresa asked many questions about living in India in a boarding school. Of course, Peter and Matthew told stories that made Theresa laugh while she did not believe some of their stories. It was a long, long dinner.

By July, Peter enrolled in a bookkeeping course while Matthew did part time work at a local chemist shop. He wanted to work in the courts; our lawyer, Mr. Das, suggested he wait until he turned eighteen and then he would recommend Matthew.

Our routines changed as our children became older with different needs and schedules, but Trinia and I were happy with our life in Kenya despite the political uncertainty, which was something we had no control of.

Part
Three

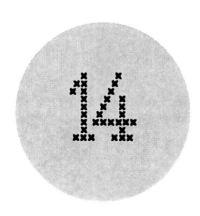

MEMORABLE EVENTS

The headlines in the newspapers were about Princess Elizabeth's visit to Kenya. The royal couple arrived on February 1, 1952. They landed at Eastleigh Aerodrome in the east end of Nairobi, very close to where we lived in Pangani. Many children lined along Juja Road and waved British flags to welcome Princess Elizabeth. Trinia, Mina and the neighbours were in the crowd. They cheered on and continuously waved the flags as the royal couple drove past very quickly. Soon the royal couple were gone on their tour of Kenya.

This visit was during the 'Mau Mau' Uprising. The newspapers reported on the special precautions taken to protect the royal couple. They were touring the newly built Tree-Tops Hotel in the Aberdare National Park in the town of Nyeri when news came of her father's death; King George VI died in England on February 6, 1952. Princess Elizabeth left Kenya as Queen of England.

During their very short visit, people crowded the city streets, if only to get a glimpse of the royal couple when they attended functions at Government House. We quietly continued sewing in the shop. Later that evening, while we sat in the living room, Trinia briefly talked about being on Juja Road when the royal car whizzed past them. I smiled and told her that the visit was more important for the British. But of greater importance was that she left Kenya as Queen of England.

We continued talking about our family. Peter had grown into a mature teenager. He was learning to drive a car and it was good as he would soon be able to drive the car we recently purchased. With advice from Nathoo and after much thought Trinia and I decided to buy the Hudson car that would fit our family needs perfectly; we were happy owners of a Ford Hudson car.

It was late February when Peter felt confident that he could take us for a drive around our neighbourhood. We sat in the car as Peter steered it down the very steep hill while we held our breath, wondering if he would make it to the bottom of the hill. Of course, he did and from that day onwards he took over the driving of our Hudson car.

It was the first Sunday in September 1952, and the entire family was on our way to visit John for a picnic at Limuru Farm—the Glovers said he could entertain us for the afternoon. Peter drove us there. Matthew sat beside him in the centre of the front seat, and I sat on the passenger side. Trinia sat in the centre of the back seat with Theresa on one side of her and Mina on the other. She brought along some snacks for the journey, which wasn't that long—less than an hour, if that.

As we drove, I gazed out at the countryside with some fear, for the political situation in Kenya was getting worse and the Kikuyu were starting to organize. The land commission had restricted African ownership of lands in favour of granting it to Europeans. Thousands of dislocated Kikuyu had, as a result, crowded into cities such as Nairobi in search of work.

My thoughts were interrupted when Peter drove through the stone gates of Limuru Farm and parked the car near the bench not far from the gates. I walked to the door, and there was John grinning at me. He gave me a big hug and followed me out to the bench. I was surprised to see him dressed up. He was in a black suit with a blue bow tie and starched white shirt with thin pleats down the front.

"John, look at you, dressed up in formal wear. Is this how you have to be all day?" I asked him.

"Yes, yes. This is it, Sabby. Now you see how I work. Since I knew you were coming, I opened the door, but usually the housekeeper opens the door. Come, come let's go to the family," he said, walking towards the bench. I kept pace with him, smiling, and feeling relaxed on this beautiful afternoon day in the country.

"Ahh, here they are," said John. "Welcome, welcome to the farm."

"Why are you dressed like that?" asked Mina.

"Mina, I'm at work, and this is how I have to dress for work. You have come to visit me at my work place." He took her hand and sat her on the bench. After a few moments of talk with the children, he glanced over his shoulder. "Aha, here comes Amish with sandwiches and some fruit."

From the direction we had just come, walked an Indian, taller than John and older by the looks of him. He was dressed as John was and carrying a large silver tray.

John said, "The Glovers are away at a tea party at the next farm and will be home at around six o'clock in time for their dinner. Mrs. Glover wanted us to have some sandwiches. I wish I could show you my flat in the farmhouse, but that's not allowed with the staff around the house."

We sat on a blanket that Trinia had laid out for us on the ground and ate the sandwiches, fruit and sipped Coca-Cola from the bottle.

It was a hot sunny day. By four o'clock, Peter and Matthew were playing catch with their sisters while Trinia cleared up the blanket. John and I helped load our small items into the boot of the car.

"It's beautiful out here, John," Trinia said.

"Yes. I wanted to take you for a walk through some of the farm. But the situation is not very good these days. It is not safe after dark, and you still have the drive back to Nairobi."

"Is it bad?" I asked trying not to alarm Trinia.

"It has become that way, yes. We are on guard once the sun goes down. A farm not far from here was attacked a few weeks ago, windows smashed and the owner badly beaten. A terrible business!"

John glanced at the shadows cast by the afternoon sun.

"You should probably think about heading back. I would have loved a longer visit, but it is best not to be on the roads after it turns dark. Better to be back in Nairobi."

Trinia called the children to the car and I embraced John. It had been good to see him. He didn't make the trips into Nairobi as often.

"Be careful," I said as I turned to John.

"Yes, said Trinia. "And thank you for a lovely afternoon. And thank the Glovers as well."

"I will," said John with the silver tray beneath his arm. He waved to the children already in the car. "And Sabby, have Peter drive straight back. No exploring, promise me."

"We promise," said Trinia and opened the door to the back seat.

Peter drove us back to Nairobi. We made no stops and met no trouble along the way.

In early October a European woman was stabbed to death near her home, and less than a week later an African chief who was outspoken in his support for the colonial government was shot to death in his car in broad daylight. On October 20, 1952, Governor Baring declared a State of Emergency that granted government forces sweeping powers in order to put down the Mau Mau Uprising. The first wave of arrests included that of Jomo Kenyatta, head of the Kenyan African Union; he and five others would be charged and eventually convicted of being leaders of the Mau Mau movement even though the KAU believed in nonviolent protest and action.

In August 1953 the State of Emergency was still in effect (and would be for years yet). It was often strange how normal life seemed to be in the comfort of the city, for there were dark whispers and rumours of killings and frightful oath-taking ceremonies in the countryside. I had tried to talk to Muturi and Karani, our Kikuyu assistants in the shop, about what was going on, but it was clear that they did not want to talk and were uncomfortable with my question.

"This is a secret we carry, Bwana," said Karani. "We are not to speak of what happens on the reserves It is true that we live in the city, but on the weekends we go to the reserves, and we must not say any more about it. I am sorry."

Muturi seemed quite anxious that Karani had said even *that* much, and I did not bring it up again. They both went back to hemming the dresses.

My European customers like the Browns and the Glovers would come into the city, regularly telling more horror stories of what was going on in the Rift Valley to the northwest of the city. It sounded terrifying to me, and yet they were convinced that Kenya would, in time, become a White Kenya. It was difficult to know how the Africans would overcome the white power that held their country, yet they were more determined than ever to take back control. I often thought of John's stories, for I knew he was fearful living on a farm that was being terrorized routinely. Nothing serious had happened at Limuru so far, but at night it was eerily quiet with guard dogs on the alert. It was very difficult to believe that this was happening in the countryside.

Even in Nairobi, we could feel that slight sense of dread of living in a State of Emergency.

"It is only a matter of time," said Matthew at the dinner table one night. "African independence won't be held back forever. The Mau Mau Uprising is a freedom movement. It won't be extinguished. The Kikuyu are taking tribal oaths, and the European farmers are terrified."

"Yes, Mr. Brown told me about these oaths," I said. "I can't make sense of it. They are vows which invite death if the oath taker breaks his word or hesitates in any way to fight. I just—"

"It is about the land," said Matthew. "The land that the British took off the Africans who lived there before any European ever stepped foot in Africa. This Mau Mau Movement will change it for the Europeans in this country."

"Yes, yes, I know what you are saying. Mr. Brown said that there are many atrocities happening in the reserves. Those of us living in Nairobi seem to be going about our daily lives while out there in the reserves there are unspeakable activities happening. It is getting out of hand. The Kikuyu want their land back while the Europeans claim that they are civilizing all of us and therefore have their rights to the land. But a lot of what is going on during the State of Emergency is far from civilized."

The discussion continued. It was strange, no doubt, for our children, being foreigners in the country of their birth. There were many questions and very few answers. There was speculation and anxiety. If the Africans succeeded, how would the British hand over power, and how would the non-Europeans be treated when it all settled down? The Goans and Indians came here in support of the British. Would that make us targets? Would the Africans succeed at all? At the moment, the British were keeping them down, but how long would that last? How long *could* it last?

It made us as a family, and a community at large, uncomfortable because we were talking about our way of life being threatened. We, the Asians (as the British called us), were being ignored in the conflict for the time being, but it would be foolish to think that we would be left unaffected if the very ground beneath the colonial government shifted.

I could see Mina drifting into her own thoughts. I was sure she could not understand our discussion. She was too young to understand this kind of political talk. And Theresa was trying to to make sense of it and eagerly listened to what we talked about; it might have been too political for her as well.

"But enough of this," I said. "For the time being let's leave the Mau Mau to the British and the British to the Mau Mau. How about a happier topic? I was thinking about our holidays this year. Peter, Matthew, you remember our holiday to Mombasa and Malindi. As you know we are taking Theresa and Mina there. We will leave tomorrow afternoon. I expect you boys will look after the place, and Peter, no dangerous driving our Hudson car."

I could tell by the looks on their faces that they were quite happy to be left alone during our vacation time. *So be it*, I thought with a smile.

Trinia looked at the boys. "Of course, keep out of any trouble while we are away."

"Don't worry Mai, we'll be good. The neighbours will tell you if we do anything wrong," said Peter. He looked at me and then looked at Theresa and Mina, winking at them.

"Girls," said Trinia. "We're going on a train journey. It'll be your first time. Stay close to Pai and I and don't run off anywhere. We must always be close to each other."

"What will it be like on the train?" Mina asked.

When no one responded right away Theresa said, "I'll tell you later," though she was just a baby the last time she was on this train.

I talked about looking at Fort Jesus and Port Mombasa for the two days we would be in Mombasa and the rest of our holiday we would be in Malindi where there were many beautiful sandy beaches to relax and enjoy the waters of the ocean. Theresa and Mina planned what they would do on the beaches—though seven years separated them, Theresa was very fond of Mina and was closer to her in some ways than she ever was with her brothers.

Peter and Matthew stood and left the table and went out to talk on the verandah to soak up the night air. *And start making plans*, I thought. It was dark out there, and I thought about John at the farm and the dangers they faced at night.

Trinia and I relaxed in the living room, I with my pipe, my cognac and she with her cup of coffee.

"Sabby, why do we always talk about politics during dinner? It makes us nervous. I don't think the girls understand the politics." She took a sip of her coffee. "It feels strange that we are living here and yet still do not really belong to Kenya. It makes me sad."

I reached over and squeezed Trinia's knee. "It is better to talk about it. We don't know all of it, but when the children have questions, we have to try to answer them. The situation is worrisome. The Africans won't give up and the government..." I took a deep breath. "Well, let's hope that whatever comes of this, is peaceful. But enough of politics. You're right. I can hear the children out on the verandah. Shall we join them?"

The children were happily gazing up at the night sky. We watched them pointing to the stars, the older three talking about constellations for Mina's benefit. Their young voices drifted into the stillness of the night. I could see that, next

　　　　　　　　　　　　　　　　　　　　　　　　　　MARIA LYNCH

door, our neighbours too were out on their veranda gossiping among themselves.

Early next morning, I arrived at the shop in a thoughtful mood. It would be a half day as the shop shut down for the holiday period every August. Behind the counter, I ran my left hand over the countertops, reflecting on the profitable year for the shop. I proudly watched my tailors finishing up their sewing before the holiday break. They began to clean the sewing machines and tidy up around their workspaces by picking up remnants of fabric and sewing bits and pieces. I walked to my worktable to tidy up. I placed the pieces of the triangular chalk together in a pile and then rolled up the measuring tapes, positioning them next to the chalk. The scissors were laid out in a straight line at the horizontal edge of the table. I picked up the design magazines and placed them on the shelf against the wall.

I walked to the desk, unlocked the desk drawer and picked up the pay envelopes that the bookkeeper had left there. I brought them out to my tailors. I spoke briefly to each one of them as I handed out the pay envelopes. I let them know how very gratified I was with the work they had done for the past year. I told them that, with God's blessings, it would continue to be profitable for the next year. They smiled in agreement and left for their holidays. I shut off the lights, placed the vacation sign on the door, locked it and headed for home.

We had a quick lunch. Trinia and I packed the luggage. By three o'clock we piled into the Hudson and Peter drove us to the railway station. Theresa and Mina were enthusiastically running around us at the station until Trinia directed them into the train to find our cabin—which of course, was in the second-class section of the train. Peter helped us settle into our cabin for our overnight journey to Mombasa.

At precisely four o'clock, the train began moving. Mina squealed when it first lurched forward. I looked out the window towards the caboose and saw the puffs of steam filling the air.

The engineer was blowing the whistle that signalled departure, and Mina came to the window. We waved to Peter and Matthew on the platform. They waved back at us. The train pulled away. Trinia yelled out the window. "Look after yourselves while we are away and stay safe."

Peter and Matthew smiled and almost together shouted, "Yes Mai, we will! And have a good time by the ocean."

The train moved faster and faster out of the station. We continued to lean out of the window until the platform disappeared from our view. We left our cabin door open. Trinia and I looked out the window from the narrow passageway, while Theresa and Mina, from the small cabin window looked at the immense fields of brown grass. They hoped to catch glimpses of antelope, or even a giraffe in the distance. I had told them that, in the past, we had seen wildlife from the train. The girls ran back and forth between our window and the cabin window, but there was no sight of any wildlife.

Dusk set in, then the night sky closed over our moving train. The girls were disappointed that they had not seen any wildlife.

"Never mind," said Trinia. "You're in for a treat now. Get dressed for dinner, and we'll take you to the dining car."

It was always a joy to eat in the dining car. This would be a new experience for our girls. Reluctantly they dressed for dinner.

"Does each class have its own dining car, Pai?" Theresa asked.

"Are we in a class?" asked Mina.

Theresa looked at her baby sister and tousled her hair. "Yes, we're in second-class, silly."

"Who's in first-class?"

"The British are in first-class," Trinia said, and I could tell that she was ready to answer more questions from Mina, but our youngest had already stopped paying attention and was fussing with her shoes.

"And yes," I told Theresa, "each class has its own dining car."

With the sound of the dinner gong, we made our way to the dining car. As we came closer, we smelled the different aromas of food being prepared. We walked in and were taken to our table with the silver place settings organized on a starched white tablecloth. Mina stared in amazement. Theresa too was amazed. I explained the use of the napkins and then picked up the menu and told them what we would be having for dinner. When the waiter came, I ordered for us.

The girls looked around in wonder. I noticed Theresa tried to act and look mature, and I smiled at her; she was fourteen. They glanced at the other dining tables with people elegantly dressed for dinner. As each course arrived, I explained the proper use of the cutlery. The dining car was crowded, and there was a buzz of conversation in the air. Mina was unusually speechless, looking around open mouthed at everything going on around her. A few times Trinia had to remind her to eat.

I directed the girls to look out the window, for there was a faint image of the moon in the distance. They turned around and smiled. Even Theresa seemed a bit shy to speak out in this formal setting.

"What do you think, Theresa?" I asked.

"Yes, it's very nice, I like being here. The food is very different, and I like the taste," she replied.

"Yes, Pai. It feels funny because the train is moving, and we are sitting here having our dinner. The moon looks like it's moving," said Mina

After dinner, we made our way to our cabin. Once inside, the girls picked up their favourite activity and the two of them played Snakes and Ladders on the top bunk.

"Tomorrow," Trinia said, "we'll have to wake up early to have breakfast and then be ready to leave the train because we'll be in Mombasa. You can't stay up too late."

"Yes, Mai," said Mina and her voice sounded sleepy already

Trinia and I continued talking in whispers. Eventually, we fell asleep on the bunk beds below our girls. The train chugged along.

The next morning, the breakfast gong awoke us at an early hour. Mina jumped down from the upper bunk and slowly lifted the cabin window drape. It was daylight.

She shouted, "It's already daylight."

"Mina, hush now," said Trinia. "Remember there are other people on the train. We are not at home."

We drowsily tidied up the cabin. We dressed and swayed from side to side on our way to the dining car again. This time, it was not as extraordinary as last night. Not being fully awake, we quietly had a light breakfast. Everyone seemed to be in a rush. The train was scheduled to arrive in Mombasa at around eight o'clock. We finished our breakfast, then quickly walked back to our cabin, packed and leaned out the window, watching the train chug towards the platform in Mombasa. The girls were joyously talking to each other.

After a rough taxi ride to our rental guesthouse—one of Nathoo's—we unpacked and went out to show Mombasa to our girls. Trinia was very good at adapting no matter where we went. She made it very easy for us. Once outside, we walked along the streets of Mombasa. We stopped for an ice cream at a local restaurant. I began a conversation with the servers and found out that the cruise ship *Ocean Winds* had docked in very early this morning. This was Menino's ship!

"We have to find our way to the port," I told my family. "We must visit my friend, Menino."

I could not contain my emotions at the thought of seeing my friend again after many years. The girls were genuinely puzzled at my excitement. We left the restaurant and walked the few blocks to the port. The heat was unbearable—the humidity was very thick that made it uncomfortable to walk. Exhausted and sweaty, we arrived at the port with the ship in full view. I told them to wait in the shady part of the port building while I went inside to enquire about visiting Menino.

After what seemed liked hours, I briskly walked my family towards the dock. We were escorted to the gangway and carefully made our way up to the ship deck. We were told to wait and that Menino would be with us shortly. I paced back and forth. I could not believe that I would actually see Menino. The last time I saw him was at my wedding. Before I knew it, I felt a slap on my back. I turned and, there in front of me, was Menino.

We greeted each other loudly and with laughter. For a moment, we forgot about the rest of the family waiting behind us. Menino stopped, shifted me aside, and then walked towards Trinia and the girls. He hugged Trinia, lifted up Mina and gave Theresa a cuddle.

"Let's go to the lounge," he said. "We can talk there, and I'll have something special for you two lovely girls."

"This is wonderful, Menino. How long have you been here?"

"In port? We arrived very early this morning. We leave tomorrow night."

He led us down the stairs towards the lounge. Menino cheerfully informed me that he was promoted to Chief Steward to the Captain and his staff.

We stepped into the captain's lounge. It was a relief to feel the cool air coming from the ceiling fan. Trinia, Theresa and Mina sat on the tan-coloured leather sofa. Menino and I sat on the wing chairs nearby. We continued exchanging our news about each other and Goa. It was incredible that we were both in Kenya talking to each other.

While we spoke, I could see Trinia looking around the lounge, admiring the oak panelled walls decorated with brass knobs and bows, the sturdy oak desk at the far corner of the room, the oak bookshelves on either side of it. Mina and Theresa were gazing down at the intricate design of the Persian carpet on the floor. We were interrupted by a knock on the door that brought in refreshments: ice cream for the girls, tea for the adults.

The girls were fascinated and delighted to eat into a three-layered ice cream square that Menino called Neapolitan.

"This is different, Mai," said Theresa. "Not like what you make."

Trinia made a delicious vanilla flavoured ice cream occasion-ally as a treat.

"Yes, I can see that. This is quite fancy. Can I taste a bit?"

"Here, Mai, have some of mine," said Mina. "I think it tastes very good."

Trinia scooped a bit of it, tasted it and admiringly agreed with the girls. I continued to share news with Menino. He looked well and seemed adjusted to his new lifestyle. He admitted that he missed his wife and children each time he had to leave them for these trips. Eventually, Menino stood up and took us on a tour of the ship. I noticed the girls were in awe at the size of the ship, the different levels, the crew who worked away at keeping the ship tidy and ready for the next part of its journey. Trinia com-mented that the ship was like a floating house.

When it was time to leave, we made our way down the gangway to the street level. I hugged Menino and I hoped we could meet again. We watched him climb up again, and once he was on deck, we waved one last time. We turned around and walked towards the bustling street.

I could not stop talking about Menino. Trinia agreed that he was doing well on the ship, with his promotion. I repeated, and not for the first time, about how Menino, Anton and I would spend time on that Benaulim beach, talking about leaving Goa. Those had been different times. We had each known that we would leave Goa, but none of us knew how our destinies would turn out.

"No one does," said Trinia. "I certainly didn't." She looked at me and smiled.

We continued walking down the street. I held Mina's hand while Theresa walked with her mother in the blazing sun. The humidity slowed our pace to a crawl.

"It is hot walking on the street. Let's go to the beach for a breath of ocean air," I said, directing the family towards the beach road. We immediately felt the cool ocean breezes as we strolled on the beach.

The children played in the sand and dipped themselves in the water to cool off. Trinia and I found a shady spot beneath the palm trees and watched the girls build sandcastles after sandcastles, only to have each successive creation washed away by the ocean waves drawing in towards them. Sometimes they stood and splashed in the water. They teased each other into the surf.

"I am glad Mina has Theresa," said Trinia. "She is very lucky. Theresa has only just turned a teenager and she seems to enjoy playing with her little sister."

"Mind you when in the ocean water and on sandy beaches we become children again. It is always magical to be by the ocean and on the sand," I said.

We returned to our guesthouse happy and sleepy from the sun and the sea air. During dinner, the girls asked many questions about the ship and Menino. They talked about the ship being like a huge house with people living there as the house floated on the ocean. Mina wondered if they would get to taste the ice cream again.

The next day, we took a bus to Fort Jesus. When we arrived, Mina and Theresa looked in amazement at the very large structure. I explained what little history I knew of the place.

"It was the Portuguese explorer Vasco da Gama," I began to explain, "who first came to Mombasa bringing with him Portuguese wealth and workers who built this fort in 1593."

Over time it became a government prison. We could only look at it from the other side of the street. We couldn't get closer as it was blocked off. But the fort was large enough that it was impossible not to be fascinated by the structure; a sandy stone coloured structure with curved and straight walls.

After a while of being near Fort Jesus, we walked in the direction of home. We stopped at a nearby restaurant for a late lunch and then went to the beach for the afternoon. Trinia and I took a dip in the ocean this time and walked along the beach with our girls, dodging the waves and splashing one another.

The next day we took an early ferry for the town of Malindi which lay approximately seventy miles north-northeast of Mombasa. We once again settled in Nathoo's guesthouse. We rented a room for the remainder of our vacation. We unpacked and went out to explore.

I took the family to Vasco da Gama Pillar in Malindi. It was in the south part of this beach town, about a ten-minute walk from our guesthouse. The sun drenched us and, with ice cream cones in our hands, we slowly made our way to the point on which the Pillar had been erected. The gentle ocean breezes made our walk bearable. Mina was very good, staying close to Theresa while we walked in the heat of the sun. The ice cream helped. When we arrived at the point, there were a few tourists walking around. I led the family to the monument, and we took our turn to walk around it, watching the huge waves crashing on the rocks in front. Mina and Theresa ran around the enormous stone-like pillar and at the same time, delighted to feel the full blast of the ocean wind.

I called out to the children pointing to the plaque stating that this marked the last stop in Africa before Vasco da Gama sailed across the Indian Ocean to India in 1498. We slowly walked towards the bottom of the monument to have a picnic of sandwiches and Coca-Cola on a bench under a tree. The girls quickly ate their lunch as they were in a hurry to go to the beach.

On our way home, we walked on the pavement while looking at the slope that slid down to the beach. We were not allowed to walk along that beach because it was a Whites Only beach. What happened next would be forever fixed in my memory. I was saying something to Trinia and Theresa turned to ask me something. That was the moment that Mina, hot and tired from walking, caught sight of the water and decided to run down onto the beach.

There was a booming voice.

"Stop, I'll shoot if you do not get out of our beach. This is not a beach for you. Get out immediately."

We turned to see Mina, frozen in her tracks, looking at this big burly white man, with a rifle pointed at her.

Theresa screamed, and before I could move, Trinia had rushed down onto the beach towards Mina.

"*Nooo. Please!* Please, don't shoot. We are leaving. Sorry, Sir."

I rushed towards Trinia and snatched up Mina and pulled Trinia as quickly as possible up the sand hill towards the street. I did not dare look at the man with the rifle. I probably looked angry while Trinia's face was pale with fear and struggled to climb upwards to the pavement. I was right there with her, holding her hand to move her along as fast as we could up this slope to where Theresa stood shaking with her hands on her face. Once on the pavement, we sat down on a nearby bench. Theresa had started to weep and Mina was inconsolable, unable to understand what she had done wrong.

Trinia was deathly still and quiet as she stared out at the water. She turned to me and spoke under her breath.

"You know he could have shot Mina, and we would have lost our youngest child."

"But he didn't. I don't think he would have. He is paid to intimidate and with the State of Emergency…" But I could tell that Trinia was not in the mood for explanations. "She is safe, Trinia. We are safe, thanks to your quick action in spotting what was happening."

Mina was sobbing in Trinia's arms.

"Why Mai? Why was the man pointing the gun at me? I only wanted to run on the sand and feel the water."

"You did nothing wrong, Mina. Nothing wrong at all. That man was not a nice man. That should not have happened. You must stay close to us from now on and not run off."

We went to a nearby restaurant. I wanted to get some ice cream for the girls and get them and Trinia out of the sun. Both girls looked worn out. And Trinia was acting as though she had seen a ghost—and perhaps she almost had. At our table, I tried my best to make sense of it for Mina.

"We must stay with our own kind, Mina. With Goans and Indians. We must not go where the Whites are, like that man with the gun. It is foolish I know; it is not right. But that is the way it is. You don't see it at home because our entire neighbourhood is for Goans and Indians. You have noticed that I am sure."

Mina just nodded. Her eyes were puffy and she had ice cream on her face. It looked as though Theresa wanted to say something, but she chose to keep it to herself for Mina's sake.

"When we get back to the guesthouse," said Trinia, "we'll take you to a beach where you can play just like in Mombasa."

"Okay Mai."

On our way back, Trinia was distracted and kept peeking in and out of the shops on the street. We bought some halva and cashew nuts. At the guesthouse, we had some with tea and then packed the rest to take home. We changed and went to our Indian beach where the children safely played in the sand. We walked along the beach, played with the girls, and helped them build sandcastles—dearly hoping that the earlier incident wouldn't cast a shadow over the entire trip and haunt their memories of our vacation.

That night when the children were asleep, Trinia and I held each other and talked about our decision to raise our children in Kenya and questioned the kind of life we would have had back in Goa. We could not help but wonder at the direction Kenya was taking and if it would be safe for very much longer.

The next day, we went back to the beach where the girls spent hours playing in the sand and splashing around in the water. We warned them not to go too far out in the water for in the distance sharks were spotted. We spent the remainder of our vacation at this beach. It felt safe and secure. There were other Goan children too. Mina and Theresa made friends with them and we with their parents and for the reminder of our vacation we spent our time on this beach. We exchanged stories about living under segregation laws. We knew that this would be our way of life no matter where we travelled around Kenya. We also looked back at what we had left behind in Goa. Most of us missed Goa, but there was no denying that opportunities existed in Kenya and not in Goa. We had come to Africa in hopes of building a better future for our families.

On the last day we met together for our last time together. We hurried the children through breakfast, for it would soon be our last beach day. We made our way to the beach and comfortably sat on the sand, under the palm trees with our new friends. We spent the whole day on the beach watching our children play their usual beach games for the last time. When it turned dark, we slowly made our way home through the cool night breezes. We walked slower than usual, for we did not want the holiday to end.

We rose early the next day to catch the early morning ferry back to Mombasa, and later that morning we were on the train that took us back to Nairobi. It was quieter than normal in the cabin, for we were thinking about the many adventures of this memorable holiday. We arrived at the station in Nairobi to be greeted by Peter. The drive home was abuzz as Mina tried to tell her eldest brother about everything that had happened. Theresa was subdued. Peter could not keep up with the conversation.

At dinnertime, we shared the many stories of our adventures by the ocean. Mina told again of the incident on the beach. And I could tell that both Peter and Matthew were angry. Perhaps Mina could sense it too, for she asked Peter why he thought it had happened. I caught Peter's eye with a look that told him to remember Mina's age.

"It's because the British rule the country, Mina," he said. "And they make these laws that we all have to obey."

"But it sounds silly. It would be nice for all the children to play together. It is sad to put people in different sections of that big beach. I think it belongs to everyone and everyone should be able to play anywhere on the beach."

I smiled at Mina. "You are right, Mina. And maybe some day that law will change and we can go anywhere we want to. Right now, there are many places we cannot go. And it is wrong. But the Africans are fighting for their freedom and for independence. In time that law will change. It is only a matter of time, I think. We must be patient and pray that independence, when it comes, comes peacefully." I was carried away with my opinions and I was sure Mina didn't understand it.

"Pai," said Peter. "You are always preaching patience. Sometimes people run out of patience simply waiting for justice to happen. The newspapers continue reporting on the unrest that is happening in the Kikuyu reserves. It could get ugly before it gets better. I read—"

"Peter, let's enjoy dinner for now," interrupted Trinia. "Besides there are many other stories to tell about our vacation. Theresa tell them about Fort Jesus in Mombasa and the Vasco da Gama Pillar in Malindi. We had a lovely time there. And then there is the visit to the big ship where we met Pai's friend. Let's talk about that."

"Yes, yes, let us enjoy dinner," I said. "Nothing will be solved over curry and rice."

They listened to Theresa relate the stories of the historic sites and most important, she enthusiastically talked about being on the beach and in the ocean waters. She observed how she felt very happy to be near the ocean; it was relaxing and peaceful.

Theresa's stories changed the mood to happier memories. Peter and Matthew responded with memories of their own from their visits to these same historic sites years before. I was encouraged to hear their memories. It was good to know that they were pleasant memories.

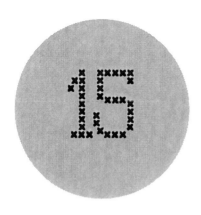

PERSISTENT FEAR AND INSTABILITY

The Christmas season always brought me joy; not only the celebration of Christmas with family and friends, but the build up to the season. At home Trinia was busy making a variety of Goan Christmas snacks while I, at my shop was busy sewing suits and dresses. This was the time when the business was most profitable. But something happened on this one particular day that I have never forgotten. It was December 8, 1953, a Tuesday around mid-morning. I came up to the front of the shop and noticed that there was unusual activity on the street. As I approached the front door for a better look, two police officers rushed into my shop shouting for the Kikuyu to come up to the front.

Muturi and Karani walked up. The officers screamed at them to put their hands up, and then they pushed them out to the waiting van. There was a deep silence in the shop. I was emotionally frozen and could not move. Luis walked up.

"What happened there?" he was confused.

"I don't know. I don't know. I guess by the State of Emergency law they have the power to do what they did, and we don't know why Muturi and Karani were taken away. Are they involved with the freedom movement? We will never know." I looked at Luis and walked back to the sewing room.

"Yes, it's because they are Kikuyu; they must be involved in the freedom movement," said Joseph, standing up to stretch his legs. He was at the sewing machine for quite a while now.

"But are they the freedom *fighters* we hear about?" asked Luis in a hushed tone. He sounded doubtful.

"We don't know," I said. "They wouldn't tell us what is going on in the reserves. They probably *couldn't* tell us. Who knows? They're gone now." There was a knot in my stomach.

"Sabby, they are *arrested*," said Joseph in a loud voice. "They are not gone."

"Okay, okay," I said. "Let's get back to our sewing. We have customers coming for their fittings."

We returned to our work, but an anxious silence had settled over the sewing room like dust. I wondered where they took Muturi and Karani and what would happen to them. The street outside was back to normal. The police and their vans disappeared, and all was peaceful again. Is this what it meant to be in a State of Emergency?

Mrs. Brown walked in for her fitting. Her lively voice broke the silence in the shop.

"Hello Sabby, is my cocktail dress ready?"

"Yes, Mrs. Brown. I'll get it. But please try it on before you take it. There may be some adjustments to it. I changed the style a bit."

I took her to the fitting room, and hoped that she would like the new design I created for this dress.

"Of course, I'll do that." She disappeared into the fitting room. I was curious. Did she know what happened a very short while ago? They seemed to know more than we did. To my surprise, Mr. Brown walked in.

"Mr. Brown. Good afternoon. Mrs. Brown is trying on her cocktail dress."

"Yes, I know. I've come to pick her up. It's getting more and more dangerous out there. I had to send the driver home. He is Kikuyu, you know. These days we don't know who to trust, even though some Kikuyu are solid loyalists for the colonial government."

He waited patiently for Mrs. Brown.

"The police were here," I said. "They arrested Muturi and Karani, my Kikuyu assistants. They came in and took them away. Why? Tell me."

"Under a State of Emergency, the government can do this, Sabby. They are doing a sweep of Kikuyu in the city area." Mr. Brown sounded defiant, defensive.

"But where are they taking them? Muturi and Karani are good workers; Muturi, especially showed a great interest in tailoring. They are taking *all* Kikuyu? Why?"

"Sabby, the government doesn't trust them. They believe that all of the Kikuyu are taking these oaths and are out to terrorize us. We've had killings of the British farmers in the Highlands. We cannot take any chances."

"Yes I understand, but where are they *taking* them? What will happen to the Kikuyu? There are too many of them. You can't take them all away." I hadn't meant to say 'you'.

"The *government* is taking them to screening camps far out. And believe me, you don't want to know about that. It's to protect us and keep us safe," Mr. Brown said softly and cautiously as if he didn't want to tell me the whole story.

"I see," I said after a moment's silence. What could I say to him? He was British and wanted Kenya to become a White Kenya. Mrs. Brown interrupted us.

"Sabby, the dress looks fabulous. I love the way you design dresses. This is perfect and looks very different from anything else I have worn. Lovely."

"Thank you, Mrs. Brown. I'm glad you like it. I created something different, and didn't know if you would like it. I'm pleased."

She exchanged a look with Mr. Brown and they whispered while I moved towards the back of my desk to write out the bill for the dress. They quickly paid the bill and left.

I walked towards the sewing room. It was quiet. No one was sewing. We looked at each other with distress and confusion.

"What is the screening area?" asked Joseph. "Do you know this place? What was Mr. Brown talking about?"

"I *don't* know," I said. "It does not sound right. Let's talk to Omondi when he comes to clean the shop. He's not Kikuyu, of course, but he may know something about these so-called screening camps." I was tense.

Later that afternoon, Omondi was surprised to see us all there. Usually, I was the only one still around checking my customer list when he came in to clean the shop. He could tell something was wrong.

"What's happened? Why is everyone waiting for me?" he said with a smile.

"Omondi, the police were here today. They took away Muturi and Karani. There is some kind of a Kikuyu roundup. They are taking all the Kikuyu from the city to some screening camp. Do you know this camp? What happens there? Is it a prison?"

Omondi did not say a word right away. He walked to the back, picked up the bucket, half filled it with water. Then he gathered the two brooms and some wash cloths. He was muttering softly as though to himself. It was difficult for us to hear him clearly.

"Omondi," I said. "You can tell us because we only want to know. We are afraid."

He looked at me and nodded, with some doubt. Then he softly described these camps.

There were many camps scattered around the countryside. Each camp was a very big open space. They made the Kikuyu dig big gutters and then they put large metal screens around this big space. This was where they remained, working all day digging gutters and trenches. Then the white men came in and talked to them about religion.

"I am told that the Kikuyu are beaten and made to work very hard there." Omondi put down the bucket and shook his head.

"They are trying to kill them. They want this land. The Kikuyu are strong, and will not let them do this. It is bad there. I can't talk any more about this. It is very bad there. Let me finish the cleaning and then I want to go home. It is bad."

We looked at each other in shock. Quietly, the tailors left for home while I went to my customer book and let Omondi finish up the cleaning. Soon he left and I locked up the shop. The car was parked nearby; Peter was waiting for me. He worked as a bookkeeper at a transportation company. He drove us in each day. On the way home we picked up Matthew who was now working at the law courts as a legal clerk. He turned eighteen in October, and he wanted to work in the courts. Our family lawyer, Mr. Das recommended him. Matthew appreciated this opportunity.

During dinner, Matthew talked again about African Independence, the Kikuyu oath-taking ceremonies and the attacks on European farmers.

"Yes," I said. "That, of course we are told about. But what are the British doing to the Kikuyu? I have my fears. They do not give us details about that, do they? The police rushed into my shop today and took my two Kikuyu assistants away. No explanation given. They were shoved into the back of a van and driven off.

Mr. Brown told me that the Nairobi Kikuyu are being rounded up and taken to screening camps. And when we asked Omondi what he knew of the camps, he didn't want to say much, but what he did say was disturbing."

Matthew looked grim. He shook his head. "And during a State of Emergency it's all legal."

"This is trouble, Pai," said Peter. "The Kikuyu are going to resist. We don't get all the news in city. Only what they want us to hear: the savage Kikuyu and how they are attacking innocent farmers and resisting civilization."

Theresa and Mina were quiet, and I could tell that Trinia was not pleased about the conversation that had again darkened the dinner table.

"What do your customers say?" asked Peter.

"I believe they think they are helping the Africans by bringing in the rule of law and imposing the British form of government to the Africans. At least some of them really do think they are civilizing them. But I don't think civilization works that way. Civilization is more like a suit. It needs to be tailored. What fits one person doesn't fit another." I thought aloud in my answer.

We were quiet for a while. Then Peter spoke. "Part of the problem is that no one talks about it except at dinner tables and in the backrooms of tailor shops, I suppose. People are afraid."

"I know I'm afraid when you talk about civilization, are they civilizing us as well? Are they making us think and be like the British? I don't understand." Theresa asked looking rather puzzled.

Matthew spoke up and gave a long "lecture" about the British rule of law—segregating us on the one hand and then insisting that we follow their laws as it was the law of the land.

Theresa listened with interest and seemed to understand what Matthew was saying while Trinia looked at me disapprovingly. I knew I should change our discussion, but the children needed to know about this political situation. It affected them as well as us. They were born in a British colony, and neither Trinia nor I were. What would that mean if the Africans gained independence?

"Let us continue this discussion another day," I said. "It is time for homework and other activities, and then in an hour we will pray the Rosary. And Matthew don't be late if you are going out."

Matthew shrugged his shoulders. "I'll be back in time for Rosary, Pai."

When Kamau came in to clear the dishes, we stood up and left the dining room—Trinia went to the kitchen to make herself a cup of coffee while I settled in the living room to light my pipe and pour myself some cognac.

Trinia and I continued discussing the political situation. She seemed more willing to talk away from the dinner table and our children, especially Mina who was seven years old; her second year in primary school. We discussed being foreigners in a country where our children were born and being raised. There were many questions to ask with very few answers. For instance, how would the British let Kenya become independent? What would it look like? Would they leave and let the rest of the non-British people decide what they wanted to do in Kenya?

And would the Africans accept *us* as Kenyan citizens? It wasn't the Kenyans who opened their doors to us. It was the British. It made us uncomfortable because we were talking about our entire way of life being threatened. I didn't leave Goa to exchange economic uncertainty for political uncertainty. I created a good life for us in Nairobi, a life I could not have created in Goa.

I noticed that Kamau never said anything to us about what was going on. He stayed in the city and did not go back to where he came from. I wondered what he thought of our conversation at dinnertime. He was much older now and perhaps was not getting involved in the independence movement. Who knew?

That night, close to midnight, I woke up to the sound of running footsteps around our house. I woke Trinia and told her to stay with the children. I grabbed my whistle from beside the bed and crept into the living room. Peering through the curtain I could see that there were many Africans surrounding our home. *This is bad.*

Trinia was with the children in the girls' room.

"There are a number of Africans outside the house. I am not sure what is happening," I said. "Girls I want you to get under your beds. Trinia you stay here with them. Theresa and Mina looked very frightened. Matthew and Peter on the other hand seemed ready to do something, but what? We waited in silence. We heard them moving about outside.

The window was slowly opening and a pole was being pushed in the bedroom. Peter moved toward it but I held him back.

"No, stay back," I whispered.

I brought the whistle to my lips and blew as hard as I could for the neighbours to hear the piercing sound. The pole dropped immediately. I continued to blow the whistle, paused only long enough to draw breath. After a few minutes I stopped blowing. Mina was crying under the bed.

We listened carefully around her sobs and could hear no sound of anyone outside our home. Peter, Matthew and I walked to the living room to check from the windows. No one was out there.

It took us over an hour to calm Mina down enough to get her back to sleep. Theresa looked brave but nervous at the same time. Both were in bed.

In silence, I continued thinking about the State of Emergency in Kenya. I thought about the Kikuyu bonding ceremonies and the taking of secret oaths inviting death. I thought of the British settlers living in fear, legitimate fear, and how quickly fear can turn to hate. Then I thought about what Omondi said about the prison camps the Kikuyu were being forced to build for themselves. And what they had to live through. Much of what was going on was not being reported. Even Omondi had been reluctant to say more than he did.

I was afraid then. Afraid for myself and my family.

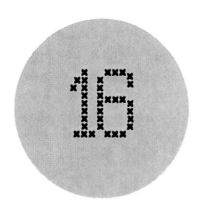

TRAGEDY

It was more than two years since the day my Kikuyu assistants were arrested from my shop, more than two years our home was surrounded by Africans in the dead of night and a window was forced open. More than two years, and yet *still* Kenya was under a State of Emergency. *How long*, I often thought, *can this ongoing situation be considered an emergency?*

In January 1956, Theresa became a trainee teller at the bank. Trinia and I were very proud of her. As a teller she had to wear a uniform. I sewed that uniform for her. After her first month at the bank, we noticed that she walked and talked with confidence.

By her seventeenth birthday on May 8, she took over the conversations at the dinner table. She challenged her brothers and often made known her opinions. It was moments like these that made us very proud of her. She was on her way to becoming her own woman. She went to the dances at the Goan clubs with her brothers as this was our Goan custom. At Sunday lunches we listened to their gossip about what happened at these dances. While Trinia and I happily attended the functions held by the Tailors' Society and for those afternoon functions, we always took Mina with us. She seemed to enjoy herself with the boys and girls of her age.

It was a cool evening in August. I was at home looking out at the fruit trees Trinia had growing on the left side and lost in my own thoughts. There was a heavy knocking on the front door and by the time I reached the living room, Theresa had opened the front door. Anton was stood there solemnly with his hair ruffled. He was breathing heavily. When he saw Theresa in front of him a look, I could not read, flashed across his face. He rushed in, grabbed hold of my hand and tried to take me to the door before I even had time to properly get into my shoes.

"Anton, I—"

"Sabby, come quick," he said under his breath. "Something has happened to Trinia. Let's go."

"What's wrong? Slow down and tell me."

"No, no, let's get in the car. You have to come quickly."

I left with Anton dragging me out to his car parked on the street. My heart was pounding. Trinia had gone to visit Natalina and Lazar, cousins of mine who lived in Eastleigh. She took Peter with her. I don't know why she insisted on going by bus and not by car. Anton was silent at first and drove very fast. Then he talked breathlessly and did not make sense. I knew something terrible had happened.

"Anton, what has happened? I can't understand you. Is Peter all right, and what has happened to Trinia? Tell me."

"Sabby, I don't know what to say. Trinia is in Natalina's home. When I left, Trinia was on the sofa lying down, and they were rubbing brandy on her and making her sniff the brandy. She fainted and they were trying to get her conscious again. I don't know. I don't know."

At Natalina's place, I jumped out of the car and rushed into the house, and there on the sofa in the living room was Peter kneeling near Trinia's feet sobbing uncontrollably. A sinking feeling opened up beneath my feet. The doctor was there, attending to Trinia. I looked at Natalina. There were tears streaming down her cheeks.

The doctor turned around and saw me. He shook his head.

"I am very sorry, Sabby, Trinia is gone."

I bent down, embraced Trinia with my hands around her shoulders, hugged her and wailed at the same time.

"No, no, you cannot leave me now. I love you. I love you. Come back, come back. Please God, bring her back to me."

Everyone was crying and sobbing loudly. It was unbearable. I was on my knees until Anton pulled me upright. He threw his arms around me and would not let go of me.

"It can't be," I said. "Trinia cannot go now. My children. Mina is still a child. They need her. Please God help me, give me courage to take this pain. It is too much."

Anton pulled me back, looked at me and, with his handkerchief, wiped my face.

"I'll be here to help you. Stay strong. I know this doesn't make sense but…"

Anton was talking but I did not hear him. I was in shock trying to figure it out. *This cannot be happening. It is not so.* I was taken to a chair. The doctor said something about Trinia's heart. Peter was being held up by Natalina. Then he was seated beside me. He was sobbing, and I put my hand on his shoulder and drew him to me. I saw Anton say something to Lazar who nodded and sat next to me. Then there was a brandy in my hand. Anton was gone and perhaps Lazar had told me where. I didn't know. There did not seem to be enough air in the room. Too much sobbing.

Poor Peter. I wished I could comfort him. I wished I could sip my brandy. I wished the room would stop spinning. This was very painful. I felt that I could not do this.

Trinia how am I to do this without you?

Anton lifted the brandy glass from my hand and took my wrists. He was back. *How long have I been here?*

"Sabby, I've told Matthew and Theresa. I'm taking you home now. It was… You need to come with me."

Peter was at my side. Anton led us both to his car.

Then Anton was driving off back to Natalina's—or no, he was just standing by his car. Was he waiting for others? What had he said to me? Somehow Peter and I were at our front door. I looked at Peter and nodded. He opened the door.

Mina ran towards me.

"Pai, what happened to Mai? Matthew says she is dead. Is this true? Why? Why?"

The sight of Mina, ten years old, snapped me out of myself. I grabbed her up in my arms.

"Yes, yes, Mai is gone to heaven."

I called the children to my side, and our tears came like a monsoon.

Then Anton was there in the background, and soon more people came into the living room. It was a chaos of weeping and voices. I saw Miguel and Fatima coming towards us. We hugged and cried as a family. More people arrived. Too many people. Everyone was crying and reaching out to touch us. At some point I realized that I had been separated from my children. Had Peter taken them off somewhere? As I turned to look around the room, silence fell across the crowd like a shroud.

Trinia's body had arrived. Anton said they needed to know where to rest… the body. I had no strength. My knees almost gave out. *My Trinia, my beloved Trinia has come home, but is not alive. How can this be?*

I walked out with Anton and saw that my Trinia was covered in a white sheet. The fellows carried her in, and I showed them the room in the back where they would prepare Trinia for her burial. Anton held me up. Miguel too was by my side. I fell on her body and sobbed uncontrollably.

The children came in. I could sense them standing at the doorway Mina was further away and stood back. I went to her, picked her up and hugged her. She didn't understand what was happening. What is death to a ten-year-old who has lost her mother? Theresa came over and took hold of Mina, and I gently put her down.

Neither did I understand this shock of loss. A massive heart attack the doctor had said. Was it also a death to a fifty-eight-year-old man who had just lost his wife and the love of his life?

Over the next two hours many people came and went. Emilio approached me and whispered that he would make the dress for Trinia. I nodded. I knew Emilio to be a good tailor and that it would probably take him most of the night to make it, for the burial would be the next day. He would make a fine dress for her. He left, and I saw Anton organizing the people who would prepare Trinia for her burial. It needed to be done quickly. They went to the back room then, and I was there in the living room with the children. We were silent, for we had no more tears or emotional strength. It was late. People gradually left. I led the children to their bedrooms.

It was very early when Anton woke me to say that Trinia was dressed and ready for the funeral service. I woke up and, in a daze, I dressed. Paulo and John had arrived, and they rushed to me, holding me up while I went over to have a look at Trinia. She looked asleep and peacefully beautiful. Once again, I sobbed. It was agonizing to see her lying there. They brought in the coffin and she was gently placed inside. That made it final. It was the end of Trinia. They carried the coffin to the living room and placed it on a table near the window in the centre of the room.

The children were in shock and looked emotionally drained. Since yesterday, relatives, friends and neighbours had begun to surround us. We had not been alone. I sat down with my children, with my tearful face. But, like them, I was speechless. We looked at each other, held hands, and then hugged each other, feeling each other's tears on our faces. We were very sad. Mina looked scared.

How am I going to live without Trinia?

Father Doyle walked in to say prayers over Trinia's body in our home. He blessed my beloved Trinia, then we surrounded the coffin and the lid was closed. I softly sobbed, as did the children. We were grief stricken. Trinia's coffin was put in the hearse. Outside, I saw the people going in the buses for the funeral. The car was waiting for us. John and Paulo were by my side.

It was then that some sorrowful looking lady came up to Mina, pulled her back and told her that she could not go with the family because she was only little and it would not be good for her to witness the church service or the burial at the cemetery. Mina screamed and pushed the lady away. Theresa ran to her and brought her along. Well-meaning she may have been, but how could this lady take Mina away from us at a time like this? I went to Theresa and Mina, threw my arms around them, and brought them to the back seat in the car with Peter and Matthew sitting in the front with the driver.

We proceeded to our church nearby. It was crowded with people. I didn't hear a word of the service. It was a blur. I only felt pain, a dreadful pain all over me. I felt the crush of people around each one of us. We moved from the church, to the cemetery and then home. John and Paulo held me up. I saw Miguel and Fatima consoling my children. This was the day the music died in our home.

The next few days were like a heavy haze that we couldn't see through. Many people drifted in and out of our home like ghosts. My children and I were filled with tears; our eyes swollen. We were not sleeping, only giving in, at times, to exhaustion. We were in a state of deep sadness beyond words. It was unbearable.

Getting back to any form of routine was not easy. How does one teach a broken heart to beat again? Trinia's absence filled the house, and we felt lost within it. How would we carry on with our lives?

People came daily to give condolences. Dishes of food were brought in, and Fatima supervised the cooking when necessary. I saw Josie and Tina as well. It was very quiet around the house for people spoke in whispers. Goan tradition meant that there was to be no radio, no music, and no news. We dressed in black for a one-year period of mourning. There was no laughter of any kind, especially when visitors came by to offer their condolences.

Towards the end of the month, the many, many visitors were reduced to a few. We could finally be left alone with our grief. But then we were more aware of the emptiness. At our first family dinner with no other people around us, I looked at Trinia's empty chair. Kamau was doing his best to make sure we were looked after. He brought in the dishes of food with quiet dignity and then faded back into the kitchen. We held each other's hands and, through our tears, said the Grace Before Meals. I tried to break the silence with general talk, but it didn't work. No one said anything for a while. Then Mina spoke up.

"Pai? You know this sadness gives me pain. But there is something funny that happened to Theresa and I the other day."

"What happened, Mina?" I was desperate to hear it.

"It was when these people were coming in. They had this look of sadness on their faces. I don't know what they said to me. I kept looking at their faces, one sad face after another. I had no more tears, and I simply looked at each face. My tears were gone just like Mai. Gone and... I don't know why Mai died... and..." She looked at Theresa.

Theresa put her hand on Mina's.

"But this lady came in," said Theresa, "and you know how we are sitting in our chairs that are in a row? She comes to each one of us, one after the other. I kept looking at her, and she was coming closer to us."

Mina said, "She looked very sad, Pai. Her face was horrible looking. I started imagining different things because it was too hard to look at her face."

"That's when I looked at Mina," Theresa said. "That's how it started."

"What started?" I asked.

"We started giggling inside of us. I could see Mina holding her stomach to stop herself from giggling. I grabbed her hand and we ran into the bedroom."

The sisters looked at each other.

"We shut the bedroom door and let out this huge burst of laughter. It seemed like our inside was telling us to get rid of this sadness. This lady's face looked funny to us with her very, very sad face. Pai, we are sorry we ran away to our room and laughed till we cried again."

Theresa looked around the dining table.

"But Pai," said Mina. "You know it made me feel as if there was something horrible inside me was coming out, and I had to get that out. Will Mai be upset that we laughed when we are supposed to be sad. I'm sorry."

I was taken aback and sat there in silence as did Peter and Matthew. They were much older and figured this out. We were filled with sorrow and did not let ourselves breathe again the fresh air of life. Trinia wouldn't have wanted that. We had to learn to live again and remember the good times we had together with her. Now we were a different kind of family, without Trinia. In silence we held each other's hands. I broke the silence.

"No, Theresa and no Mina, you did not do anything wrong. It was good for you. Mai would be very proud of you. She's looking at us and smiling at us and telling us to breathe again and to learn to live without her."

"I miss her very much already," said Matthew.

Peter had been very quiet and had not spoken much since Trinia died. He had been with her and it probably affected him the most of all. But he spoke then.

"I keep looking for her. She is missing. She is nowhere. I even miss her telling me off when I sneak out to have a smoke. I keep seeing her everywhere but she is not there."

We nodded in agreement and there was comfort to be found in that.

"This is the way it is," I said. "You will hear words that she would use, and yet she will not be there saying those words. You will see her on a street where she walked, and yet she will not be there. You will hear laughter and be sure it is her laughter only to realize it is not. My children, this is our grief and our tradition gives us a whole year to mourn, dressed in black. That doesn't mean that we'll forget Mai after a year of mourning or even stop missing her We will always remember her and what she was, your Mai, and my beloved wife. It will be a difficult year for us."

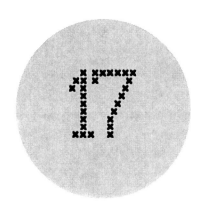

AFTERMATH OF LOSS AND MORE POLITICAL UNCERTAINTY

For the first month after her death, we visited Trinia's grave every Sunday. Then we went every other Sunday for a while. It was too emotional for us, and then it became a once a month visit. Over the years we visited her gravesite on her anniversary date.

By October, fewer people came to visit. I kept looking for Trinia. I wanted to talk with her and saw her image in everything I did. It was like a piece of my heart had been wrenched out of me. Her health had not been perfect for a few years before her death, but she had managed to stay cheerful and never complained. She had faithfully taken her medication and walked for exercise whenever she could. I had never thought she would go suddenly. No one had.

It was a Saturday afternoon; there was knock on the door. To my surprise I saw Nathoo and Ali. I brought them in the living room. They each grabbed hold of me and expressed condolences. I was speechless and we sat down. They talked quietly to my children who soon left us to ourselves. They spoke about their memories of Trinia. Each Christmas, our Goan snacks would be decorated on a tray and brought over to their homes. Their wives and children were thankful and enjoyed the different samples of Goan Christmas snacks.

"Thank you. But I remember both of you bringing in trays of Indian sweets. We enjoyed those very much; Nathoo during Diwali and Ali during Eid. But then Ali you brought meat during your second Eid which usually happened around our Easter time. Yes, Trinia appreciated those gifts very much."

"Sabby, remember when you, Trinia and I think you brought Mina along to my son's wedding. That was an elaborate affair, right? Trinia looked beautiful and your family enjoyed our type of wedding festivities. I was very happy that you came with Trinia."

"Yes, it was Mina who came with us. Mina could not stop talking about the banquet of food and Indian sweets for the crowd to eat and enjoy. We talked about it for a long time after that wedding festivity."

Theresa brought in tea and biscuits while we continued speaking about Trinia and her very short life. She was only forty-five when she passed away. They sorrowfully shook their heads. They left wishing me well over this mournful period.

The next Saturday, Mr. Rana and his wife came by with similar memories of Trinia. They remembered the exchange of Christmas snacks and Diwali Indian sweets. It made me smile when I thought of those happy times that came to mind by these visits from my Indian business friends. It was very kind of them to bring these joyful memories back to me. Yes, we attended the weddings of their sons and daughters. I forgot about those times with Trinia. She loved those festivities that were quite different from ours.

At the shop, the sympathy cards had been slid under the door. I gently picked them up and carried them back to my desk. I opened each card and read the beautiful words of sympathy some from customers who had never met Trinia. *How will I ever get over this loss?* It was like a deep wound. I was weak emotionally and physically. My tailors were good to me. They talked about different activities at the Clubs and Sunday gatherings, and I tried to add my voice to what they said—though some days I could not manage to keep up with the conversation. Most of the time I did my sewing. During lunchtime, friends dropped by to console and help in whatever way they could. Mostly they spoke about Trinia and how she had brought that special joy in my life.

As the weeks went by, I concentrated on the business to get back to some sort of routine. I worked to the deadlines for the suits and dresses. I missed Trinia very much. She had become my right hand partner of my business and my life—both seemed permanently changed with her passing. On our way home, we stopped to pick up letters from the post office box, and there were many letters from Goa—especially from Trinia's family— each expressing shock, condolences and prayers for her soul and for my children and I.

In the evenings we arrived home to a quiet house. It seemed none of us knew what to say to each other. I observed the children walking about in silence, and it seemed sad. Dinnertime was not what it used to be, but I tried to talk about different situations. Each time we talked about anything, we inevitably looked to Trinia's chair and, finding it empty, we became silent again.

Matthew often expressed his opinions about the ongoing political uncertainty. He wished that it would move forward and resolve itself—as though his resolution of political uncertainty could be applied to the resolution of grief. We talked aimlessly and without the passion that we had before.

Once in a while, we would coax Mina into talking about school. She did not like wearing black and envied the school uniform of her classmates. She stood out in black, and everyone looked at her with sorrow or—worse by far—pity. It bothered her.

I comforted her by telling her that the mourning period would come to an end and to stand tall until then and be strong. Sorrow would pass.

"But we will never forget Mai. She was the soul of this home, and we must hold onto her memory in whatever we do now and in the future."

We had the first anniversary Mass on August 16, 1957. Once again there was a big crowd of people. We put away the black, for our year of mourning had come to an end. I saw the relief in the faces of Theresa and Mina—it was easier, perhaps, for men to wear black than women. When we returned home, Peter turned on the radio.

It seemed strange, haunting almost. The sorrowful silence had been broken by the sound of music in our home. At dinner-time, after our usual prayer before our meal, I said a few words in memory of Trinia. The children glanced at me. Mina smiled; a smile that I had not seen in a long time.

"Pai, that is very nice what you said about Mai. Can we do that every time before dinner?"

"Yes, that is good," I said. "Every day, each one of us will think of what to say about Mai and then we will say it before we eat or even during dinner."

We agreed, and that night during dinner we talked about Trinia. It was wonderful to hear the memories of their Mai—some were funny memories that made us laugh. It felt good to laugh.

We will be all right, I thought. *Time will heal the wound, but will leave a permanent scar on each of our hearts.*

"Listen, one more thing," I said. "The mourning period was hard. I know that. Wearing black every single day… none of us liked it. I didn't like it. We didn't listen to the radio and denied ourselves music. The silence was difficult. It was not nice for us. I honestly don't think Mai would have wanted that for us. I could feel her telling us to stop, but we stuck to our traditions, and did it for a whole year."

Peter looked around the dinner table, and nodded in agreement.

"Pai, it was difficult, especially for Theresa and for Mina wearing black dresses to the bank and school. Theresa could not wear her bank uniform and that made her stand out in the bank and of course Mina could not wear her school uniform either. I understand that it was tradition but, well, I don't know."

"Next time when we experience such a loss," I said, careful not to say, *when I die,* though that would be what would usually happen next. I did not want to put those thoughts in their minds that night.

"Let us promise ourselves that we will not wear black for one whole year, let us remember the lost one with happy memories and thoughts and play the music that our loved one enjoyed. Promise me that."

We leaned in over the table and held hands in agreement.

"It was a year of deep sorrow," said Peter. "But now we have to live our lives without Mai. Let us remember those happy times we had together."

Theresa said, "I keep looking for her, even a year later. She is missing. She is nowhere. On weekends, I loved it when we used to be in the garden. She talked about the different fruit trees and flowers, and how important it was to water them regularly. I miss that." Tears welled up and rolled down her cheeks.

Mina was silent and far away, Theresa took hold of her hand and squeezed it. They both exchanged sorrowful glances.

After dinner, we moved to the living room. Music was playing in the background. Peter and Matthew joined me in the living room. I picked up my pipe, lit it and began puffing away. I watched the children listen to the music, and tears streamed down my face.

This used to be our quiet time together, when we talked for an hour or two before going to bed. The children moved to do their individual activities and were into their nightly routines. It was different and still very sad. We were still heavy hearted. I turned in for the night. This time, I picked up my rosary and offered it up for Trinia, my beloved.

It was October when John and Mrs. Glover came into the shop—John for a new butler suit fitting and Mrs. Glover for a dress I designed and sewed for her. Mrs. Glover spoke first, while John stood behind her and winked at me.

"Hello Sabby," she said. "How are you doing today? It is good to see you doing what you love to do. It will ease the pain of your sorrow. It'll be different without Trinia."

"Yes, yes, I miss her terribly and the children miss her. I pray that we can live with our loss. It is still very painful. I have your dress ready for your fitting. Please, try it on."

She went into the fitting room while I talked with John; he would drop by on Sunday. Mrs. Glover came out, saying how much she loved the dress. The fit and length were perfect; she was very pleased and asked to come by the next day to pick it up.

"Of course," I said.

John then went into the fitting room to try on his suit. Joseph looked after him while I attended to Mrs. Glover.

At that moment Mr. Glover rushed in.

"Excuse me, Sabby, I don't mean to interrupt, but we ought to be going. Things have taken a bit of a turn on the reserves, and we need to be back before twilight."

He pulled Mrs. Glover aside towards the front of the shop. I could only hear their whispers: the government was getting into more serious action to suppress the Kikuyu.

"Sabby, can you tell John that we are in a hurry?" he said. "We really must leave."

"Yes of course," I said as I walked to the back of the shop. "Joseph, quickly finish with the fitting. The Glovers must leave soon."

Joseph hurriedly worked on the necessary adjustments on the suit, while I continued my conversation with Mr. Glover.

"Mr. Glover, do you know what is going on in the reserves? We hear very little about what is happening there, and it is very troubling to hear bits and pieces of news from you and my other European customers."

He gave me a hesitant look before he gave an answer to my question.

"There is another government roundup of the Kikuyu, and the feeling is that it may turn out to be bad."

"I remember the roundup they did in the city a few years back. The police took two of my Kikuyu assistants. That same night our house was surrounded by Africans. We scared them off with a whistle, but it was quite frightening."

"The cost of having European customers like us perhaps. Who knows? It could be because your son works in the courts where they tried Jomo Kenyatta who was sentenced to prison. They are constantly on the watch; then they terrorize by surrounding our homes. We have to be careful."

"But how long will this State of Emergency last? It has been years after all."

"I know, Sabby, it's bloody ridiculous, but we simply have to stop them from taking oaths. Once they take the oaths, they become different—they go savage, and then they terrorize us and even murder us. They come to our homes during the night and some of our farmers have been killed. You told me how they surrounded your home. They do that with us almost every night. We are trying to civilize them and make them work for us as we develop their land. Anyway, we have to get home quickly."

"What about these camps I have heard people talking—"

"Sabby, don't worry about the details. The government is taking care of it all. We must go. You be careful, and make sure you get home before it gets dark. It won't be safe to be out after seven o'clock."

John walked up to the front and stood beside Mrs. Glover.

"Thank you, Sabby," Mrs. Glover said. "I'll come back tomorrow to pick up my cocktail dress."

"*That* depends entirely upon what happens today," said Mr. Glover.

As they left, John gave me a nervous wave.

For the first time since Trinia's death, my thoughts returned to Muturi and Karani. I wondered what became of them, whether they were still being held in a camp, or if they were still alive.

"Yes, Bwana, I know," said Makori. "The people in my village talk about these camps. It is not good there."

Makori was a new assistant, and though he was African, he wasn't Kikuyu. A few days after the Glovers had been in, I asked him if he knew anything about the screening camps.

"Very little food for many Kikuyu and little water to drink. It is very bad there. They are killing them. No spirit. But the Kikuyu are strong."

"Makori, this is not good. These methods aren't working. It is five years of being in a State of Emergency."

It didn't matter what we thought or how frustrating it was for us. The British controlled Kenya. I blew out my breath in frustration.

"Bwana, the Kikuyu will be okay. They are very strong. I heard that in these camps they are not allowed to talk, but they find a way to talk with signals and signs that the British do not understand, and most of the time the British don't even see them making these signals. But the Kikuyu are beaten and many die. Then the British make them bury their own in the trenches. It is bad, very bad, Bwana. Not good there."

"Yet the Kikuyu will continue to fight them," I said. "I can see that, Makori."

"Yes, Bwana, the Kikuyu will fight. There are many of them. They will not give up. They are fierce leaders. They are fighting for the freedom of the Africans."

"I hope it will happen peacefully and without too much violence."

"Bwana, there is already too much violence but mostly on the Kikuyu reserves and in the camps. And we don't know how bad it is there. It is very bad. I will go back to finish the hemming of the dresses, okay, Bwana?"

During the months of September and October, most of my customers were the Europeans from the White Highlands. They would have their tea or garden parties and there was always a dress or a casual pair of trousers to sew. There were no fittings for the day at the end of October. The tailors worked silently, and I was lost in dark thoughts that moved from the loss of Trinia, the ongoing sadness of my children, and the rumours of torture and death in the camps. Everything seemed uncertain to me.

I was distracted by this loud voice coming from the front door.

"Sabby, how are you doing?" It was Paulo. "You okay. I see you are busy sewing. That is good. How are the children?"

He sounded cheerful, and I was grateful for that.

"Paulo, good to see you. Yes, I'm busy as I usually am. But you know how I miss Trinia. It's very difficult to explain what it feels like. But day-by-day, I feel my painful wound becoming a permanent scar. The children are fine, I suppose. They miss their Mai very, very much. I'm doing my best."

I have had this conversation many times with different people over the past months that it sounded repetitive. But I was glad to see him, genuinely cheerful for my sake. Before long the conversation turned to the ongoing State of Emergency. Neither of us understood the violence and hate in the countryside.

"…and yet we are silently going about our business here in the city," I said.

Paulo shrugged but his face was grim. "What else *can* we do? We have no control; the British have the control. It's not that we don't care, it's that we're powerless. They are civilizing us, that's what they say."

Civilizing, I thought. There was nothing civilized about colonial rule. In Britain, a big part of their civilization was based on their democratic traditions. But there is no democracy in a colony. Africans lived under a dictatorship. It was dressed in the pretence of a benevolent dictatorship perhaps. Everyone knew the true shape of things in Kenya these days, but no, certainly no one in our community spoke out about it—not during a State of Emergency.

"The Kikuyu are human beings just like us and the British. This land *belongs* to the Africans. They have been here since time began, and now the British think… bah! Enough of politics as Trinia would say. Do you want to stay for lunch? I expect Kamau to bring in lunch shortly."

"I'd love to. But I only came to see how you were doing and keep you company for a while."

The other tailors had gone for lunch already. Tears streamed down my face. I put down my sewing.

"Here in the shop, I do the sewing, and that helps me accept the pain, but when I'm home the pain comes back. I look at Mina and seriously think about how I will help her become a responsible adult. It is tragic to have this happen to us. But I am picking up and trying my best. That is what I need to do."

"I am here for you, Sabby, and are the other fellows. We will always be around. I keep thinking of your children." Paulo shook his head.

Kamau walked in with lunch, and I thanked him. I wondered, as I often did those days, what he thought of my dressing European customers. He was hard to read, quiet and reserved. Paulo and I split the meal and talked. It was good of him to visit. After lunch, he left me to my work and said that he would see me on Sunday.

At closing time, my tailors left, and wanted me to have a good night. Omondi was there cleaning up and was quiet as he worked. He had grown more troubled over the last year—who knew what he faced on a daily basis as an African working in Nairobi. I made a point of thanking him as well when he was done. As always I would say, "Keep well, Omondi. I will see you tomorrow."

As always he gave me a nod when he left. Peter walked in moments later and drove us home.

That night at dinnertime, I informed the children about Trinia's will. I thought that it was important for them to know what Trinia and I did some years ago when we built our home, especially as it affected them.

"What will?" said Peter. "I didn't know that Mai had one?"

"When we built this house, we made a will, and so *this*," I said pointing to the walls around us, "is all in Mai's name. I know we didn't follow our tradition, but I was advised to keep the business separate from our personal home. The business is in my name and we decided to put the home in Mai's name." It sounded very business-like. They watched me in silence and waited for me to continue.

"I went to the lawyer two days ago, and he went over the will with me. He thought it would be a good idea to explain the will to you."

The lawyer had suggested it would be a good idea to discuss the will. In *the event of my death* the children would know the state of affairs; but I didn't tell them that.

"What is a will?" asked Mina.

"It is a legal paper that describes Mai's wishes when she is no longer with us," Matthew responded.

"Let me explain the most important part of the will. We cannot sell or move from this home or administer what's in the will until Mina turns eighteen," I said. "I have the will with me. After dinner we'll go over it in the living room. Peter, you can read it for us."

"Yes of course," said Peter. "I'm curious about it I must admit."

Matthew, however, seemed distracted and didn't show much interest. Something had been bothering him all night.

"Matthew," I said. "Is everything all right? Are you upset that I hadn't brought this up earlier?"

"No, nothing like that," he said. "It's just I was hoping to discuss something else after dinner. It's not important."

But it was important. I could tell.

"What is it, Matthew?"

"Mai never liked it when I brought up politics at the table." Matthew looked down at his plate.

"Well that's true. She felt uncomfortable because the situation threatens our security and the life we've built here in Kenya. But we must continue to know what is happening in this country. Go ahead, Matthew, what have you heard?"

It looked like a weight had been lifted off his shoulders.

"You know the newspapers are revealing more about what is happening in the reserves. Much of it is ugly, though they try their best to justify their actions. They want to bring the Kikuyu down. After years of emergency, there is a lack of confidence in the government. I heard that they recruited Kikuyu loyalists to work with them and inform on rebels in order to bring down their own people."

"Matthew, this is troublesome, and I did hear it from one of my customers. This will cause more tension, for if it is true, the Kikuyu will not be able to entirely trust each other. They won't be able to speak openly to each other because they won't know who is a traitor or not. If they speak out they could be turned in to the British. This makes it worse than ever because it would cause a great deal of anger."

I always thought that the British were doomed to lose Kenya and that it was only a matter of time, and yet I would not say it at the table. Matthew's support for the Kikuyu plight made me anxious. He was young and brash, and the British were growing, in my view, ever more desperate and vicious. I was unsure how to respond.

It was Peter, almost as though he read my thoughts, jumped in.

"We have to be careful as well," he said. "We mustn't ask too many questions or express too many opinions. We could get into trouble as well, couldn't we, Pai?"

"Yes, Peter. But we must keep our eyes and ears open, and we mustn't be *afraid*, instead we must stay informed and act accordingly. Your Mai and I talked many times about this uncertainty. But you know, it doesn't do any good talking about it. We have to learn to live with it. I only hope it won't break out into fighting. That will be horrible."

Once again, I noticed that Theresa and Mina didn't like political talk, just like their Mai. They drifted off in their own thoughts when we talked politics.

Matthew seemed to know more, but he held back and became silent. He worked in the courts and probably heard more than he was saying in front of us during dinner. I had to respect that. Kamau came in to clear away the dinner dishes, and we moved to the living room.

The children sat on the sofa while I took my usual position in my favourite chair. I lit up my pipe. Peter picked up the will and started reading through it.

"Peter," I said. "Read it aloud. It concerns all of us."

"Oh, right. It's legal writing and a little complicated in places but... let me read."

We listened attentively, and since it was not a long document, we were able to concentrate. I watched each one of them as he slowly read through the document. I could see Mina being confused and did not really understand what was being read.

Maybe, I brought this out too quickly. But what if anything happens to me suddenly like it did to Trinia. They must know.

Peter came to the part where nothing could be done with our home until Mina turned eighteen. Peter stopped and pointed to Mina. Jokingly, the children turned towards Mina and together they practically shouted:

"Nothing can be done until you turn eighteen."

With all eyes on her, Mina smiled, as though happy to be at the centre of attention. She had some power that she did not quite understand and because it came from her Mai that felt good.

I smiled.

"Yes, that is what is written, and Mina, by that time you will clearly understand the meaning of it. I remember the day we sat down with the lawyer to draft this will. It was difficult for Mai to see the need for it. But we did it. The lawyer explained it very clearly to Mai. And now years later I am very glad it is here for us. We will always have a home, no matter what happens, even after you turn eighteen, Mina. That's what it says in the will."

I glanced at my children. They were in agreement.

Matthew said, "This means that we put the will away until Mina turns eighteen, Pai?"

"Yes, Matthew. The lawyer has one copy, and I'll put this copy in the safety deposit box at the bank and it won't get lost with my business papers."

We were suddenly sad again. We wanted Trinia here and not her will. I hid my tears while everyone else moved about. I went to my bedroom, picked up the Rosary and began the prayers to myself. At the end of the Rosary, Trinia's presence was around me. She was smiling and looking after us. This had become my nightly routine.

I cried myself to sleep.

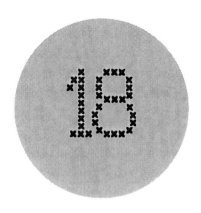

INCIDENT IN CHURCH AND MOVING FORWARD

Sunday mass at St. Teresa's was always special. Trinia and I were committed to our faith and the church. It had been over three years since her death, and though the rough edge of pain had dulled, the deep sense of the loss remained. I thought of how we used to walk to church together in the cool early Sunday mornings. Run by Irish Holy Ghost Missionaries, St. Teresa's was nothing like the Catholic churches of Goa with their high pointed steeples, carved wooden pulpits, intricate altars and stained glass windows. Still St. Teresa's had been our parish church, mine and Trinia's, and that made it all the more sacred to me.

Anton joined me outside, and we waited together until it was time to go in. It was a simple interior with a high ceiling and a plain altar set against the far wall—there were also two side altars. Anton and I sat in the last pew as the church filled up in front of us. The gleam of the golden tabernacle in the middle of the central altar was visible from every pew.

Mass began, and soon I brought out my handkerchief to wipe the tears from my face. I missed Trinia not being by my side. She had a strong faith and believed deeply in God and the Blessed Virgin Mary. She did all the novenas and attended Benediction regularly. I wasn't regular. I remembered the times when I used to bring dresses home to be sewed on the weekends—Trinia didn't like it when I worked on the hand stitching on a Sunday, for it was a day of rest and no tailoring should have been done on that day. It was forbidden by the church to do paid work on Sundays. I had these thoughts through the Mass until Father Ryan's raised voice forced me to listen to what he was saying towards the end of his sermon.

He didn't seem too happy. He loudly complained about us, the parishioners. According to Father Ryan, we were not contributing our required amount of our church dues. He raised his voice even louder to announce that he had listed the names on the bulletin board, and that these people were to pay up soon. I looked at Anton, and we both were dismayed and angry. This was not right.

There was a funny kind of silence in the church as Father Ryan stepped down from the pulpit and continued the Mass. At the end, when we walked out of church, I heard people whispering to each other. I could sense that they were furious as they gathered around the bulletin board. Mr. D'Costa stood in front of it and announced that this was not right. The Church Committee would be meeting to discuss this matter with Father Ryan. Anton and I walked outside and shared with other fellows our frustration. Anton invited me over to his home for a coffee. We talked about the list, a blacklist, really.

"How can he do that? Some people can't afford to pay their dues." Anton was angry.

Comfortably seated on the sofa in his living room, Tina brought in cups of coffee.

"I know, Anton, this is very bad of Father Ryan. Why did he do that? There are some of us who give more than our share of church dues, and he *knows* that. That should be enough."

"These priests want too much. Besides they never tell us how *much* is collected each week. They should let us know, don't you think, Sabby?"

Tina came back in.

"Sabby, you'll stay for lunch I hope," she said.

"No, no, Tina. Thank you very much. I have to go back to my children. They go for the later Mass and then we will have *our* Sunday lunch. You know, how Trinia used to fuss about Sunday lunch and always made a big thing out of it. We had to be present to enjoy her delicious special Sunday dishes and we used to get into loud conversations and discussions. Now we have memories, but we still do the Sunday lunch with quieter conversations. Maybe that will change over time."

Tina came over and gave me a big hug.

"Yes, of course I understand. Trinia loved entertaining and preparing food and loved having people around. We had many conversations, ate, and laughed. Those were wonderful times. I too miss her and those happy times with her, Sabby."

"She was a wonderful woman," Anton said. "Happy and kept *you* happy, Sabby. I miss her being around you." Anton sipped at his coffee.

"It is very painful to be without her day and night. You can only imagine how much I miss her. I keep repeating how much I miss her. All we can do is live through it. Enough talk. I have to get back. Kamau is very good. He prepares the dishes just as Trinia taught him how to do it. He's been with us for a long time now."

I finished my coffee and stood up. Both Tina and Anton came to the street to see me off.

I walked home slowly, thinking of what would give me the courage to carry on living with my children. I felt Trinia's presence in every bit of my being. She seemed to be guiding me along. As long as she was there in spirit, I would find the courage to continue with life as it would turn out to be. I arrived home to find Peter, Matthew, Theresa and Mina waiting for me.

"Pai, where have you been? Mass was over a long time ago?" Theresa said in a half-annoyed voice but with a smile on her beautiful face.

She led me into the living room.

"Don't worry, I met Anton at church, and then I went to his home for a coffee. I thought it was a short visit, but I guess it's almost lunch time." I smiled at them.

Theresa grabbed hold of my arm. "Lunch *is* ready, Kamau is waiting to serve it. Let's go eat."

Matthew turned to me as we made our way to the dining room. "We want to talk about what Father Ryan said at the end of his sermon. It sounded bad coming from a priest."

"I know, Matthew. He will have to change that. Let's talk about it."

We were in our usual chairs around the dining table. I took away Trinia's chair months ago because I couldn't bear to see the empty chair at the table. We had spread our chairs out a bit more to fill the gap. Kamau brought the dishes to the table. Theresa looked proud, for she now supervised Kamau, almost as though she had taken over the kitchen. She proudly said that she liked cooking and that she learned from Mai about preparing, cooking and serving the dishes. Kamau left as I led the prayer before meals. I had barely finished—we had not even started serving ourselves—when Matthew spoke out.

"Father Ryan was cruel. That was very unkind."

"There is no need to list the names of those who did not contribute the money that is supposed to be given to the church. It is insulting to those who cannot afford the money. What is the *matter* with Father Ryan?" Peter was outraged.

"Mina and I couldn't believe it. We sat there looking around at the reactions from the crowd. People were shocked. Why did he make such an announcement?" Theresa questioned turning in my direction.

I kept silent for a while, knowing it was going to be a difficult conversation. I knew Father Ryan was wrong, of course. Some of the Catholic priests took advantage of us and thought they could get away with being unjust and inconsiderate.

I carefully observed my children and they wanted answers. They knew I cared about my faith and believed deeply in the church. And now I had to discuss the injustices coming from the priests—were Trinia still alive the conversation around the table would be quite different. She would have responded immediately and then I would have added my opinions which were sometimes different from hers. These priests were supposed to lead the way and show us how to live with each other with honour, in peace, justice and most importantly with respect for the human being in both body and spirit. This action of Father Ryan showed no respect for the human being.

"Yes, I agree that Father Ryan embarrassed some people, *especially* those who cannot afford to pay what the church says we have to pay. It is not right what he did. Mind you, I heard Mr. D'Costa of the Church Committee say that they are going to have a meeting."

"What good is a meeting *now*?" said Peter, still angry. "There are people there who see their names on the list. It is already public and the damage is done."

"Peter is right," said Matthew. "These priests look like they are greedy for money. How could they do that, Pai? They should be *helping* us, their parishioners, and not embarrassing us."

"Pai, it didn't sound right, and it wasn't right to post names on the bulletin board." That was Mina's objection, who was now thirteen and growing up to be a beautiful teenager.

"I know, you are correct, and Father Ryan has embarrassed our people. But we must remember that these priests are human beings as well. They do not have super powers. They are like us, and they can make mistakes too." Trinia, I thought, would have liked that comment.

There was silence for a moment and we ate our lunch. Each dish was very well prepared—but it missed Trinia's touch, or maybe it was her presence I missed most of all.

After a few bites of food Matthew said, "Pai, you are too kind. You know these priests do *other* bad things."

I shot him a warning look and glanced to Mina.

"But Matthew, Pai is right; everyone does something that they should not have done and so long as they correct it, we must forgive them." Theresa defiantly looked at Matthew.

Matthew looked away and was eyeing Mina's reaction. She listened with curiosity.

"Theresa that is a very sensible comment and yes, I've heard those *rumours*. But again, remember they are human beings. We make mistakes, and they can make mistakes as well. We must learn to forgive them. There are always people to tell them when they are wrong. That's why we have the Church Committee."

Peter looked at me in disbelief.

"Let's hope they will do something about this list on the bulletin board, quickly."

"Yes, I'm sure by next Sunday, the list will be gone and that Father Ryan may even apologize to the people." I said with sincere hope that the Committee would get this situation under control. *Wouldn't it be nice if Father Ryan apologized?* I didn't think that would happen. Matthew was angrily doubtful.

"They should take it down immediately and not wait any longer," said Theresa eyeing us. "Some of us go to Church during the week days, like *me,* and we don't want to see that list there until next Sunday."

"You have more faith in him than I do, Pai," said Matthew. "I'll be surprised if he apologizes. These priests get away with so many—"

"Okay," I said, a little sharply. "Let's not talk about the priests. Mina, tell me something about your week at school, now that you are in secondary school—"

"Actually," said Peter unexpectedly. "I have some news. You know that I have been dating Jane D'Souza and she has been here a few times. Well, we want to get married—we don't want a long engagement. We want to be married by next year."

We were pleasantly surprised for a moment. Then we stood up, grabbed hold of Peter, and congratulated him. He explained that he met Jane's parents and that they talked about an engagement party next month at their place. I knew Jane and her family. They were good people. Peter would be happy.

After lunch, Kamau came to clear away the dishes and we left the dining room. The house seemed quiet, and then I heard Peter turn on the radio. It filled in the gap while everyone gathered around the living room—a program about the latest musical hits. I didn't understand it, but it was good to see the children cheerfully listening to it. I saw their spirits being uplifted. I took my favourite chair, picked up my pipe and, after many tries, managed to get a good light coming from the pipe. I puffed away at my pipe and thought about the upcoming week.

My peaceful thoughts were interrupted with a knock at the door. Matthew opened the door and in walked Anton and Emilio. Peter turned off the radio and the children disappeared. I brought out the beer and noticed that this was going to be a different kind of visit; they were very upset.

Before I even had a chance to hand him a beer Anton repeated what we discussed earlier that morning. "What the priests are doing is serious. They have *no* right to embarrass *anyone* in our parish. That is wrong!"

"Sabby, how could they be unkind?" Emilio was angry. "Did you notice when he made that announcement there was silence in the church? The congregation was shocked. We treat these priests very well. We invite them to our parties, you know, christenings, marriages and sometimes our birthday parties. What is the matter with them?" Emilio was outraged.

I shrugged. "They need more money than they are getting, I suppose. They looked at their accounts and checked how many people are not making their contributions. And when they calculated the money they could be getting they decided to do what Father Ryan did on the pulpit."

"I don't know," said Anton. "They look well fed and clothed to me. I don't see them starving. Many of us volunteer at the church. That Mrs. Fernandes sews their vestments and altar cloths. I'm sure they don't pay her like they would have to pay you, if you made them. Right, Sabby?"

"I think their vestments come from Ireland," I said. "They are specialized garments. But the altar cloths and other small pieces are done by Mrs. Fernandes. But you must remember, it is a business running the church. They need more money. Being missionaries, they get some money from Ireland, but the rest comes from the parishioners. It's not enough for them." I took a gulp of beer.

"Okay, okay, I accept that they need money to run the church and their house, but to talk to the parishioners the way that Father Ryan did during Mass was disgraceful," said Emilio. "That is not the way to do it. He could have gone to the Church Committee and found a way of getting the parishioners to pay their dues. Father Ryan did wrong." He sat back in the sofa.

"Emilio is right," said Anton. "And some of our parishioners may not be able to afford the required amount. They give what they can. You know there are a few who are supported by St.

Vincent de Paul Society. I hope they are not on the list. I didn't check the list. I was too mad to see who was on the list."

Anton took a large gulp of beer. Then he leaned forward.

"I heard that Father Lawlor visits Mrs. Fernandes fairly regularly. Who *knows* what goes on during these visits? People are gossiping about that. I don't even want to say it."

"Now, now, Anton. Let's not gossip, okay? I heard that too. We mustn't spread this gossip."

Emilio said, "There you go, Sabby, being forgiving to these priests. Some of them do wrong. They are not setting a good example for our children. I'm sure your sons have heard the gossip, haven't they?"

"I don't know about the gossip," I said. "But at lunch we talked about the list. They were very upset and condemned the priests. As usual, I told them that people make mistakes and that Mr. D'Costa is looking after this list. They weren't satisfied with my answer either, especially Matthew. I think he wanted to bring up the gossip, but he didn't. Mina has just become a teenager and is still too young for that kind of talk."

We were silent for a while and drank our beer. Theresa brought in samosas. She put the plate on the coffee table and left quickly before any of us even had the time to talk to her. She knew that, when my friends came over, we could talk and talk about everything and anything. I hoped she didn't overhear any of this conversation.

"Okay Sabby, enough about the priests," said Anton as though reading my thoughts. "I know what you're thinking. All we can do is pray for them, right?"

I smiled at both of them and nodded in agreement. "What else *can* we do? Pray for them about the gossip and hope it is not true, whatever is going on there. But the list has to be removed, and I know Mr. D'Costa will see to it. He is a good man."

"These samosas are good," Emilio said. "Is it that lady at the corner who makes them?"

"Mumtaz," I said. "Trinia was fond of her and always bought samosas from her whenever we had friends and family visiting. Now Theresa does it and seems to automatically know what to do. I know Connie, our neighbour, helps out with my girls. She was a good friend to Trinia. They helped each other with the children."

"Sabby, it's been three years now," said Anton. "And I know how much you loved Trinia, we thought she was very special, and I know you cannot imagine life without her. I think you should consider those marriage proposals you told us about. You need a woman." Anton had that caring look on his face.

They quietly waited for my response. I drifted away into my thoughts of one particular marriage proposal. I liked Anna. She was a widow with two children, twins—a girl and a boy. I took Mina there for a visit to see how she would adjust to these children around her age, but she sat there and didn't even speak to them or look at them. That had been when I knew it would not work out.

"Sabby, did you hear what I said?"

"I heard you, Anton. I have to think about Mina and how she, her brothers and sister would adjust to another woman as their mother. I'm not sure it'll work out. I had a peaceful and joyful life full of harmony with Trinia. Getting someone else in here will be… difficult."

"Ahh…" said Emilio with a smile. "Good! you *have* thought about these marriage proposals?"

"Yes, I even visited one of the women. No, I won't tell you who. There is too much gossip around already. Very nice woman, I like her. But it would be a difficult adjustment and not just for me. I turned it down. I'm not the only one who misses Trinia." I said sadly.

They looked at me with their mouths open and did not respond. I could see that Anton understood more than Emilio, for I'd known him longer. I knew they both cared about me. The conversation moved on to other topics. Jomo Kenyatta's sentence of seven years' hard labour, for instance, had just ended and yet he was still being held prisoner by the colonial government; that made them appear desperate. While in India, the Nehru government was increasing its pressure on the Portuguese to give up their hold on Goa.

By the evening, they both left, telling me that they hoped that the church list would be removed soon.

After spending an afternoon with them, I knew, even more clearly than before, that my business had become my priority like it had been before I was married to Trinia. The children were grown up and even Mina would be a young woman. Peter would soon be married and living with Jane in a flat nearby. My thoughts went back to the time of my arrival in Kenya. I was young, full of energy and alone. Now, I was older and with children. I had a beautiful time with Trinia. We enjoyed life together as a family.

There were many weekends when we drove to the drive-in outdoor theatre to watch movies. I was very surprised that we could watch movies in the open air with a large screen in front of us with speakers brought inside the car. It was wonderful. Then there were those times when we visited the Nairobi National Park. I'd wake the children very early on a Saturday morning. We drove into this Park and saw the wild animals in their natural habitat; the giraffes, the antelope, impala, zebras, elephants, hippos and rhinos. The children loved the lions sitting as a family in their shady spot under an acacia tree; the cubs being playful while the male lion protected them. Those were lovely memories of our life as a family.

I went into a state of sadness to find that she was no longer around. Trinia had left a large gap in our lives. She was not there when I needed her most. But she was ever present in spirit. At night, alone in my room, I still had long conversations with her. And though there were no responses from her, I would imagine her responses. I thought this was my way of coping with my loss.

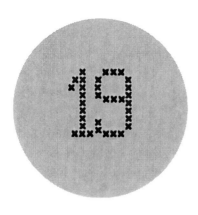

CHANGE

The decade of the sixties brought in a variety of changes. On January 12, 1960, the Kenyan Colonial Government ended the State of Emergency. It had become clear, after seven years of ruthless suppression, that the dream of a White Kenya was not going to happen and that there would be change of some sort. In February, there were nationwide calls for the release of Jomo Kenyatta. By the fourth year anniversary of Trinia's death, a petition of over a million names had been presented to Governor Renison—and in May, Kenyatta was elected President of the Kenyan African National Union *in absentia*.

Our family was moving forward. Peter had married in 1959, and in July 1960, made me the grandfather of a beautiful boy, named Richard. Matthew dated a few women. One who he truly wanted to marry was a brahmin and he was turned down because of the caste differences. In September, Theresa joined the convent in Ireland to become a nun, and by her first few letters, she seemed to be adjusting to her religious life. Mina turned fourteen with two more years left of secondary schooling. She was intelligent and independent, and—perhaps only because she was the youngest—I worried the most about her and her future and my need to protect her. I continually advised her that she had to learn to look after herself. She missed having a mother around. I knew that. Our neighbour Connie helped out as much as she could without interfering. Her husband, Xavier, was very supportive and always came by to chat with me. He and Connie had two children of their own.

In August of 1961, Jomo Kenyatta was released. He subsequently led the two KANU delegations to the Lancaster Conferences in London where Kenyan Independence was negotiated.

In December of that year, Indian troops crossed the borders of Goa ending over four hundred and fifty years of Portuguese rule. Letters from Trinia's family were about India's annexation. Some of the Goans were truly disappointed because they wanted Goa to remain a Portuguese Province. Goans were used to their life under Portuguese rule. Menino wrote long letters about the changes—Indians moved in and Goans were afraid that they would take over the jobs. The State of Goa had its own government within the Government of India; very similar to other states like Kerala. While the Goans in Kenya talked endlessly about the Indian takeover of Goa, there was no real action; possibly because our lives were entrenched in Kenya.

Change was happening everywhere. Change is the way of world. Nothing stays the same.

Kenya, of course, was moving closer to getting rid of British rule. The Kikuyu were persistent, which was why, despite the British suppression and the collaboration of Kikuyu loyalists, independence was likely.

MARIA LYNCH

The colonialists finally realized that the sixties would be a different time period indeed. I liked the African leader Tom Mboya from the Luo tribe. He was very smart, and I had hoped to be alive to see him become eventual President of Kenya. Most of the talk was about Jomo Kenyatta—a Kikuyu—becoming the first President. He deserved this honour as he fought vigorously against the colonialists.

In December of 1963, elections were held. During the pre-election period, there was a fair amount of anxiety in the Goan community. We saw the small lorries on our streets carrying people with loud speakers, blaring their messages of how they would rule Kenya. It made me restless. Some of the Indians were campaigning to become part of the newly formed Kenya Legislature. There was a Goan too—Pio Gama Pinto—who had been active in the independence movement. Pinto campaigned to be elected in the new government as part of Kenyatta's KANU party; he won a seat in the Kenyan Legislation.

Ultimately it was the Kenyan African National Union that won the elections. The British Government transferred the reins of power to the newly elected Government with former political prisoner Jomo Kenyatta at its head. The ceremonial hand over took place on the Parliament Hill grounds and was considered a great day for Africans. Yet there were many non-Africans who were uneasy and thought they had an uncertain future ahead.

The British Government agreed to buy out any settlers who wished to return to Britain. But what would happen to people like us? We came from India. Though I was born in Goa, I did not want to return. My life was in Nairobi and was very different from Goa. My life was rooted in Kenya. Trinia was buried in the Nairobi City Park Cemetery and it was my wish to be buried with her one day. Our children had been born in Nairobi; it was the only place they had ever known. What rights would they have?

"Sabby, you certainly seem far away this morning. Nothing serious, I hope."

It was February 1964, and I was at the shop, routinely sewing a pair of trousers; I was lost in thought. I had not heard John walk in. I smiled at him as he came to my sewing room.

"Ahh, John, good to see you. Where have you been? It has been a long time. I was miles away I'm afraid, trying to think of some kind of pathway for our future that could make sense. Like everyone else I suppose."

I put my sewing down and brought a chair out for John.

"What is the news with you?" I asked.

"Well, the Glovers say they will stay on as long as they can. But you know, they can always go back to England. They have a home there. They've promised me that, if they leave, they will recommend me to their few friends who are definitely staying here to help the Kenyans. That will be another adjustment for me. Who knows, we'll see?"

"Yes, another change for you. You've been with the Glovers for... What has it been?"

"Almost forty-five years. I could no more go back to Goa than you could at this point. We made a good life here, didn't we, Sabby?"

"Yes, yes, we did, no question about that. I am happy for you, John, and glad the Glovers have your interests at heart after all the years you've spent with them. I'm thinking of my children. How—"

"They're hardly children any more, Sabby," he said with a big grin. "Even Mina is grown up."

"She's eighteen," I said, "and looks to me for direction. But what direction to take. I don't know. Do I take a British passport?"

The Indian and Goan population of Kenya were offered the opportunity for British citizenship. My children were born in a British colony after all. We wouldn't be able to stay with British passports. We would have to go to Britain, and that I didn't want to consider, not at sixty-six years old.

John looked alarmed. "I can't even think of trying to live in Britain. What will you do?"

"My mind's made up. I will get an Indian passport, and if I have to go back to Goa, I will. But I can't think of that. I want to be with my Trinia—be buried with her. We created a beautiful life together here with our children. Even without her, it is a good life. I cannot imagine going to Britain."

"Surely your children will be better off in Britain though. They won't go to Goa, will they?"

I gave John a sad smile.

"No, I don't think they would make a good living in Goa. I cannot expect them to go to Goa. They don't know Goa like we do. It'll be different for them. They'll have to get British passports. I don't know how I'll cope without them near me."

"Sabby, we never thought it would end up like this, did we? I'm thinking of the time when we first came to Kenya; we created a good life for ourselves. It's the politics that changes everything. Now we look like the bad people who didn't give the Africans the opportunities they deserved, at least that's what's written in the news. We 'Asians' took over the trades, the businesses and government offices, as though the opportunities we were offered were our fault."

John waited for my agreement with him.

"Always, someone has to be blamed. Why not blame the Indians? John, the British have to keep peace. We went through a terrible time with the Mau Mau. I don't even want to think about those times. After the very long and bitter Kikuyu struggle they had to give Kenya back to the Kenyans. This is a very good thing. But what happens to people like us?"

We were caught in the middle. Those who were born in Kenya could supposedly apply for Kenyan passports, but people like John and I would not have that choice. My children would have the possibility to try for Kenyan citizenship, but it was unclear if it would be automatic. There was a great deal of uncertainty.

"It's true. We knew there would be uncertainty when we came here, but who could have guessed that we would still be facing it as old men." John shook his head. "What about Nathoo? I can't remember, was he born here or not?"

"He was," I said. "And so was Ali, the man in whose shop I first started tailoring. They will be granted Kenyan citizenship and their children will have no trouble at all. I have discussed it with both of them, and they will both stay on. They visit India often, but like us, they consider Kenya their home."

"Ah Sabby, how long have we been talking about the politics over here? It's never been simple has it? Anyway, I have to go back. I only came for a short visit. Mrs. Glover is meeting someone in the city. I have to meet her soon. I better go."

"John, come over on Sunday. Paulo and Anton will be there, in the afternoon. Can you come?"

"Good, I'm free on Sunday. Yes, I'll see you at your place."

I continued with my sewing. My world was changing once again, but this time it was not through a choice of my own. The politics of the situation forced this change on us. My children would have to take British passports; they would manage the change better than I could. I was too old for that kind of change. Miguel and Fatima were worried too. They didn't know what they were going to do, for they didn't want to go back to Goa. They were thinking about going to Britain since their sons, Albert and Joe, would be going there.

"Good day, Sabby. Is my suit ready? Is it the one you are working on now? It doesn't look like mine. It is a different cloth, yes?"

Once again I had not heard Mr. Brown come in. Perhaps my hearing was going. I smiled.

"No, no, Mr. Brown, this is another customer's suit. This is gabardine. It is a very nice cloth. Feel it."

I encouraged him to smooth the cloth, squeeze it and feel the texture. He looked at me in a curious way.

"Do you think I could wear this kind of cloth? It feels a bit heavy and maybe a bit too smooth."

"Ah, Mr. Brown, now you understand the different kinds of cloth. Yes, you are right. It would be good for those cool evening functions; some of those outside functions you have at your home during June and July when it is colder at nights. Think about it for your next suit. Now let me get the suit you came for."

Mr. Brown tried on the suit, and I watched as he smiled and turned in front of the mirror. I was pleased with his reaction—I made many suits for him and many dresses and outfits for his wife. They were my loyal and regular customers.

"Good job as usual, Sabby. How much do I owe you this time?"

With that, he paid for the suit, and I walked him to the door. Even though I wanted to, we didn't talk politics this time; it was just business. That was fine with me; it was best to keep it that way with too much uncertainty in the air.

I did not expect any more customers. It was time to close shop. My tailors had left. I could see Peter parking the car outside the shop. I went to the sewing room and saw that everyone did their bits of tidying up. I quickly collected the bits and pieces of cloth and re-arranged my worktable, making it ready for the next day.

"Pai, it's me." Peter called from the front door. "Are you ready to go home?"

He helped me with closing some of the glass cabinets that I had left open.

It was a silent drive home. I didn't want to talk in the car. We would talk after dinner. It was over a year into Kenyan Independence and some of the Europeans had already left for their homes in Britain and other places in Europe. But many had stayed behind, claiming that they wanted to help the Kenyans build their country. This sounded funny, of course, after so many years of trying to make this country a White Kenya. Now they were being forced to think differently. There were *some* British people who were in favour of independence, and maybe they were the ones who had decided to stay behind. They would continue to do well and would make their deals and compromises with the Africans.

It was quieter than usual at dinner. Peter was not with us and neither was Theresa; only Mina, Matthew and I. After dinner, I talked with Kamau; he was getting older and had been in my service for a very long time. I noticed his slowness. He told me that his son, Matu wanted to work for us. I was happy to hear this news. He quickly added that he wanted to continue living in the housekeeper room with Matu. I thought about it for a while and then agreed. He added that he would train Matu. I smiled with gratitude. We shook hands and we both walked away from the dining room.

Peter, Jane and little Richard were in the living room as well as Matthew and Mina. With Richard on my lap, I showed them Theresa's latest letter from Ireland. She was settled in the convent and was doing well. Peter, Matthew and Mina took a quick look at the letter and then it was put aside. Though I sensed that none of them really understood their sister's decision. They knew that Theresa at least was free of some of the hard decision that now faced us. It wasn't long before the talk turned to the passport issue.

"I've not seen these British passports," I said. "But they won't make you British. I'm not sure how it will work. A colony is not Britain. I think it'll be a different kind of passport, a colonial British passport. Matthew, what have you heard?"

"Pai, I heard the same thing," he said. "In fact, I saw one. Bandhu at work has one. We examined it carefully. It has a D in front of the passport number, and we joked about that. It'll be a signal to anyone looking at the passport that we're not the real thing." Matthew gave Mina a wink.

"Matthew, this is serious. How will you be treated if you're not the real thing? What does it mean? What do you want to do, Matthew, Peter and Mina? I don't know what'll happen to Theresa. She'll probably stay in Ireland. She now belongs to the convent. It's too early to tell about her. But what do each of you want to do?"

There was silence again. This was a difficult decision. How could they decide? Kenya was their home. They were born on Kenyan soil. I supposed they would take British passports and eventually move to Britain—whenever the Africans were ready, they would simply force them to leave by making Kenyan citizenship a requirement for working in Kenya.

"The question is, Pai, what are *you* going to do if you will not take the British passport?" Peter looked at me with great concern and I could tell that the children had talked about this. "Tell us. This is important to us. We need to take care of you and each other."

I suspected that Peter would be pleased if I would simply consent to take the British passport offered and move to England where he and Jane would look after me.

"Look children, I'm in my sixties. I cannot move to Britain. I'm too old to try to adjust to another country at this stage in my life. Business has slowed down. I get contracts to make uniforms with a few orders of suits and women's clothes. It is not as busy as it used to be when you were younger. Those were good days for us and for my business. And besides my eyes are failing. I cannot see as well as I could when I was younger. You know the big part of tailoring is fine work and now I do less. The tailors do the uniforms."

I looked at my children, and saw three capable, intelligent individuals who would cope and succeed wherever they went.

"No, I will take an Indian passport," I said. "And if I am forced to leave, I will go back to Goa. I will be comfortable there. Many Goans my age and younger are going back, even Connie and Xavier have said that they are prepared to return to their home in Goa. This time I will leave not out of my choice like I did when I left Goa, but because of the decisions of the political leaders. But my heart is here in Kenya. Mai is buried here, and my wish is to be buried with her. That is really what I want. But who can tell the future?"

"Oh Pai, please don't talk about dying. I don't know what I would do without you. In fact, I don't even know what I will do regardless. I don't want to leave Kenya at all. I don't *know* any other place," Mina said as she shifted in her chair uncomfortably.

Matthew looked irritated, perhaps because—despite his confident manner—he knew that it would not be easy for either him or Peter and his family to make a life in Britain.

"Well, now is the time to make decisions for yourself, little sister."

"Matthew, there is no need to talk to Mina like that." I said.

I felt bad for Mina. Theresa leaving had been like losing a second mother in a way, and I knew she was unsure of her future.

"Pai, I—"

"No, she is still a teenager. It is difficult for her," I said. "Mina, you are my youngest, and I will always be here for you whatever you decide, remember that."

"Mina," Matthew said, "I am sorry, but you will be eighteen in a few months. You're not a child."

"Listen this is a difficult decision," I said. "The situation and the politics are forcing us to make a decision. When I came here, it was my choice. No political situation threatened my lifestyle in Goa. This is very different."

They nodded in agreement.

"It's very strange to feel that you don't belong to the country of your birth," Mina said. "It doesn't make sense."

Jane did not say much and listened mostly and sometimes nodded in agreement. She made sure that little Richard behaved and played with his toys that she brought with her.

"We're not the Africans' responsibility, Mina." Matthew's tone was harder that it needed to be. "Pai came to a British Protectorate, and we were born in a British Colony. Kenya belongs to the Africans now, and they don't feel that they owe us a thing."

Peter put down his water glass with a thump.

"Matthew, you have a sharp tongue. No need to scold Mina. She is trying her best. Do *you* have good suggestions for her? Jane and I think we know what to do. Let's hope time will be on our side, right Pai?" He smiled at Mina to make her feel better.

"Yes, Peter let's hope it'll take the Africans sometime to adjust to ruling their own country." I looked at my children and was glad for the new opportunities they had before them.

Little Richard was restless. We stopped to give him some attention, and then Jane took him to my bedroom and put him in the carry cot as he was ready to fall asleep.

My thoughts turned to Theresa in the convent. She joined as a grown woman and she knew what she wanted. I had been reluctant to let her go, but she wanted to do it. Certainly her letters to me had shown that she was happy with her decision—though I often wondered if her letters were censored. Either way, I had to accept it.

What would Trinia have thought about our family? In the eight years since her death, our children had grown up. Sitting in the living room, listening to them thinking about their future decisions, I felt that she would have been proud of them.

"But what about the passports?" said Mina.

"Yes, Mina, Richard is asleep. Let's continue." I said. "You know my decision, now it's time to tell me your decision or what you think you will do."

"I'm taking the British passport," said Matthew.

"Peter?"

"Yes," said Peter, "Jane and I decided that we will take the British passport."

I turned to Mina. She could not make up her mind; perhaps I had to make this decision for her.

"Mina it looks like you should do the same," I said. "I know you're young and that this is a big decision, but I advise you to follow in your brothers' footsteps. They will be on this earth far longer than I will."

She was about to object to thoughts of my death, but I held up my hand.

"When you, my children and grandson leave, and who knows *when* that will be, you will be able look after each other in Britain and that would put me at ease. Right?"

I knew I would be fine in Goa, if it came to that. I could build a small home on the property I owned there. I knew it would be a difficult re-adjustment for even Goa was not the Goa I left as a teenager. There would not be many people that I knew, though Paulo and Anton were talking of going back. Of course, Menino was still there, nearing his retirement. In some ways it would be like our teenage days—only we'd be moving *a lot* slower. I smiled at that thought.

"Pai, if we were to move apart, I'd miss you very much." Mina's voice quavered, and I could tell she was close to tears. "I will come to visit you every year."

"Mina, you have to think of your future. There's not much for a young person in Goa. And with the annexation things are even less certain. You will be better off in Britain. You are working as a Secretary at the Insurance company, and that will be of great benefit in Britain, far better than in Goa. I can see you working in an office where you will become the Executive Secretary. You will be confident and you will do well. Right, Mina? And every year when you come to visit me, you will tell me your stories of the life in Britain and you too, Peter and Matthew. My little Richard will be a big chap as they say in Britain."

Mina wiped her eyes and looked at the floor.

"Yes Pai. It makes me sad to think of visiting you and not living in the same place as you. But I'm excited to think of exploring a city like London. There is much to think about. It makes my head spin."

Matthew reached over and touched Mina's hand. Then he glanced at me.

"You can be sure, that I won't leave Kenya till the very end, when I absolutely *have* to leave, not until it is impossible to stay. I think it'll be a while. Maybe as long as ten years, I hope."

"I am with Matthew, it will be that long for me as well," said Peter with a big smile on his face as he cuddled Jane. It was time for them to leave for their home. They picked up Richard and left.

It still didn't feel secure. I could see Mina looking uncertain, but with a look of adventure in her eyes all the same. She would be fine. Of course none of us knew what the years ahead of us held, but that was always the case, no matter the circumstance. Ten years? Perhaps we would have that long together. Still, I could not imagine leaving Kenya and my beloved Trinia behind.

BEYOND CHANGE

The newspaper headlines reported the assassination of our Goan Pio Gama Pinto on February 25, 1965. He was shot while in the car in the driveway. Gama Pinto was a passionate politician and actively fought for Kenya's independence. I thought, as Goans, we had to recognize and honour his service to Kenya.

In August of 1966, I marked the ten-year anniversary of Trinia's death and could scarcely believe it. Each year of Kenyan independence had become more and more tense for non-Africans who had built lives under the British Colonial rule.

Luis and his family left for Goa; it was sad to see him go. He was a long time and loyal employee of S. Mendes Ltd. Tailoring Establishment. I had fewer customers and was back to two tailors, Joseph and an African by the name of Okello. I trained him. He was very good and did the occasional suit order. But by that time the orders were mainly uniforms for government workers. I did not enjoy doing this kind of tailoring. Still, I cut the cloth while the other two worked the machines sewing the uniforms. It was busy work because it was volume tailoring. There was very little designing or fitting to the person's size. It had become three sizes: small, medium and large. There were very few orders for made-to-measure clothing.

"Sabby, how are you?"

"Anton, good to see you. How are you doing?"

Of course, I mostly knew the answer already. It was tense at home.

"The same as the last time we spoke," he said. "Tina still wants to go back to Goa. She has family there. She is ready to go back, but I don't know, Sabby. We made a good life here, didn't we?"

We had this same conversation before, but Anton needed to go through it again. He was struggling with the decisions ahead of him.

"Yes, Anton we did. We did indeed, but it's all changed. Still, you have made frequent trips to Goa and you have built a nice home for yourselves there. I know you were thinking of retirement in Goa. But now you have to go there sooner. What about your children?"

"The children will go to Britain. They say that our grandchildren will not have a good life in Goa. You know, Goa is still backward compared to here. You know that."

"Yes, yes, I know. When the time comes to leave, it'll be Goa for me. Right now, I don't know where I'll live in Goa. My property there is a coconut farm. Some relative will take me in until I decide what to do. Houses there take a long time to build, right?"

"I told you about that. Tina's family helped with making sure it was built. You remember my stories, some of them were quite funny and some were terrible. Now we have a nice house. Your children are going to Britain then?"

"Without question. Peter, Matthew and Theresa know what Goa is like, but Mina has never set foot on Goan soil. There were many reasons—our parents were no longer alive and then Trinia's brothers and sisters moved to Bombay. My wish is for her to do that, visit Goa someday. But I don't think it will happen in the near future. She is working as a secretary. She loves her work and is happy. They have taken British passports. When the time comes, they will go to Britain and make lives for themselves there."

"Just like we came here to make lives for ourselves, I suppose." Anton gave an unusual smile. "It's very hard to accept. We came here, followed the British ways, and had a good life. Now it has changed, and we don't belong here. At least we can say we belong to Goa, but our children where do they belong?"

I took Anton aside, and we walked out to the Indian snack shop for lunch. We sat at a table overlooking the street while we waited for our lunch. Everything appeared normal, and yet we both knew that there were difficult decisions for almost everyone around us.

"Our children have followed the British laws and don't know anything else," I said once our samosas came. "Let's hope they will adjust to Britain." We ate the samosas and drank sips of water.

"They will have to, won't they? What's the choice? We did our best in raising them here. We gave them a life very different from anything they would have had in Goa. Much better here, and they know it. They will adjust to Britain. They are older and better prepared than we were when we came here." Anton picked up his glass and had another sip of water. His mood had lifted, and I was glad of that.

"Of course, you are right," I said. "You know, Anton, I want to stay here as long as I can. That's what I want."

"I know. It's different for me. Tina is already making plans for Goa. We may leave sooner rather than later. Remember, when the time comes, you can always come live with us in Goa until you get settled."

"That's good of you, Anton. Thank you. We'll see. This is all we talk about these days. I feel as though we have lost the joy of living here. Maybe that's just the way of old men like us," I said with a wink. "I have to go back to the shop. See you on Sunday? Paulo and John will be there."

When I returned to the shop, Ali and Nathoo were waiting for me. They wanted suits made. I loved it when my regular customers came in. Nathoo chose his suit length, while Ali handed me his suit length from his shop. They left to return in a week for their fittings. Both were born in Kenya and had no intention of ever leaving. They were in their seventies and had their large extended families firmly settled in Kenya. They were very actively involved with the independence movement and were regarded quite highly among the African political elite—Nathoo even brought two of them to have their suits made with me.

I had hoped that Okello would have brought in more African customers, but it had not happened. He was very good at making suits, but it seemed that lately there was something suspicious going on with him and I couldn't figure it out. He seemed distracted and didn't talk as much as he had before. There was something wrong. I told myself a couple of times, that I would have a talk with him, but I couldn't seem to figure out how to approach him.

My yearly stock-taking was in June of 1967. Peter helped me do an inventory in the shop. It was early on a Friday before the shop opened. I knew it wouldn't take long with Peter's help. The uniform bolts of cloth were stored in the cupboards in the sewing room, ever since I started taking uniform orders. The suit lengths were in the cabinets in the front. My business had changed, but I kept the front of the shop the same as before because I would still get a few customers coming in for made-to-measure clothing—mostly my Goan customers.

After doing the inventory, Peter said that there were three missing suit lengths. He thought that Okello had been taking them, but I wouldn't believe it because he was honest and kind, and I could not see him stealing from me. Peter was determined to find out because, for some reason, he didn't trust Okello. He had met him many times, coming to pick me up after work, and he always said the same thing; there was something not quite right about him. Peter, being unable to figure out Okello had decided that he was responsible for the missing suit lengths. I suggested that we talk to him (as I had been meaning to for the last six months), but Peter had felt that nothing would come of such a talk. He wanted to know where Okello lived. Unfortunately, I didn't know.

At the end of the day when the tailors left, Peter and I were in the car ready to follow the bus we knew Okello took each day. It was easy to simply follow the bus at a distance and watch at each stop for him to get off. Before long we saw him step off at a stop not far from the shop. Peter stepped out of the car and walked after him. In a few minutes he had returned to the car and we drove home. Now he knew where Okello lived.

I asked Peter what he intended to do now that he knew where he lived. He thought for a moment.

"I am going to pay him a visit on Sunday afternoon."

And true to his word that is just what he did. Later in the evening when he dropped by our home, he told me what happened when he visited Okello.

Peter knocked on the door to Okello's home in the early afternoon. A lady opened the door, Okello's wife Peter presumed, who was very surprised to see him. Looking beyond her, he saw Okello at the sewing machine. Peter pointed to him and told the woman that he came to see him. She stepped aside.

Okello leapt up and came towards the door with a forced smile on his face, and tried to guide Peter out onto the front step as though to talk outside. Peter pushed past him and walked in the room, at which point Okello stepped back, stood aside, and looked down. There were two suit lengths on the bed. Peter had asked him if the suit lengths were from the shop, but he wouldn't answer. Instead he slowly walked to the bed, picked up the suit lengths, and gave them back to Peter. No words were exchanged. On the way out, Peter told him not to come to work the next day.

"You fired him there and then?" I asked.

"Yes, I had to, Pai. We don't know how many suit lengths he would take from us in the future. And maybe he stole others that we didn't account for. He looked busy sewing a suit. I didn't stop to ask about *that* suit length. That was probably the third missing suit length. I had to leave quickly."

"Yes, yes. It is in an area that we cannot stay around too long. You did the right thing, but I'm so very disappointed with Okello. He was my hope for getting African customers. He acted like an honest man."

Peter shrugged and patted me on the shoulder.

"I'm sorry, Pai."

He left me alone in the living room with my pipe smoking and my own thoughts. Peter had seen him at his own sewing machine, and I tried to think when he would have bought it. He certainly hadn't told me about it. Okello was a good tailor. I had trained him well. He was a quick learner and very willing to learn from his mistakes. I had hopes of letting him expand the business with the up and coming African customers. I knew then that there was no point dwelling on it. In my heart I wished him well. *Maybe he will get African customers after all.*

The shop was different without Okello. He was a reliable tailor who worked attentively. Now it was only Joseph and I. The uniform orders were still coming in, and when I went back to sewing on the machine we managed to meet our deadlines.

Miguel came to visit regularly. He and Fatima would not be leaving Kenya. They didn't like the tension either but what could any of us do? More and more Africans were coming into the city and there were less and less non-Africans every day. Long time residents emigrated to Britain or India or America and Canada. Many of the Indians, involved with the independence movement, were planning to stay.

The Kenyatta Government had implemented a rigorous Africanization policy soon after it took office, and by 1967 every non-African in the country was affected by this policy. It meant that Africans would fill all vacant jobs and would be given preference for all future jobs. Africans would be the priority in every part of the country's economy. The Indians were the business owners; from small shops to big companies, and there was an unspoken opinion that the Indians stood in the way of the Africans progressing into the business sector. There was growing pressure for the non-Africans to leave so that the Africans could take over.

And of course, all of that was their right, for it was their country. No one was denying that any longer. Still I was hurt at being pushed out. After all, in many ways I silently supported African Independence as it was their country.

I suppose none of that matters now.

Changes were happening in our family as well. Matthew was now married to Cathy from Nakuru. They both were very happy, and I could not have been happier for them. They wanted to stay in Kenya as long as they could. Matthew too moved into his own flat, in the same building as Peter. Both were close enough to our home. Peter had another child, a girl named Alice. I spoiled both grandchildren by making them clothing which they proudly wore. Mina and I occupied our home which seemed large for only two people. Kamau's son, Matu, was still with us and looked after us very well; Kamau was around in his aged state.

I continually thought that our days were numbered and that we would soon have to leave. It made me quite sad. Anton and Tina had left for Goa. Paulo had retired (though not from playing cards), and his wife controlled him more than ever. He had slowed down quite a bit. John still visited regularly and was always as jovial as ever. He kept my spirits up and seemed quite satisfied with his new job at the Johnston residence. They were Kenyan born and had influence in the government. John had said he would stay on until—as he always put it—we all disappeared. Unfortunately, like me, he was getting on in age and not as quick off the mark as we once had been. We were both approaching seventy.

It had been a good life despite the sorrow of losing Trinia and despite the knowledge that my children and I would soon have to part ways. They would create their own lives in Britain. Often I thought about my own parents, dead many years, and how Miguel and I both left to start our own lives in faraway Africa.

We received regular letters from Theresa. She would be finishing her nursing course at the hospital soon and then she would be sent back to Nairobi to the hospital run by the Sisters of Mercy. It would be good to have her back in Nairobi.

Mina was still anxious about her future. She had seen more and more of her friends leaving with their families. Some had gone to Goa, others to Britain or Canada. Each day brought news of another Goan family leaving. Scattered like seeds in the wind. The whole atmosphere had changed, and would not be changing back. We moved through our days with increasingly heavy hearts.

MARIA LYNCH

SUNSET YEARS

By September of 1968, Theresa was back in Nairobi, living at the convent and working in the hospital in the southern part of the city. It was good to see her on weekends or whenever she had the time to visit. She was very happy, and that was good to see with my own eyes. When she arrived back in Nairobi, she commented on the many differences—the increased number of Africans and less Europeans and Indians; this after all was the reality of the changed independent Kenya.

On July 5, 1969, Tom Mboya, a prominent Member of the Kenya legislation was assassinated in broad daylight. I was truly disheartened; he was the one person I thought would one day become the President of Kenya.

I was no longer keeping too well. I had started feeling my age. I had two minor strokes the previous year from which I recovered quite well. But I was feeling the strain on my health. We had fewer uniform orders at the shop and Joseph was doing most of the work. I made enough from the shop to get by, but I lost my enthusiasm and was not as energetic as before.

Mina was as bright and lively as ever. She had an adventurous spirit about her. She wanted to travel and see different places. I advised her that she could do that when she lived in England, and that she could explore much of Europe. I encouraged her to always live within her means. She consistently was very cute when she listened to me with her wide open eyes, the way she would take in what I said to her. Sometimes she looked at me in a way that told me that she figured out that I had grown tired and couldn't keep up with all the changes around us.

In January 1970, I found myself in the hospital. I was disoriented and afraid. Theresa was next to me and told me, I think, that I had another stroke—her words didn't make sense. She comforted me, and I knew I was at the Sisters of Mercy hospital where she worked.

I tried to smile and turned away to look out the window. I could hear Mina, Matthew and Peter in the room, though they weren't there moments before. Were they? I turned to look for them and could make them out, but their images swam slightly and I couldn't bring them into focus.

What is happening?

I called them to come closer and reached out my hands to them. They placed their hands on mine. I could feel each one of them. It was my time to go.

I'm going to Trinia. I can feel her presence. The children will be okay.

And then I let go and fell into nothingness.

I could hear Mina crying, Peter and Matthew calling to me, and Theresa closing my eyes as I disappeared into a bright light.

I am here with my children in a hospital room that has come into clear focus.

Theresa looks around and, without words, pulls out her rosary and begins the prayers. The others join in, and I am immensely proud of them. They say their goodbyes and then turn and leave the room, Mina looking back with tears in her eyes. I feel at this moment, nothing but love and gratitude. The door closes and I am now alone in a hospital room with the body that held me for seventy-two years. Dust motes dance in the air.

xxx

The marble edging around Trinia's grave has been broken up and laid aside. The metal cross is next to the stones and the gravesite has been opened up to make room for the casket housing my body. It seems a trivial, sentimental thing now; the idea of where my body is buried. Trinia is not there anymore than I will be. Still these things are important for the living. I understand that.

Trina is with me in a way that cannot be put into words—but with me nonetheless. Our children stand together holding hands as the Archbishop starts the burial service with a prayer and the moment stretches on forever like a vast ocean whose unimaginable tides swell and recede and swell once more. And so it is that I can now look back over all that has happened and see the pattern of my life and the lives of my wife and children chalked out in careful strokes beneath the African sun.

CPSIA information can be obtained
at www.ICGtesting.com
Printed in the USA
LVOW10s1756311016

511029LV00005BA/675/P